A TERRORBELLE™ NOVEL

PATRICK THOMAS

PADWOLF PUBLISHING INC.
WWW.PADWOLF.COM

WWW.PATTHOMAS.NET
WWW.TERRORBELLE.COM

FAIRY RIDES THE LIGHTNING
© 2012 Patrick Thomas

Book edited by Alycia J. Mellgren

Cover Art by Patrick Thomas and Roy Maurtisen

Cover Design by Roy Maurtisen

Special Thanks to Dr. Howard Margolin for find that which others did not

10-digit ISBN 1-890096-50-4, 13 digit ISBN 978-1-890096-50-2
Printed in the USA
Third Printing

Congratulations to Joe McKeon
for winning the
Healthy Families, Happy Lives 2012 charity auction
for a chance to be written into one of my books.

He makes his appearence in the bar scene at Snake's.

For Erin
again because without her I wouldn't know
Terrorbelle's hair is supposed to be pink

and

For Colin
because he's just as big a
Terrorbelle fan as his sister

"A bartender named Murphy once told me to be careful when I hit the road because sometimes the road hits back. He was right."
-Terrorbelle, agent of Nemesis & Co. and former Daemor soldier

Not being able to fly stinks. It's the one thing I don't like about living in New York. Otherwise, Earth is great. I love TV, fast food, and firearms, but there's nothing here that equals taking to the sky under my own power. Sadly, there's just not enough magic for me to pull it off.

There are other compensations, not the least of which is motorcycles. It's nowhere near as fun, but I can go faster and further without tiring out my wings.

Riding for the fun of it is something I don't get to do enough of. I hang my hat and the rest of my clothes in Hell's Kitchen. The place is not exactly abounding with open roads, but there's enough traffic and lights throughout Manhattan to make sure I can't go anywhere fast.

Of course, I get out of the city all the time, but it's almost always work related. My job at Nemesis & Co. takes me all over. And by all over, I don't mean the East Coast or even Earth. Add in that my job generally involves dangerous activities like taking down some monster, mystic threat, or bad guy and you can understand why my boss considers even a souped-up motorcycle way too slow. Instead I get to utilize alternate forms of transportation including a magic elevator and a flying horse. There are others as well, but they tend to be worse and one is outright terrifying.

To say the least, I was thrilled about having a weekend off to relax. And considering who was riding on the back of my bike… well let's say it made my excitement seem a little odd.

Months ago I'd never have imagined willingly going away for fun with Rudy. If anyone had tried to tell me otherwise, I'd have said they were nuts. Sure I trusted the Valkyrie with my life, but I had been a soldier in Faerie. I didn't have to like a Daemor to know she'd have my back when it counted. And working for the boss is a lot like being a soldier.

The party princess and I were about as different as people come. Rudy was good in a scrap, but we didn't hit it off at first, nor did we hang out much outside of work. But things changed and I started to like the hard-drinking-good-time-girl once I saw there was more to her than that.

This getaway was her idea. My bike was pointed due north and away from the city toward Ulster County. We were paying Rudy's dad a visit.

I realize on the surface it sounded a bit hum drum, but that's because

I hadn't named dropped who her father is yet. Guy is known for carrying a war hammer and calling down lightning to smite his enemies. Vikings loved him big time.

Yep, I was spending the weekend with Thor, the Norse god of thunder. Not bad for a girl from Ogre Rock.

Even though we were heading to the same place, I was still surprised to have my passenger. After all, a motorcycle is fun, but doesn't really compare to riding a winged flying horse.

"So why didn't you ride Morningdour?" I said. As a Valkyrie, Rudy had a red winged horse which could not only fly, but move unseen among the living. The Norse princess had insisted that her horse match her hair. Since her grandfather Odin, the king of the Norse pantheon, was the one in charge of handing out the horses, Rudy got what she wanted.

"Morningdour wanted to go on ahead, so I let her. Why? Do you mind me riding up with you?" Rudy said. She tried to keep her tone light, but I could feel the shift in her body. The idea bothered her.

"Not at all," I said. "I just figured Morningdour would get you there on the quick."

"Then we couldn't have a girl's road trip could we, Terrorbelle?" Rudy said.

"I guess not," I said.

Poor Rudy had been through hell a ways back during a particularly nasty case. It was a type of hell I could relate to, having been there myself at the tender age of eleven. Rudy came to me for guidance on how to get through the mental and emotional aftermath of that level of violation. I'd mentored soldiers in other ways of being a warrior, so this wasn't that different. Except that it was.

The fall leaves had just started to change along the Taconic. The bright colors reminded me a little bit of home. There were times I still missed it, but not enough to leave my new life here. That and the Faerie I remembered as home was destroyed when the soldiers killed my mama in front of me.

Sad when something so beautiful makes you thinks of something so dark.

I turned my mind back to the road. Riding was relaxing, especially when I fell into a rhythm. I hadn't been this stress-free in ages. Like most things in my life, it was too good to last.

The sound of engines modified to drown out all other noise came up behind us and blasted away my serenity.

Three bikers were riding alongside us, checking us out. I guess it was unusual to see two women on a bike, but that doesn't excuse rudeness. Can't blame them too much for checking out Rudy. The Valkyrie was lean and muscular and taller than my six feet. Her long red hair was out of its typical braid and was flying behind us almost like it was alive and dancing. She lived in tank tops, had perfect skin and looks that made models in her vicinity feel plain.

These jokers were looking at me too. While I've never considered myself terribly attractive, I do draw some male attention. What I lack in quality of looks, I make up for in quantity of certain female attributes. Let's just say that I'm well-endowed to the point that strippers stop me to ask for my surgeon's name. Only rarely will they believe me when I tell them my huge chest is natural. I usually don't bother to explain my mixed Faerie heritage.

So I'm used to men paying me, or at least a couple of parts of me, unwanted attention. I could deal with a guy sneaking a covert look from time to time, but the ones that outright stare like I'm a piece of meat that exists just for their jollies tick me off.

Luckily, while not as big as my front, the rest of me sports some pretty large muscles. I'm more than a bit stronger than the average human. If my bike broke down, I could carry it to the next exit.

Rudy could do it with one arm while skipping.

Normally, I'll look at the offending jerk, frown and flex and he'll head for the hills.

It was a challenge to glare at these bozos without having the bike swerve, but I managed to do it.

None of the putzes took the hint. From the way they were behaving, I'd guess that the only way they'd take a hint was after beating the crap out of it first.

All three wore colors with the name Hogg Huns embroidered on the back.

One was on a low rider with his hands above his head. A beard went from his chin to his ample belly and his helmet looked like it could have once graced the head of a German soldier from World War I. He wagged his tongue like it was trying to get away so it could lick us.

"You shouldn't be driving a bike, sweet thing when you belong on the back of mine," said another who had long hair pulled back in a ponytail. A black leather vest rested on bare skin which showed off an impressive amount of body ink. Ponytail seemed to believe the helmet laws and rules of etiquette when speaking to women didn't apply to him.

The last of the rude trio sported a bushy goatee and a black helmet and seemed to think Ponytail was hilarious.

"Sorry, I'm only interested in men," I shouted across the road.

That got some laughs from his fellows Huns, Bushy and Longbeard.

"Ditch that bike and I'll show you how you're supposed to ride," he said with some pelvic thrusts.

I always did enjoy a challenge. "Okay, you've got a deal. If you can outride me, I'll go for a ride on the back of your bike, but if I win, you and your little friends scoot off and leave us alone."

"Deal. A race then?" he shouted, stopping to spit a bug that had flown in his open mouth.

"Race? That's for wimps. I'm thinking more stunt riding," I said, then whispered to Rudy. "Hold on."

I revved up my bike and popped a wheelie, rode on the back wheel for a quarter of a mile, then spun 360 degrees on the back wheel before landing back down on both. I wasn't exactly a stuntwoman, but I was built strong thanks to the combination of my pixie and ogre genes. I could lift my bike over my head, so making it perform like it was a bicycle wasn't much of a stretch.

"Hold it steady, T-Belle," Rudy said as she stood up and bent down to put her hands on the seat. The Valkyrie lifted her feet up into air and stayed in a handstand as we rode. Pushing with her arms, Rudy propelled herself up into the air, jackknifed and landed back in the saddle, so to speak.

I was impressed, but shouldn't have been. Rudy had been riding flying horses since she was a kid, so doing a few little stunts on a motorcycle wasn't much of a stretch for her. I slowed down so Ponytail could catch up.

"If you can beat that, I guess I better get ready to go for a ride," I said.

The other two riders laughed and Ponytail frowned. "Come on, let's get out of here."

The three of them sped off. Rudy blew them a fake kiss.

"Origami is one of life's most underappreciated art forms."
-Terrorbelle, agent of Nemesis & Co. and former Daemor soldier

The next few miles passed uneventfully, at least until the red winged horse pulled alongside of us and kept pace with my motorcycle effortlessly. Unlike me, the horse had its own magic which let it take to the skies unseen by most of the living.

"Hi Morningdour," Rudy said. The flying horse whinnied, then dropped a piece of paper in the Valkyrie's hand. "It's a note from Dad."

"What, he doesn't know how to text?" I said.

"Dad doesn't even own a cell phone," Rudy chuckled. "It's a menu. He wants to know if we want steak or fish for lunch."

"Fish for me," I said. I tried to watch my figure for all the good it did. My muscles were so large that even male bodybuilders could look puny standing next to me.

"It's tilapia, so I think I'll have the same. He also wants to know if we want lobster bisque or Italian wedding soup."

"Might as well stick with the seafood theme and have the bisque," I said. The paper had a pencil taped to it so Rudy leaned on my back and wrote down our orders. She put it back in the horse's mouth and gave Morningdour a kiss on the side of her head. The horse pressed her forehead to Rudy's, then took off back into the sky.

"What's with your dad and the menu choices?" I asked.

"Dad's appetite has always been legendary, but over the last few years he's learned how to cook more than the basics for himself and he's become very particular about what he serves."

"I've had his cooking. I'll gladly eat whatever he puts on the table." These days Thor could qualify as a god of gourmet food. It was one of the reasons I so readily agreed to the road trip, instead of staying home to play with my goddaughter Pixie. She lives in the same building and is named in honor of me. However, her mother Lucinda felt giving her daughter the name Terrorbelle might give her some issues when she was old enough to go to school. I couldn't argue with her on that one.

I noticed there was a minivan up ahead that was pulled over along the side of the road with its hazards on. A family was standing alongside the van.

"Those people might need help. Should we stop?" Rudy said.

We got closer, I was able to make out our three biker friends standing in front of the family. The father had protectively positioned himself in front of his wife and two kids. It was obvious he was scared, but wasn't letting that stop him. I liked him already.

I felt my jaw tighten. "I think that would be best."

I slowed down and pulled in behind the van. The three bikers turned to look at who was joining them. Seeing it was us made Ponytail frown.

"You folks need some help?" I asked.

The father nodded. "We had a blow out and I didn't realize we didn't have a jack or tire iron. We've got a spare, but we can't put it on."

"You ladies can move along. Me and the boys are the local representatives of the Triple A and we got this covered."

One of the kids, a boy of about eleven stuck his head out from behind his father. "I don't think Triple A asks people to empty all the money in their pockets before they change a tire."

Ponytail smiled evilly at the child. "Shut up kid and stop making up stories."

I put my hand on the biker's chest and gently shoved Ponytail back a few feet away from the family. "No need to worry about your Triple A card. Rudy and I will be happy to help you out. Free."

Ponytail laughed. "How're you going to change a tire without a jack? I doubt you got one on your bike."

The hatchback was already open so I reached in and pulled the tire out one handed. Rudy moved to the left rear of the car which was the side with the flat. I tossed the tire about ten feet in the air in an arc towards her. The Valkyrie plucked it out of the air one handed and placed it on its side on the ground. I then bent over with my right arm and lifted the back of the van off the ground.

"I don't need a jack," I said. "Why? Do you?"

Ponytail and the biker boys were suitably impressed, at least if their open and hanging mouths were any indication. Ponytail wasn't giving up. "You still don't have a tire iron. You'll never get the lug nuts off."

Rudy bent down on one knee. Ponytail saw her finely manicured hands and smirked, at least until she started twisting a lug nut. Ponytail's jaw dropped even further when it came off.

In short order, all five were removed followed by the tire. Rudy replaced it with the full size spare and quickly tightened the lug nuts back in place. I gently lowered the car back down. My arm was sore. I should have used both. My own fault for showing off.

"There you are, folks. Good as new," I said.

"Thank you so much. Can we pay you something for your help? We would have been stuck here. There is no cell service," the mother said, waving her smartphone in the air as if to demonstrate that it wasn't working.

"No need. Just a good deed from Terrorbelle and Rudy's car repair service. Next time you're in a position to help someone else, do it and we'll call it even," I said.

"I like your pink hair," the little girl said.

"Thank you. It's my natural color," I said.

She turned to her mother. "Can I get pink hair"

"We'll see, dear." Which was grownup speak for no. Judging by the deflated look on her face, this was something that the girl had already learned.

The family got into the car, but Ponytail grabbed hold of the father's arm before he made it into the driver's seat. "Wait a second. You still owe us."

"For what? You didn't do anything," the father said, yanking his arm away and inching toward the safety of the driver's door.

Ponytail followed after him. "Doesn't matter. We stopped, so you gotta pay for a service call regardless."

The father tried to get inside, but Ponytail threw him against the van and grabbed him by the front of his shirt.

"If you don't got the cash, we can take it out in trade," Ponytail said, leering at the woman who was already in the van.

"That's my wife!"

"Don't worry. We'll let you watch," Ponytail said.

I lived through soldiers manhandling my Mama up to and beyond the point of death. And they made me watch.

No child was going to see someone hurt their parents while I was around.

I yanked Ponytail's hair back so hard he probably got whiplash. It was enough to make him let go. I reached forward and grabbed him by his large metal belt buckle. A second later I had lifted him over my head. I used my left arm this time.

I turned to the father and smiled. "Don't worry about this, sir. We'll take care of it, too. You and your family go ahead and get back on the road."

"Bless you," the father said gratefully, but that didn't stop him from locking the doors of the van once he was inside. The kids waved from the back row as they pulled away. I waved back with my free hand.

The other two biker boys moved towards me, having taken issue with me laying hands on their friend.

"Put him down," Longbeard said.

"Before we hurt you," Bushy added.

They weren't the only ones taking issue with the way things were going down. Rudy came up behind them, spun them around and grabbed their oversized belt buckles. She bent her knees and, with a clean and jerk, got both men over her head.

"Show off," I said.

"Well if you got it, flaunt it. I have lots, so please notice the flaunting. But don't despair, Terrorbelle. If you spend years working out and practicing, you still won't be as strong as me, but you will be better off then you are now," Rudy said with a smile.

Sadly, she was right. I was strong, but the daughter of Thor had me beat. Not by a tremendous amount, but it was enough that any strength contest would come out in her favor.

"Yeah, but I can take you in a fight," I said.

"Keep thinking that if it helps you get through the night," Rudy said.

"My nights are fine because a Daemor –" My old unit in Faerie. We were the elite female soldiers of Mab's rebel army. "Will kick a Valkyrie's butt any day of the week and three times on Sunday."

I guess we were spending too much time on friendly bickering and not enough concentrating on the bikers we were teaching a lesson to. Like most men, they needed to be the center of attention or they just weren't happy.

Showing them up on the road and changing the tire wasn't enough humiliation for the day. Nope, Ponytail was hungry for more slices of degradation pie. That was the only explanation I could come up with why he would be dumb enough to take a swing at my face from the position he was in.

Sometimes you just can't save people from their own stupidity. And sometimes you don't even want to try. I didn't bother to try to block the blow, instead smashing my forehead into his fist. It hurt me a little, but I heard a crack and it didn't come from my skull. Ponytail grabbed his broken hand and screamed like a baby.

I've got a very hard head.

"Wait your turn. We would have gotten back to you eventually." I lowered Ponytail down and held him in front of me so our eyes met. "I don't like you. I especially don't like bullies who prey on innocent people. What you were doing to the family was positively repulsive."

"You don't like it, then call the cops. That family will never testify or press charges. And if the two of you try, the Hogg Huns will go after everybody you care about," Ponytail said.

"Most of the people I care about can take care of themselves. You'd be making a serious mistake in even trying." Actually, I'd love to see him go after Nemesis. My boss is the daughter of Nyx, the embodiment of night herself. Among the boss' abilities is being able to shadow step through a realm of absolute darkness. It's a place of pure terror. I speak from personal experience.

Nemesis would grab hold of this loser, take him into the shadows and leave him there for a few seconds. When he came out, he'd be babbling incoherently and trembling uncontrollably. Or maybe he'll choose to go after Gani, who was the other third of Nemesis' trio of agents and the twin sister of Merlin. Our white haired partner might turn him into a toad. If he was lucky.

"Sadly for you, we don't need a cop to take care of things. We're more hands on kind of gals," I said, turning towards Rudy. "Up for a Dagonet special?" Dagonet was the jester knight of the Round Table and sometimes boyfriend of Gani. They met back when she was a mage for Camelot and the Round Table.

Dagonet has some interesting training techniques, including the use of juggling to promote hand and eye coordination. We've trained with him a couple times, despite the fact that beside being extremely long lived and an exceptional acrobat, he is no stronger than any other man. To survive as long as he has, he's developed some interesting martial techniques.

Of course, Rudy and I took them to the next level.

"I'll give it a try, but if they get any vomit on me, you're getting my dry cleaning bill," Rudy said.

The Valkyrie threw Longbeard towards me and I tossed Ponytail towards her. Then she threw Bushy and we kept the pattern going, juggling the three bikers. When they started to scream, we threw them higher and faster, making them spin in the air as cars whizzed by. After a couple of minutes of begging and screaming fo rus to stop, we finally obliged, dumping them on the grass shoulder.

"Have you learned your lesson yet?" I said. Ponytail flipped me off and pulled a knife. He was so dizzy that he stumbled when he stood and I was able to easily take the blade away from him.

"I guess not. You leave us no choice but to teach you a lesson that you will find it impossible not to learn from. You will not intimidate, hurt, steal or try to force yourself on anyone, ever again, because if you do, we will find out about it and we will come back for you," I said.

"So you can throw us around a little bit. Big fricking deal," Ponytail said. "Next time we won't leave our guns in our saddlebags."

Rudy moved quickly and removed four handguns from their bikes. She handed two to me.

"This is what we like to call gun origami," Rudy said, twisting the gun barrels into odd shapes. Not one to be out done, I did the same. It's not as easy as we made it look. It takes a lot of hand strength and coordination.

"What do you think?" Rudy said, holding out one of the guns.

"Great elephants," I said.

"They're ducks," she said.

"That was my second guess," I said, holding up mine. "Not bad, huh?"

"Excellent geese," Rudy said.

"Actually this one is supposed to be a dragon and this one's a rat," I said.

"Now that you mention it, I can almost see it," Rudy said.

We tossed the bikers our artwork. Each picked up one and tried to un-bend it. Rudy and I smiled as we watched them strain and turn red without being able to change the shapes we twisted the guns into. Rudy did a quick frisk of the men to check for more weapons

"Now back to your lesson. Since you're so keen on people riding on the back of bikes, it seems to me that you really don't need yours, now do you?" I looked at Rudy. "Ready for some more origami?"

Rudy started stretching her arms behind her head. "I will be once I've warmed up."

We moved toward Ponytail's bike. It was a beauty and I felt bad about what we were about to do to it. I grabbed the back wheel and Rudy grabbed the front. We twisted in opposite directions, effectively turning the bike into a pretzel. We kept bending, twisting and pulling. When we were done it looked like a piece of modern art that looked like it had been run through an auto compactor at a junkyard.

"Ta da. A swan," I said.

"I thought we were doing a horse," Rudy said.

We tossed the newly made hunk of junk at the biker's feet.

"My bike!" Ponytail cried. The biker pulled a snub nose revolver out of an ankle holster on Longbeard's leg and leapt up facing me. I let my yellow trench coat fall to the ground, revealing my razor sharp pixie wings. I spun in a circle so that my wing cut his wrist, making him drop the gun as well as having blood spurt out of the wound. I turned again, leading with a roundhouse kick into his gut that sent him flying ten feet.

He lay on the ground holding his stomach and moaning. I turned to the other bikers with a smile. They understood the implied threat and raised their hands over their heads.

"Bad idea. As my friend Hex would say, this is your only warning. You better hope we never see any of you again or have to come after you."

I put my yellow trench coat back on and Rudy got on behind me.

"Sorry I missed the gun," Rudy whispered.

I nodded. It was a pretty big screw up, but it wasn't like I'd never made a mistake. "Be more careful next time. Neither of us is bulletproof."

I revved my bike and spun out so gravel pelted the three men. As we got back on the highway, Rudy waved daintily and said, "Toodles."

She does like to make an exit.

"Home is where the hammer is."
-Thor, Norse god of thunder

Be it ever so humble, Thor's place was his home. And the simple farmhouse seemed especially humble for the Norse god of thunder, even if he had twenty five acres and neighbors barely close enough to wave to.

When we pulled in the driveway, Rudy's father was multitasking. Thor was jogging in his fields, but apparently that just wasn't enough exercise for the thunderer, so he decided to till his fields at the same time. Strapped to Thor's back was a large set of plows that normally would be hooked to a tractor, wide enough to work an acre in a few passes.

Thor had his mane of thick red hair pulled back and braided. Normally, not a good look for men, but it worked for him. It brought to mind a Viking, which seemed only logical. The look was only helped by the fact he was shirtless. Despite the exertion, Thor hadn't seemed to work up a sweat yet, which was a pity. He had the type of body that should be glistening in the sun, if for no other reason than to let women passing by truly appreciate his muscles and broad shoulders.

Thor spotted us driving up the road and sped up into a sprint. Upon reaching the field's edge, he unstrapped his harness and continued running until he reached Rudy, who had barely made it off the back of my bike in the same amount of time. Thor lifted his daughter off the ground into a fierce bear hug, then swung her around like she was a little girl. I guess to him, she still was and always would be.

"Welcome my little Thrud." Rudy's actual and most unfortunate real name. We changed it to Rudy when she joined Nemesis & Co. "It's so good to see you. I've missed you so much." He was probably one of the few people that would call the six foot two beauty little. The thunderer was not only taller, but probably more than double as broad.

Not that I was going to be left out of the fun.

"And my favorite pink haired righter of wrongs. Welcome Terror-belle." Thor lifted me up into a bear hug of my own, but no swinging. It was nice to be hugged by a guy who can actually lift me off the ground, even if he was shirtless and was actually a little bit sweaty. Or maybe even because of that. Thor was hot in a hulking massively built barbarian kind of way. If you liked that kind of thing. Who was I kidding? What woman wouldn't like that kind of thing? I could have stayed wrapped up in his arms for hours, except for the fact that he was my friend's father. That sort of put a damper on things. That and my attraction was purely physical. My heart had already chosen another, even if Murphy wasn't exactly returning of the favor.

And I had another guy courting me, whom I rather liked too. And Joe Hannk was a movie star to boot. Not that that played a factor for me, but it impressed the hell out of some of my girlfriends.

As soon as my feet hit the ground, I returned the favor and lifted the thunder god with a hug of my own. That got a hearty laugh from Thor, who probably was even less accustomed than I was to having someone lift him up, especially if that someone was a woman that he wasn't related to.

"I'm so glad you girls could make it," Thor said.

"Me too. Getting a day off from Nemesis is like pulling teeth. Getting a weekend off is even worse," I said.

"How was your ride up?" Thor asked. Rudy and I looked at each other and grinned.

"We stopped to help somebody with a flat tire and turned somebody's motorcycle into origami," Rudy said.

"Motorcycle origami, huh? It seems like it would be a little difficult for most people to master, so I'm not sure it will catch on with the masses," Thor said, as his eyes darted over our shoulders and his face lit up.

Rudy and I turned to see what was there. It turned out to be a who – a well-dressed woman in her late fifties was coming toward us carrying a tray loaded with a pitcher of lemonade and four glasses.

"Hello, Isabella," Thor said with googly eyes.

"I see your daughter and her friend made it up," Isabella said, looking at Thor with googly eyes of her own. "I brought fresh squeezed lemonade."

"This is my daughter Thrud."

"Daddy!" the Valkyrie whined.

Thor grinned. "Who prefers to be called Rudy and her friend Terrorbelle. Girls, this is Mrs. Humphrey, my neighbor."

"Please just call me Isabella. Rudy, It's such a pleasure to finally meet you. Your father has told me so much about you, I feel like I know you already."

Rudy smiled slyly. "That's funny because Dad hasn't mentioned you."

I elbowed Rudy in the ribs.

Isabella was unfazed. "Well there is no reason why he would, dear. We are just neighbors. Would any of you like a cold drink?"

"I'm thirsty. I'd love some," Thor said, rubbing his hands together.

Rudy and I both said we'd like some too. We each got a normal size glass, but Isabella gave Thor what was basically a pitcher full.

"I know you're always very thirsty," Isabella said as she handed it to him.

Thor took a sip, then a gulp and ended up chugging the entire glass. "Thank you. That was delicious."

"You are very welcome. I'm going to go back home so you can visit. You can give the glasses back to me some other time. Pleasure to meet you girls," Isabella said.

"Same here," I said.

"Bye," said Rudy.

"Bye," Isabella started to walk away and then turned. "I'll still see you at the bake sale right?"

"You know I wouldn't miss it. I have been baking all day," Thor said. "And don't forget about tonight."

"I don't want to impose," she said.

"No imposition at all. It wouldn't be the same if you didn't join us," Thor said.

"I guess I'll see you then," Isabella said, then walked back across the street. Thor didn't take his eyes off her until she went inside and the door closed behind her.

"Looks like you've got a female admirer," I said.

"Isabella is a very sweet, kind, and wonderful woman," Thor said with a soft smile.

"Looks like you're interested in her too," I said, taking Rudy's and my bags off the back of the bike where we had secured them.

"Isn't she a little old for you?" Rudy said, with a frown. Thor hadn't even been married to her mother, a giantess, but she had issues with him dating. In fact, the Norse gods' idea of marriage differed greatly from the human. It apparently let the men horndog around to their hearts content, but who am I to judge?

Thor laughed. "My life has been measured in centuries. She has barely made it passed half that. How do you figure she is too old for me?"

"I'm not talking human years, I'm talking Asgard years. Look at the shape she's in. If you were going to get romantically involved, you might break the poor thing," said Rudy.

"I've taken that into consideration. We go to the gym together. She is taking yoga to increase her flexibility and Pilates to increase her strength," Thor said as he walked toward his house. "Come inside and I will get some hors d'oeuvres ready,"

I followed after, being careful to look around and above me.

"T-Belle, what's wrong? Are you looking for Morningdour?" Rudy asked.

"No. The goats," I said. Toothgnasher and Toothgrinder and I did not get along well, especially since they were able to fly on Earth and I wasn't. Since I was the one with the wings, they found this terribly amusing.

Thor opened the porch door and motioned for us to go in first. The door led into a huge eat-in kitchen that would be the envy of any cooking show. Matter of fact, it was set up so a cooking show could have been filmed there. Although most food programs don't have two goats sitting at a table and eating. The goats apparently got into what looked like some stuffed vegetables and had devoured most of the tray. I expected the god of thunder to be upset and yell at the animals, but he barely paid them any mind except a small shake of his head that came across as a halfhearted scolding.

"So much for our hors d'oeuvres. I guess," I said, as I hung my yellow trench coat on the coatrack. No reason to hide my wings here. The goats actually turned and glared at me. I stuck my tongue out at them.

"Nonsense. I have to leave something out for them to find and steal, otherwise they will go after everything else."

Walking up to his refrigerator, I noticed it had a keypad alarm system. Thor covered the keyboard with one hand while he pushed buttons with the other. There was a loud beep and he opened the eight foot wide refrigerator door outward and took out five trays of hors d'oeuvres already on cooking sheets. He had pre-heated the oven before he went out into the fields so he just popped the trays in.

Now five trays of appetizers for three may seem like a lot to most people. Then again, most people have never seen Thor and Rudy eat.

"And while they are cooking, I will show you to your rooms," Thor said.

He really didn't have to. Rudy visits frequently and I'd been here before. Each of the farmhouse's extra bedrooms was made into a guest room. Mine was quite nice. Simple, with a twin bed and rustic red color. The only unusual part was all the rooms had pictures or paintings of storms, although for the lord of thunder that would likely be what he considered art. The one in my room had a tornado and a midnight blue sky with lightning bolts flashing behind it.

I unpacked my bag, put my stuff in the dresser and the closet before heading back out to the kitchen.

The kitchen door was halfway open and Thor was looking out the window. "Oh no. The goats are over bothering Mr. Needles' farm animals again." Thor turned to me. "Terrorbelle, would you mind rounding them up? I don't need to be upsetting the neighbors any more. And if I leave now, the hors d'oeuvres and dinner might be ruined."

I have been to four and five star restaurants, as well as those that should get no stars. Thor's cooking would rate at least a seven on any normal scale.

"Well, I certainly don't want dinner ruined," I said, my mouth watering at the smells wafting through the kitchen. I didn't need to mention the antagonistic relationship between myself and the goats, because the thunder god knew it well from my last visit.

"Honestly, I think they do it because they like you, Terrorbelle," Thor said. Obviously I didn't hide the look of disbelief on my face very well. "I'm serious. The goats are foul tempered. They don't get along with practically anyone, but when you come, they go out of their way to cause mischief. I think they enjoy playing with you."

"I think they like messing with me. But as long as you're going to feed me all weekend, I'll put up with it and go get them."

"Thank you," Thor said, putting on an apron that said "Kiss The Cook." In place of the normal crossed utensils, this one had a fork crossed over a hammer.

I put my hand on the doorknob and paused a moment longer than I should have before I went out.

A while back I won a bet with Thor and ended up with an amulet that controlled the wind for twenty-four hours. It was designed to give someone like me the ability to fly. Because Earth is so poor in natural magic and I was so big, flight was not an option for me on most parts of the planet. The best I could usually manage was a hover or to slow a fall. And a good wind could help me or send me crashing.

I was hoping that Thor would have made me another amulet. But none was forthcoming, so I finally opened the door, then stopped another moment to look at the coat rack.

I decided not to bother covering up my wings. First off, I could still jump while using the wings which gets me a lot further than using just leg power. Also attitude is helpful when trying to catch critters that can fly. And since Isabella didn't seem the least bit put off at the sight of Thor plowing the fields without a tractor, I doubted the sight of me without a coat was going to upset her.

In fact, if the neighbors were used to flying goats buzzing their properties, I doubted the sight of a pink haired, pixie winged woman was going to cause too much commotion.

As soon as I got to the road, the goats spotted me. The troublemakers flew from Mr. Needles' farm over to Isabella's property, where she was working on her hands and knees in her garden with a big wide sunhat and dark glasses. The goats dove down like they were going to knock the poor lady over. Instead they stopped in front of her and she petted the two horned beasts. She reached into a box next to her and gave each of them what looked to be a dog biscuit. Each goat was bigger than a great dane, so maybe the snack made sense to her.

I knew they knew I was there, but I tried to sneak up on them anyway. As I made it to Isabella's white picket fence, the pair simultaneously turned toward each other and then me. I swear the little monsters grinned. I leapt over the fence in an attempt to grab them, but they took off flying and I barely managed to touch Toothgnasher's tail.

I landed on my hands and knees next to Isabella.

"Come to help me with the gardening my dear?" she said with a grin.

"I'm not much of a gardener, but I prefer that to rounding up those two," I said.

"Nasher and Grinder aren't so bad. They are just looking for attention. And poor Nasher has a little limp," she said. Isabella handed me the box of dog biscuits. "They love these. Maybe you can use these to entice the goats to go home."

"I'm willing to try anything," I said, filling my pockets with the treats. I would have taken the box, but needed my hands free if I had any chance of catching these two.

I leapt back over Isabella's picket fence and tried to walk slow and determined down the street, like a gunfighter in a western. I knew I was beyond intimidating the goats, but it made me feel better to try.

The pair were dive bombing Mr. Needles' livestock. The chickens were running and fluttering around the yard, not flying that much better than me. The pigs in their pen were squealing and trying to get out. The cows in the field had run to the far side, except for one bull that looked like he was hoping the goats would get low enough for him to get a shot at them. I admired the bull's attitude.

I saw an older man, probably in his late sixties, run out of the house with a shotgun in his hands.

"Get off of my property, you flying varmints," Needles said, punctuating his demand with a blast from his double barrel. The goats flew out of range.

This was getting ugly quickly.

"Mr. Needles, please put down the shotgun. I'll take care of the goats," I said.

"And who are you, little missy?" he said. I smiled. It had been a long time since someone called me little and at six feet, I was a good two inches taller than the farmer. "I'll have you know that I shot those flying varmints dead more than once and the next day they show up again, good as new. That ain't natural. What makes you think you can deal with these demon goats?"

"My name is Terrorbelle. My specialty is handling the unusual."

I popped my wings up behind me and went into overdrive. My wings buzzed faster than a hummingbird and I slowly lifted off the ground. Needles had a wooden plank fence, the kind that had a post every ten feet or so with two boards lengthwise attached to each post. I went forward over the fence and lowered myself down onto the ground.

"That sure was impressive," he said. I thought so too. Sadly that was about the upper limit of what I was going to do without a really good updraft. "I guess I could give ya your shot at rounding them up. How's ten minutes sound? If you ain't got 'em by then, I'm gonna do me some skeet shooting. They come here so often, I stocked up on ammo."

"Thank you for you indulgence, Mr. Needles," I said.

The goats had been hovering nearby watching the exchange.

"Ya hear that ya blasted varmints, she's gonna get ya," Needles said, waving a fist in the air at the goats. As a team they flew over Needles' sage green pickup truck and did their best pigeon imitation, covering his windshield in manure.

Needles pumped the shotgun and again emptied both barrels in the goat's direction, but they were already flying away and escaped unscathed.

I put a hand on the shotgun and gently pushed it toward the ground. "Please Mr. Needles, I said I would get them."

"Well, who's gonna clean off my truck?" he said.

I sighed. "I'll take care of it."

I got a shovel from the shed and scooped the goat poop off the truck. Next I got the garden hose and sprayed it until the windshield and the truck were both clean.

As I was putting away the shovel, I walked in front of the open barn.

There were a bunch of old tractor parts hanging from the rafters in a fish net.

"Sir, do you mind if I borrow your net and a few of those stakes?" I asked.

"I like the way you think, missy. Help yourself to whatever you need long as you put it back where you found it when you're done," Needles said.

I jumped up near the ceiling and used my wings to hover there as I unhooked the net from the hook it was hanging from. I carefully placed the tractor parts on the floor and got the feel of the net. Decent quality, although not anywhere near the strength of the nets folks used for catching game or people back in Faerie. Still, it would do.

"I wish you had two nets," I said.

Needles grinned and went to another part of the barn that had a couple of saddles.

"Back in my day I did some rodeo work." He likely did more than some. He sported a gaudy belt buckle that only a rodeo champion would want to wear. "These days I only keep the one horse, but I have a couple of these." Needles held out a western style lasso. "You want to borrow one?"

I grinned. "Yes, I do."

Needles put down his shotgun in the corner, clicked the safety, and handed me one lariat, taking the other for himself. "I think maybe I have been looking at these varmints all wrong. Instead of seeing them as nuisances, I should have been looking at them as a challenge. I use to be able to rope cattle with the best of them. I even won the national hog tying competition 'bout twenty seven years ago. I may be a little rusty, but I never tried to lasso something that could fly before. I trust you wouldn't mind me lending a hand?"

"As long as the shotgun isn't involved, I'd be happy to have the assistance."

We walked out of the barn. I had the net laying across one shoulder, held the bulk of the rope in my left hand with the lasso part in the right. Needles went ahead. The goats floated mockingly in the air in front of us. I heard Needles laugh as he swung the lasso around a couple of times and threw once. To my amazement it went right around the neck of Grinder.

"You're goin' down, ya flyin' varmint," Needles said.

The old man pulled and the goat came down about two feet. Then the goat pulled back and started flying. Needles didn't let go, instead dug his heals in. The problem is that a magical goat is a lot stronger than a horse or a bull. Needles was dragged through his yard, leaning back like he was waterskiing. Dust flew up around his boots. The old man wasn't frightened. As a matter of fact, he was yelling yee haw as he bolted across his farm and was having a grand old time.

Despite his upbeat attitude, I didn't want him to get hurt so I ran after both of them. They came to the end of a fence. Needles let go with one hand and looped the rope around the fence post as he went by. The goat got pulled backwards and jolted like a dog running fast and reaching the end of his leash.

The fact that the lasso was around the goat's throat limited how hard he could pull. If it had been around his chest, I had no doubt he would have been able to yank the fence post right out of the ground. Even as it was, the fence post was rocking. I caught up to them and threw the lasso. I missed by about two feet.

"No missy, you got to use your hand on the inside of it to keep it open and use the movement of your arm to throw so the circle stays that way. As soon as you get it around you've got to pull it tight quick."

I followed his advice and got Grinder on the second try. I yanked the rope tight quick, then started pulling down. So did Needles. Slowly, the goat descended, but it was like the two of us were trying to handle a balloon in the Macy's Thanksgiving Day Parade by ourselves.

When we got Grinder low enough, I was going to grab hold, but Needles beat me to it and hog tied the goat.

"Nice work," I said.

"You too missy. We might make a rodeo gal out of you yet," Needles said, then ducked as the brother goat dive bombed him.

I took the net off my shoulder and waited. It didn't take but a couple of seconds before Nasher decided to dive bomb us again. Throwing a net is something I'd been trained to do repeatedly. Earth military tends to train soldiers in guns and knives. In Faerie there's a much wider choice of weapons one has to be proficient in.

I caught goat number two on my first toss. I grabbed the ends of the net, closing it with him inside. He tried to fly off and pull me across the yard like his brother did Needles, but I pulled the net and swung it like a sack of potatoes until he hit the ground. Not hard enough to hurt him, just enough to knock the wind out of him. I thought about staking the net to the ground, but as he pulled against me, I realized it wouldn't hold him. Instead I took one of the dog biscuits out of my pocket and gave it to him. He calmed down, so I tossed Grinder one. Both seemed content to nosh for the moment.

"Missy, you've got to be the most impressive gal I ever met. You're welcome to come by my farm anytime. Hell, if I'd known these varmints could be this much fun, I'd have invited 'em back sooner," he said. "Can you manage to get 'em back by yourself? We can put 'em in the back of the pickup and take 'em back to Thor's."

I slipped the troublemakers another biscuit each, then grabbed the netted goat with my left arm and the hog tied one with my right. They may have been the better fliers, but I was stronger.

"No thanks. I can manage them. I appreciate your help Mr. Needles," I said.

"Happy to oblige. Most fun I had since I retired from the rodeo."

"I'll be back to clean up later," I said.

"Don't worry your pretty little head about it. I'll take care of it," Needles said.

"Thanks," I said.

I may have been stronger, but that didn't negate their gravity defying magic. They may not have the muscle power to break my grip, but they could still fly. With me holding onto each of them they took off into the air. I could hear Mr. Needles below me yell, "You ride 'em girl!"

I used my wings to try to slow us down, but that's about all it did. I have four sets of razor sharp wings, two on either side. The joints where they attach to my back are extremely flexible. I put a wing on the back of the neck of either goat and dug it in a little.

"You know you're not going to be able to throw me. You also know that I may not be able to fly as well as you around here, but I can certainly lower myself to the ground." That was only a mild exaggeration. I could usually glide and slow my fall, but it depends on how high they went. If we got to parachute height, my wings wouldn't be strong enough to stop me from hitting the ground like a pink haired meteor. "If you even try it, I'll cut both of you through the neck and cook you up for dinner tonight myself." Not that I was being cruel. Another part of the goats' magic allowed them to be killed and eaten then brought back to life the next day so long as all their bones were put in a pile before sunrise. Thor did it on and off for centuries. Couldn't be pleasant. I figured it was part of the reason they were so ornery. The reason Nasher had a limp was one time someone broke one of his bones while they were eating and he regenerated wrong. "Are we clear?"

Magical animals like the tooth brothers and Morningdour had enhanced intelligence. Some of them were smart, even smarter than people.

The goats were bright enough to nod yes in unison.

Even when I wasn't the driver, flying was a wonderful thing, once I got over my fear of falling. I was pretty sure I had the goats intimidated enough not to try anything. And despite our rough and tumble relationship, they had done nothing more than be mischievous, never doing me any actual harm. And killing them would only be a day's inconvenience.

"How about we do a couple loop-de-loops before heading back? I bet Thor has those appetizers ready."

I swear the goats smiled as they did a dozen loop-de-loops. It was enough to make even me nauseous. I learned a long time ago as a soldier in Faerie to never show signs of weakness, so I didn't say anything as they flew down and into Thor's yard.

But I didn't let go of either of them until we were inside Thor's kitchen and Rudy had locked the screen door behind us.

"I've heard that the way to someone's heart is through their stomach. It's not the only way, although you do have to make sure to go to your right and toward the head. And it does save the trouble of having to crack open the rib cage."

-Terrorbelle, agent of Nemesis & Co. and former Daemor soldier

When I lived in Faerie, I was raised mostly by the ogre side of my family. Cooking basically consisted of putting meat over a fire until it stopped moving or the moldy or rotten parts turned black. When I visited the pixie relations, most meals consisted of fruits, berries, nuts and some meat, mostly a lot of squirrel and bugs. Admittedly, the pixies did slow roast their meat, maybe even put some spices on it, which was a little better than having to eat around the burnt bits like the ogres. Neither was terribly extravagant.

Then when I was a Daemor in Mab's Army, we lived off of rations and other food cooked for the masses. Nourishing, but not exactly a gourmet's delight. I'm not saying I've never had a good meal, but the ones I did have in the old days were few and far between and each stuck in my memory. On Earth, the food is much better.

Thor's cooking was like arriving in culinary heaven. The appetizers were so good, I wanted to lick my plate. In fact, Rudy did. So did the goats, but to them I was a little more understanding. They couldn't use silverware.

Then came the soup. A lobster would gladly die to make the bisque if he was given a taste first. Next was the salad with homemade almond vinaigrette dressing.

That was followed by duck with some sort of mixed fruit sauce I couldn't identify, but made me practically drool from the smell alone. I figured Thor had decided to change the main course. After the first bite, I was totally fine with that. I finished an entire duck myself. Thor had cooked a dozen. The goats had one each. Rudy had four and her father had five.

Turns out I was wrong. The duck was only the final appetizer. The main course was only starting. The fish was in a green cream sauce that was better than what had been on the duck. I had thought I was full, until I took a nibble. I couldn't help myself. I finished the entire thing, along with sides of asparagus, garlic roasted potatoes and fresh baked rolls.

Next came dessert. I had to unbutton my jeans. It was something called English Toffee Pudding. It didn't strike me as much of a pudding and I really didn't see any toffee in it, although it might have been English.

It would have made my pixie relations flutter in ecstasy. Hell, at the first bite, my wings shivered in delight.

By the last bite—and I did finish every last bit— I was so stuffed I was ready to go to sleep. I had exceeded my recommended calorie intake for the weekend in one sitting. I was going to have to go on a diet when I got home, but it was so worth it.

"Better dishes than latrine duty."
  -Daemor saying

When dinner was over, Rudy and I waddled to help Thor with the dishes, while the goats retired to the living room and seemed to be playing a game of chess. Neither Rudy nor Thor found this odd, so I didn't comment on it.

When the dishes were done, we went for a walk and ended up by a big empty field on the edge of Thor's property.

"Dad, would you give me a ride?" Rudy said, batting her eyelashes at her father.

"Sure. We haven't done that in ages," Thor said. He reached in his pocket and pulled out a tiny hammer. It was Mjollnir. One of the charms placed on the mystic weapon let it shrink small enough that Thor could actually keep it in his pocket. Since it is normally too heavy for most people to lift, I wasn't sure how it didn't rip though his clothes. Probably part of the enchantment.

As the hammer grew to full size, Rudy ran across to the far side of the field.

"How are you going to give her a ride from over here?" I asked.

"Watch," Thor said, tossing his hammer across the field. It flew like a missile, passing Rudy, then stopped in midair and flipped itself around. It came back, slowly at first, then picking up speed. As it passed Rudy again, she jumped up and landed on the hammer like it was a skateboard. When it got close to Thor, he raised his hand above his head so the hammer was going at an angle mimicking that of a ramp. Before it could smack into the thunder god's hand, Rudy leapt up. The momentum shot her up into the air where she did a flip and landed like a cat.

"Awesome," I said.

"Dad's been doing that with me since I could walk. We call it riding the lightning. Asgardian slang for doing something really brave or extremely stupid," Rudy said. "You want to try, T-Belle?"

"Heck yeah, if Thor doesn't mind," I said.

"Why not?" Thor said.

Rudy grabbed me and dragged me across the field, holding my hand like we were a couple of schoolgirls. As we've gotten closer, I've learned more about Rudy's childhood. Nowhere near as brutal as mine, but she was put in what passed for Valkyrie school as a young girl. In Asgard, they didn't have things like summer vacation and spring break or six hour days. And corporal punishment was a given. My childhood was torn from me at eleven, but Rudy didn't have much of one at all. I'm rarely giddy or anything approaching it, but around Rudy I'm about as close as I get. She is one of the few people I know who can actually make me giggle. Maybe it's because after her attack, we have that tragedy in common. Whatever the reason, our dark and serious boss finds the rare times when we've giggled on the job disturbing.

We stopped in the field and turned back.

"Ready?" Thor shouted.

I gave him the thumbs up sign and he threw the hammer. It passed me, then turned around. I leapt for it, got one foot on it and fell off. I turned and raced after it, but it sped up. I leapt for all I was worth and my toe just grazed the handle. I landed on the ground and walked back.

"The easiest time to jump on is the moment after it's turned around, because it stops," Rudy said.

I gave Thor the thumbs up and he tossed it again. I listened to what Rudy said. I ran to it and leapt on it as soon as it stopped. Problem is, it hadn't turned and when it flipped over, it tossed me on my butt.

Rudy giggled and I glared, which only made her giggle more.

"You want me to show you how to do it again?" she said.

"No, I don't. I'll get it on my own," I said. "Third time is the charm. Let's go again."

Thor was chuckling as he threw his hammer. This time I waited until after it turned around before I jumped. I landed with my left foot on the hammer, my right on the handle. It was slow at first, which let me adjust my footing. I was determined that I wasn't going anywhere.

And I didn't, but that was only good for so long. As I got closer to Thor, I realized I was so intent on figuring a way to stay on that I hadn't figured out how to get off.

Thor realized this and didn't lift his hand up. Instead he put it low and in front. As soon as the hammer hit his hand I became airborne and slammed into him, which should have been like hitting a brick wall. Instead, Thor went limp and fell back onto the ground, cushioning my fall.

I landed on top of him in what at another time could be considered an intimate position.

He felt good under me, so I lingered a bit. "Come here often?"

"Surprisingly not as often as one might think," he replied.

"A pity," I said as I pushed myself up.

"Which? Having to move or my unfortunate lack of certain kinds of activity?" he said.

I looked over at Rudy, who even across the field was glaring with her hands on her hips.

"A little of both. Thanks for being my air bag," I said.

"Anytime. Next time, remember to jump.

I did and it was beautiful. I had enough momentum to fly. It wasn't far, but even a little air time on my own is beyond wonderful.

"There are many kinds of celebrations. A soldier should enjoy them all, whenever the opportunity arises because soldiers don't always live until tomorrow."

    -Daemor saying

We returned to Thor's farmhouse over an hour later. I was slightly battered and bruised, but happy. Riding the lightning was fun. I figured we'd be calling it a night, but the god of thunder had other ideas.

"So are you young ladies ready to head out for a night on the town?"

Rudy and I looked at each other and then back at Thor. "Sure." we said in unison.

My last visit here had been for Thanksgiving with the rest of the team. It was a brief overnight stay. This go round was for the whole weekend and was just the Valkyrie and me. The stories of Thor's partying have been legendary for thousands of years. I've seen Rudy party and she's started a few legends of her own in New York City. The girl can drink entire groups under the table and even she admits that she can't come anywhere near what her father can do. Even though I wasn't a big partier myself, how could I turn down what was sure to be a night to remember with the lord of thunder himself?

"So where are we going? Seedy pub, some international drinking contest or maybe a place that is known for epic bar fights?" I said.

Thor smiled. "Even better than that. Karaoke night at Snake's!"

Okay, I admit it. My jaw dropped. The last thing I expected from someone with Thor's reputation was a night of singing into a microphone.

Thor had a pickup truck, but it didn't have the extended cab. He walked across the street to get Isabella to join us. She rode with him in the cab, which meant Rudy and I were in the back end.

We rode past Mr. Needles' farm. He was outside fixing his fence and waved to us.

Thor stopped the truck. "Evening Ray, heard you had some fun with my goats."

"I did indeed. It was fantastic. The best time I've had in ages. I'm not as young as I used to be, but give me a couple days to rest up and you send those goats back. I want to see if I can catch 'em without the little lady's help next time," said Needles.

"I'm sure they'll enjoy the challenge. We are heading down to Snake's Bar. You care to join us?"

Needles paused for a second then looked out of the corner of his eyes at me. "I'd love to. I will hop in my newly cleaned truck as soon as I'm finished here."

"See you there then," Thor said.

As we pulled away Rudy leaned over and whispered in my ear. "Looks like you've got yourself a gentleman admirer. Wonder if Murphy or Joe will be jealous?"

"Very funny," I said. I wished Murphy would be jealous and to be honest Joe might be, but I wasn't so sure Needles was actually interested in me. And he was a little old for me.

With a name like Snake's, I was expecting a dive. It wasn't. It was owned by a guy called Snake and had been a seedy dive for years until the place ran into some financial trouble. Snake's daughter offered to help out and save the place. In doing so, she gave it a makeover, turning it into a place that folks with money to spend on drinking wouldn't be scared to go into.

According to the sign on the door they had trivia night, game night and of course karaoke night, which was already in full swing when we arrived. They had a TV screen that listed the singer's name and song. Some guy named Joe McKeon was pouring his heart into the song, but I really wasn't buying him as a love machine, but it didn't stop him from trying to convince the audience.

A woman name Viper, the daughter of Snake, came around and took our orders. Another singer finished telling us he was too sexy for his cat among other things before she came back with the drinks. Isabella got a strawberry daiquiri, Thor had what looked like a mini keg with a handle on it. It was bigger than his head. Rudy had a line of a dozen drinks that included four jello shots, an Alabama slammer and a Blue Whale. Needles' and I had beer, although mine was of the light variety. I'd taken in enough calories for one day. A clipboard came around and everyone at the table started signing up for a chance to get up and make a fool of themselves.

"T-Belle, what are you going to sing?" Thor asked.

"I'm not really much for singing," I said.

Thor grinned. "Singing? Who said anything about singing? It's karaoke. There's a difference." Which was true. I'd been to karaoke at Bulfinche's Pub. Having witnessed just a few song selections at Snake's, I could state without fear of contradiction that the mystic and non-mystic communities had a lot in common when it came to karaoke. Each had people who enjoyed singing without any discernible talent, but with plenty of enthusiasm.

I hated to admit it, but Thor was right. It wasn't about how good a singer somebody was, but about how passionately they belted out a tune and how much fun they had doing it.

"No one expects you to be able to do it well. That would just be a bonus," Thor said.

"You could dedicate your song to my dad and sing 'You Are the Wind Beneath My Wings'," Rudy said with an evil grin, remembering the amulet I won off Thor.

"Rudy, did anyone ever tell you that you're hilarious? Because if they did, they were lying to you," I said.

Viper came back bringing refills for Thor and Rudy without even being asked. Thor was a regular and apparently Rudy had been here before. Thor was floating a tab for the group. Viper looked at me not signing the clipboard. "Well, we do have rules here on karaoke night. Anyone who comes in the door has to sing. You don't want to sing or join in the fun, you have to leave. You can do it as part of a group if you like."

I rolled my eyes.

Rudy grabbed the clipboard and scribbled her name and mine along with a song title. I took the clipboard and looked at what she wrote. "'Bullet With Butterfly Wings?' You've got to be kidding me."

"How about 'Brick House'?" she said.

"Funny," I said. Because of my extreme proportions, I have been called a brick house and worse.

The guy who sang about being a love machine came up and high fived Thor. The god's red hair suddenly took on blonde highlights.

I leaned over to Rudy. "What just happened to your dad's hairdo?"

"Joe McKeon's a comic geek. Nice guy, but big time into the comic Thor. That representation of him is blond and there are a lot of people who know about it. Gives dad a lot of extra power, but geeks like Joe tend to focus all that energy. Around them Dad's hair tends to get a little lighter."

Made sense I guess. Few of the old gods had worshippers, but could still pull manna from humans knowing about them. Popular culture only helped matters out and made Thor one of the most powerful gods still around.

Needles was the first of us to get called. He did some old country tune I never heard of called 'Dropkick Me Jesus through the Goalposts of Life.' He actually did some sort of skipping motions and a couple of yee haws for good measure.

Next up, Thor and Isabella did a duet. It was only Thor's first number.

He had signed himself up for no less than seven turns.

The song they chose was "Don't Go Breaking My Heart."

Isabella could carry a tune, but I wouldn't say Thor was a great singer. He had a low booming voice, not unlike thunder. What he lacked in skill he certainly made up with enthusiasm. In the middle of the song a group of men came into the bar looking for trouble. Trouble tried to sneak out the back, but was drunk and fell at our feet. Typical.

I tapped Rudy on the leg and motioned with my head for her to look at the door. Twenty men wearing Hogg Huns colors were filing into the bar.

I guess maybe our biker friends didn't learn their lesson back on the Taconic.

The first one in was a mountain of a man with long black hair and a matching beard. He had on a leather vest and his exposed arms were so filled with tattoos that I couldn't spot any uninked skin. The guy was probably even bigger than Thor. My money would be on him being the gang's leader.

"I think it's a little too late for that when you've already went and broke my heart," the big man said interrupting the song.

"You tell her, Mayhem," another one of the bikers shouted.

"You led me on. You promised me love and security and then you tore it all away," Mayhem said, with a mix of intimidation and mocking in his tone.

Isabella had stopped singing as soon as she noticed the men. The poor woman had actually started to tremble.

With the microphone still at her mouth, she said, "We were pen pals when you were in prison. Everything you told me was a lie. When I found out the truth, I wanted nothing to do with you and I still don't."

"That don't excuse how you treated me. I deserve to be compensated for my heartbreak and my time. I know you got money. You give me ten grand and I'll go away," Mayhem said.

"I'll give you a countdown of ten to go away," Thor said, frowning.

Mayhem looked at Thor and realized he wouldn't be a pushover, but wasn't intimidated. After all, he had nineteen other guys watching his back. "You must be the new man in Isabella's life. Red, man to man, I'm warning you that it's only a matter of time before she breaks your heart too. Some women are just built that way. Her name should be Jezebel, not Isabella."

"Three. Two. One," Thor said. "You're still here?"

Snake and his daughter moved up to Mayhem with baseball bats, but the other members of the gang stepped up and the two of them backed away slowly.

"I told you I need to be compensated," Mayhem said. It was obvious this was some new twist on the extortion game.

"You took advantage of a lonely, widowed woman with sweet talk and lies until she saw through it and you're upset over it. Get over it and get gone," Thor said.

"Tough guy, huh? You going to get rid of all of us?" Mayhem said.

"So not only are you a liar, but now you're a coward? Too afraid to take me on by yourself, so you've got to bring a whole bunch of friends?" Thor said, his smile and easy going manner confusing the bikers. Most people would be afraid and looking for a way out at this point, not pushing matters.

"Are you challenging me to a fight?" Mayhem asked.

"I'm not sure how much of a challenge it would be, but yes," Thor said.

"Since you seem to be making this a duel, what kind of contest should this be?" the biker asked.

Thor jumped down from the stage and grabbed Mayhem as if he was going to tango with him.

"Dance contest?" Thor asked.

"No," Mayhem said, trying to push Thor away, but he couldn't break the thunder god's grip.

"Oh well," Thor said as he spun Mayhem around twice and then let go. The biker spun out the door and out of the bar. Thor turned to wink at Snake and his daughter. They nodded their thanks back. A bar fight would wreck their place, which is why the thunder god took it outside.

Thor followed Mayhem outside with a mess of bikers on his heels. I was more interested in Ponytail and his two friends who were bellying up to the bar, choosing not to join the rest of the Huns. Rudy looked at them and at her dad.

"Go," I said. "I got this."

"Give me a beer and a shot of whiskey. And a bag of ice for my hand," Ponytail said. "I've had a hell of a day."

"And it's not over yet," I said. "What did I tell you would happen if we ever met again?"

"Listen sister, I've had a rough time and I don't need some skank giving me grief," he said as he turned toward me. When he saw my face, his jaw dropped. "I didn't know it was you. I didn't even know you would be here."

"Pity. You should have looked inside first," I said slamming my fist into my open palm. Ponytail and his two friends bolted out the door.

Viper gave me a raised eyebrow and a wry smile. "Friends of yours?"

"Pretty close to the opposite of that," I said and followed them out.

The Norse god and the biker were facing off in the parking lot. Ponytail and his two friends tried to make their way around the crowd of bikers to get away from me. And they were trying to do it casually so none of their biker buddies would see them fleeing from a woman with pink hair.

"You want to have a what?" Mayhem said, confused at whatever Thor had suggested.

"A joust. Like with knights of old, only using motorcycles instead of horses," Thor said.

"You got a bike?" Mayhem asked.

Thor shook his head. "Got a truck."

"If you think I'm going play a game of chicken with you in a truck and me on a bike, you've got another thing coming. And we sure as hell ain't loaning you a bike."

"Fair enough. How about we make it interesting then. You get the bike. I'll just stand on my own two feet. You get to try to run me over and knock me down," Thor said.

"I though knights used lances," Mayhem said.

"You're welcome to use one if you have one. If you don't, there are a couple of 2x4's over in that dumpster that you're welcome to have at. I hope you will allow me to use this to defend myself," Thor pulled out his tiny hammer, holding it between his thumb and forefinger.

Every biker laughed.

"Let me get this straight. You're going to let me ride my bike with a 2 x 4 in my hand, which I will use to run you down or knock you over and all you're going to use is a Cracker Jack toy?" Mayhem asked.

"I wouldn't call it a toy. It's a hammer, but I guess you can call it a toy if it makes you feel better. So do we have a deal?" Thor said.

"Hell, yeah. This is going to be fun," Mayhem said, rubbing his hands together.

The road outside Snake's Bar was largely deserted at this time of night. Thor took up a position on the blacktop near the far exit of the bar's parking lot. Mayhem rode off about a quarter of a mile down the road.

"We need a lovely lady to start us off. Rudy, would you do the honors?" Thor asked.

"Sure, Dad." Rudy grabbed a bandana out of the pocket of one of the bikers and went halfway between the two men. She raised her hands above her head and brought the bandana down. "Go!"

Mayhem had propped the eight foot long piece of wood underneath his armpit and on the bars of his bike. He sped down the road, aiming the end of the piece of lumber directly at Thor. The thunder god didn't flinch at the approaching danger. Instead the hammer grew in his hands to full size. When the bike was about twenty feet away the thunder god threw Mjollnir. The hammer went straight into the bike's headlight and kept on going, pulverizing the metal into dust as it hit. The bike stopped short as if it had hit a brick wall, but Mayhem didn't.

The biker flew forward and into Thor's outstretched left hand. He caught and held the biker over his head. The hammer kept going for a good half mile and then turned around and came back. Thor lifted his right hand over his head and the hammer smacked right into it with enough force to crush a human skull. The thunder god just smiled.

"That was fun. Why don't you grab another bike and we'll go again?" Thor said.

At this point I lost track of what Thor was doing because of some commotion behind me. I had stopped to watch what was happening on the road, but still kept an eye on Ponytail and crew. The biker was sneaking up behind me with a knife in his hand. I saw him coming, but decided to let him get closer. We had done this dance already, but I guess he figured he was safe from my wings since I had my long yellow coat on.

His mistake.

As Ponytail stepped within striking range, one of my wings shot out and cut his wrist again, making him drop the knife. My trench coat had special Velcro openings that I had undone the moment the bikers walked into the bar, like a cop loosening the strap on a holster.

I had shredded enough clothes using my wings to defend myself that I finally came up with the bright idea to start designing them with defense in mind. Bruce, my tailor down in the Village, did a great job putting a few coats together for me. He was having some trouble doing the same with my bulletproof ones though. Body armor makes it more of a challenge.

Ponytail screamed, but I hadn't touched him. I spun to face him, but before I could connect my fist with his face, Needles was there. The old man acted like he was back at the rodeo and put the biker's hands behind his back and took him down to his knees. Needles planted a booted foot in the biker's back and kicked him onto his stomach. He held an extension cord he must have grabbed from inside the bar and used it to hogtie the biker.

"That ain't no way to treat a lady, Hoss," Needles said. "I think you best apologize."

Which is when the biker's two friends grabbed a hold of Needles arms and yanked him off Ponytail.

Needles pulled away from one with an elbow to the gut. Not one to let a man or anyone else fight my battles for me, I joined in by leveling an uppercut to Bushy's jaw, knocking him down. I took Longbeard and threw him over the heads of the other bikers. A few of them turned to look back at me. Now I had their attention and none looked happy. In retrospect, it was probably not the best place to have tossed him.

Several bikers moved toward me. More appeared torn about whether they should risk helping out their leader or coming after little old me. I was the easier target, so about eight of them encircled me, looking tough and trying for bad ass. They succeed, but I could do bad ass too.

I took my jacket off. The sight of my wings made them stop short and exchange confused looks. Not realizing what the wings could do, they pulled their guns and knives and kept coming toward me.

Great. I'm good, but not good enough to beat eight armed men without major risk of getting shot. As Thor was still busy and Rudy was watching him, I was left to deal with the eight gunmen by my lonesome. Boy, I wished I packed the bulletproof coat. On days like this, I swear I'll never leave home without it. Then I end up lugging the extremely heavy thing around on a hot day, getting all sweaty and I forget about my vow until the next time I have a gun pointed in my face.

Of course, I wasn't exactly unarmed. I leapt sideways to draw them away from Needles as I pulled my gun. Nemesis was going to kill me if she had to come out to the boonies to deal with the state troopers if I actually shot any of these jokers. The gun had multiple types of ammo, including stun bullets, but the moment I pulled the trigger, so would they. Best save bullets of any kind as a last resort.

Across the way, Thor only had eyes for Mayhem, whom he was still holding off the ground. "We can still settle this like gentlemen, but you'll have to do a few things to make up for your transgressions here. First, you're going have to buy the bar a round," Thor said. Mayhem answered by punching him in the jaw. Thor didn't move, didn't flinch, because apparently his head was even harder than mine. Mayhem yelled a second after contact. Even from where I was standing I heard the bones in the biker's wrist crack. Fortunately, so could the eight bikers coming after me and they turned to see what happened. I used the distraction to kick one in the knee, grab his gun and elbow him in the side of the head.

"So it's going to be like that, is it?" Thor said. "The hard way it is. All right, Hogg Hunnys, please give me your attention. Each of you is going to strip down to your birthday suits."

The seven bikers saw their laid out brother and decided I was the more immediate threat. They pointed their guns at me, then were smart enough to realize because they had encircled me any stray bullets might take out fellow Huns. Didn't stop them from pressing their attack though. Their fellows had also pointed their guns, but not at me.

A huge grin grew across Thor's face at the sight of the firearms. "Let me thank all of you so much for pulling your weapons. It means I won't feel so bad about doing this." Thor lifted the hammer above his head and out of a clear sky a lightning bolt shot down into his hammer and split into twenty jagged fragments, each of which zapped a different biker. The men convulsed and fell to the ground. Well, one was already there. Amazingly the lightning left Rudy, Needles and myself untouched.

Moans from the bikers filled the night air. The lightning had shocked them, but left them conscious. From the smile on Thor's face, it was on purpose. One of the prone bikers lifted his gun and pointed it at Thor. Another lightning bolt came down from the sky into his hand and out his back, blowing out flesh by making both entrance and exit wounds from the electric attack. The biker's eyes closed and didn't reopen. He was still breathing, so he was alive, but when he woke up probably will wish he wasn't. Electrical burns are nasty.

"Strip. Anyone who touches a weapon gets more of the same," Thor warned.

Mayhem wasn't doing as he was told, so Thor simply grabbed a hold of the head Hun's clothes and ripped them off. The biker screamed as the tearing fabric bit into his flesh.

"The lot of you are going to leave here and never return," Thor said.

One of the nude bikers said, "How are we supposed to ride our hogs naked?"

"That's easy. You aren't going to have your bikes anymore."

"That's not fair," the biker said.

Thor shrugged. "Neither is twenty grown men trying to extort money from one lone widow. I gave you to the count of ten. If you had listened, you could have rode off with your bikes, none of you the worse for wear. Now, I decide what happens. You are going to walk down that road and never come back again. You are not going to bother Isabella. As a matter of fact, you are never coming back to this town again because if you do, you're not going to leave. Have I made myself clear?"

Despite all that had happened, the bikers were used to fighting. They weren't going to give up their most prized possessions just because some guy with long red hair and a hammer told them too.

Thor realized this and swung his hammer over his head three times. A tornado, small at first, literally leapt off the top of the hammer and grew. It went down the parking lot, scattering bikers in its wake. Then it came to the portion of the lot where they all parked. The tornado went to the first bike and literally sucked it up into its funnel cloud. It went down the row repeating the process until every bike was in the twister, making it look like some sort of bizarre junkyard blender.

"Your bikes are now scrap." The tornado started moving down the road. "I could easily call the tornado back and then you could join your bikes if you prefer to leave town that way."

The tornado had also gathered all their clothes into a single pile. A lightning bolt shot down into the heap, setting it on fire.

"No," Mayhem said, accepting he was outmuscled. As he shook his head, I realized that hair was falling out. And not only the hair off his head, but off his entire body. I scanned the lot and the other bikers were also suddenly bald. Their chests, legs and backs were as bare as that of a baby.

"Our hair! What the hell did you do to us?" Mayhem yelled.

"A little electrolysis is nothing compared to what I am going to do. Of course, I am willing to give you another count of ten to get out of here and bring those that can't walk with you. You came as a group, so you'll leave as a group."

"But…" Mayhem said. Thor threw him down the road and he landed so his bare back and backside got some fairly serious road rash.

"Nine. Eight."

The naked bikers got up, carrying their wounded brethren and started running down the road. By the time Thor got to one, they were just about out of sight.

It would have been perfect if Thor's idea of celebrating our victory hadn't involved him, Rudy, Needles, and I going back inside and actually singing the song "Celebration."

"Knowledge is the most powerful of weapons in the right mind."
-Daemor saying

I'm fond of libraries, just not so early in the morning. I would have enjoyed things much more at a later hour, although everybody else in the place seemed to be okay with the unreasonable time of 9 am. Not that I wasn't normally up by this time on work days. It's just we had a late night of it. After Thor sent the bikers running, there was karaoke and more karaoke.

We were singing on stage until after four in the morning. And by we, I mean I was dragged up there more than once. Still nobody's ears seemed the worse for wear. When we got back to Thor's place, he, of course, had to make us a huge early breakfast. I didn't get to sleep until seven and they woke me up at eight. I wouldn't have even moved if not for the smell of Thor cooking brunch.

Lack of sleep does not make Terrorbelle a happy camper. Not that anyone else seemed the worse for wear.

And we were raising money for a good cause, the local public library.

When I came to Earth from Faerie there were a lot of things that I found odd or amazing. Sometimes both. One of those things was public libraries. In Faerie, books are extremely rare and the idea that someone would loan one out to anyone who asked seemed absurd. Yet there it was.

I was lucky in that Gani helped mystically teach me many Earth customs and languages, as well as being able to read English. My first few weeks in New York, I spent most of my free time reading. That is until I discovered TV. Not that I stopped reading by any means, I just split my time. TV was a window onto my new home.

I still had a soft spot for libraries. The big one downtown with the stone lions was my favorite. It seemed shocking to me that any library would have to have a fundraiser, that people who lived in the community it served wouldn't reliably fund it. Such was not the case.

Thor had made fifty varieties of cookies and twenty varieties of cupcakes. Each one was better than the last. The cookies were two for a dollar and the cupcakes a buck a piece, which in my opinion was underselling them. This stuff was better than the gourmet shops in Manhattan. And they could get upwards of five bucks a cookie.

The bake sale itself was not actually in the library. The town building was huge and housed the town hall, town court, constable's office, the volunteer fire department –of which Thor was a member – and the library. The place had a long three pronged shaped hall that lead to each of those sections. There were three main entrances into the place, so tables with baked goods were set up at each. I was given the back door and a table full of one hundred cookies to sell. The cupcakes were apparently for the front table only.

Several people looking as groggy as I felt walked by and ignored me and the cookies, on their way to their jobs. Not paying attention to me I could understand, but to not notice the way those cookies smelt? Something had to be wrong with them.

"Morning, little lady," Needles said, as he moseyed my way from the front of the building.

"Good morning, Mr. Needles," I said.

"I told you to call me Ray," he said. "How ya feeling this fine morning?"

"Tired," I said.

Needles leaned in to get a closer look at my eyes. "You don't look hung over at all. I like a lady that can hold her liquor."

"I didn't have much to drink." I didn't really. With my pixie metabolism, it takes more than a little bit to get me drunk and my size doesn't hurt either.

"I heard you were helping out the library and I thought I would do my part. How much for the cookies?"

"Two for a dollar," I said.

"No little lady, you misunderstand me. How much for the entire table?" he said.

"Fifty bucks," I said.

Needles pulled out his wallet and handed me a crisp new fifty dollar bill. "I'll take them all then."

"Thank you," I said. "I'll pack them up for you."

As I started putting them back in the box I had just taken them out of, the back door opened and a leather wearing woman rode in up the steps and through the door on a custom built motorcycle. I was impressed that the doors were wide enough to let the sidecar through. I pulled Needles back out of the way and the biker woman gave me a wink as she rode by and down the hallway. Her head sported a biker helmet with molded metal wings attached to the side.

"Is that another one of them bikers from last night?" Needles asked, puffing up like he was getting ready to do battle.

"No, we know her. She's a friend," I said. Although I had no idea what Mista the Valkyrie was doing here.

I quickly followed in her wake.

Thor and Isabella had taken up the bake sale station at the front door of the town hall. Mista made straight for them, or at least Thor, riding right up to him.

"Excuse me miss, there are no motor vehicles inside the town hall. Please take your bike outside," Isabella said politely.

"I'll take it out when I'm good and ready to take it out," Mista said. Her tone was not belligerent, more boarding on aloof. Apparently there were not enough winged horses to go around, so Odin had arranged for some of the Valkyries to get flying motorcycles instead. Mista was the only one to be allowed both, but she preferred the cycle. "Thor, I bring tidings from your father."

"That's nice Mista, but the lady asked you to take your bike outside."

"Excuse me?" the Valkyrie said, not seeming to process the simple request.

"Isabella told you motorcycles are not allowed in the building and to park it outside. When you have done that I will be happy to hear about the tidings," Thor said. Mista sat on her bike, apparently too stunned to move. "Is there a problem?"

Mista shook her head. "No problem." She revved up the engine and started to drive off, but Thor put a hand on the front handlebars stopping it in its path.

"There are people trying to work here. And I don't need you to get into trouble with the local constable. He is actually a nice guy. Turn off the engine and walk it out. Please and thank you," Thor said.

The Valkyrie did as instructed.

"Terrorbelle dear, we are okay up here. You can go back to your station," Isabella said.

I held up the fifty dollar bill. "Actually I'm sold out thanks to Mr. Needles." I turned to Thor. "What does Mista want?"

"I haven't the slightest idea. This is one of the reasons I don't have a cell phone. People tend to save up the important stuff and send a messenger, so nobody bothers me with all the picayune nonsense."

Rudy came from her station on the other side of the town hall. "I thought I heard a motorcycle. Those bikers from last night aren't back, are they?"

"No, one of your spear sisters is here with a message," Thor said.

Rudy frowned.

A minute later Mista walked back in the building. The Valkyrie was always pretty easy going, but then I realized I only knew her in relation to spending time with the folks at Bulfinche's Pub. The way Paddy ran the place tends to bring out people's better natures.

Mista had returned with an attitude so big that the two of them almost didn't fit through the door. As she got closer to the god of thunder, who was effectively the second highest ranking god in the Norse Pantheon, it was obvious Mista was doing her best to rein it in.

She had been the leader of the Valkyries until recently and her demotion still stuck in her craw.

Mista stopped in front of the table that was covered with baked goods and reached down to pluck a cookie off the plate and flipped it into her mouth. "Delicious," Mista said.

"And fifty cents," Isabella said.

Mista did a slow turn to glare at the woman.

"Excuse me?" Mista said.

Isabella pointed to the bake sale sign listing the prices. "We are raising money for the library. You ate a cookie, so you owe the library fifty cents."

"I don't have time for this. I have a message for Thor from his father," Mista said. "It's important."

"So is raising money for the library," Isabella said.

Mista sighed loudly rolled her eyes back in her head and took her wallet out of her pocket to hand Isabella a twenty. "Keep the change. I might feel peckish before I leave and grab some more."

"Thank you very much," Isabella said with a smile.

Mista stood in front of Thor, bowed her head and beat her fist against her large chest. Nowhere near as large as mine, but still impressive. "Lord Thor, as I have said, I bring you a message from your father. Is there some place we can go to speak in private?"

"Everyone here knows. You can just tell me," Thor said.

Mista nodded. "There is trouble in Valhalla. Father Odin has summoned you back to Asgard."

"Has Loki escaped? Has Twilight begun?" Thor said, color actually draining from his face. Norse gods, unlike most of the rest of us, knew exactly how they were going to die. It was the when that was troublesome.

"No, my Lord. There is something … altogether different. I can take us on my bike immediately."

"Nonsense, I will take my chariot. You can return and tell Odin that his favorite son will be arriving shortly."

"And his favorite granddaughter, too," Rudy said. "Terrorbelle, you want to come?"

I've done many things and been to many places in my life, but I had never visited the home to a pantheon of gods. "I'd love to."

Mista frowned. "No offense guys, but I think it's best if just Thor came."

"Excuse me?" Rudy said with serious uptown attitude. "No one tells me when I can and can't go home."

"And Terrorbelle is a friend to us all and as such is welcome in Asgard," Thor said.

"Thor, it really would be best if you came alone," Mista said.

"Why?" Thor asked.

Mista blushed and looked at her boots. "I am not at liberty to divulge that."

"Then Rudy and Terrorbelle will be coming with me. End of discussion."

"Very well. I will return and give Odin the news," Mista said.

Mista exited the same doorway she came in, but with much less attitude. In fact, I'd say her body language now projected great sadness and I had no idea why.

"Isabella, I am sorry but I'm going to have to bow out on the bake sale," Thor said.

"Of course. We all have families we need to take care of. Thank you so much for last night," Isabella said.

"It was my pleasure, literally," Thor said. He wasn't kidding. On my way to the bathroom, I saw Isabella doing a walk of shame from the shower to Thor's bedroom, only she seemed more thrilled than embarrassed. "I'll stay until you can get replacements."

Isabella made some phone calls and a few minutes later a couple of ladies showed up to handle the tables. The pair exchanged a kiss and we left to the giggles of middle-aged women who were impressed by their friend's love life.

"You can go home again, but when I do I always end up asking myself why I bothered."
-Thor, Norse thunder god

Thor tried to play it like being called home was no big deal, but it was obvious from his change in mood that it troubled him. We made it back to his place in record time. Rudy and I even got to ride in the cab this time.

We climbed out of the truck and started looking around for the two horned troublemakers. They were nowhere to be seen.

"Do you want me to round up Nasher and Grinder?" I asked.

"No need." Thor said, putting his right thumb and index finger in his mouth and blowing out a shrill whistle that seemed louder than it should have been. Seconds later the two goats were overhead and landing in front of us.

"We are going home, boys. Get ready," Thor said. The two goats went into the barn and somehow managed to get on their own harnesses.

Thor also went into the barn and rolled out what looked suspiciously like a mini-parade float that was painted with lightning bolts on the side like an old time car.

"That's your chariot?" I asked, without being able to stop from snickering.

The thunder god shrugged. "Have to keep with the times."

"So when does the marching band get here?" I said.

"Sadly, it's their day off," Thor replied. "So Terrorbelle, would you like to ride with me or with Rudy on Morningdour?"

The redheaded Valkyrie was in the process of saddling up her winged horse. She would put one strap on and the horse would undo another. At one point the horse even got one strap on Rudy's holster loosened.

I shook my head. They were like a couple of kids. However, I wasn't real keen on going on horseback. Morningdour and I had a little bit of a history. She was a good horse, but she was mischievous just like her owner. Nowhere near as bad as the goats, but she liked to pull aerial stunts which made me nervous, especially on Earth. Like I've said, if I fall off from high enough up, my wings won't do me much good.

"I'd never ridden in the chariot of a god before or the parade float of one for that matter. I'll give it a try," I said.

Rudy climbed on Morningdour and Thor and I stepped on his parade float. The animals all lifted up into the air. All three of them were special not only in that they could fly, but in that they had the ability to travel between dimensions.

It's something I've done before, but usually using a portal or a path. Traveling between Faerie and Earth is as simple as walking. Well not exactly, as passing the veil between the worlds can make one extremely sick. I had a tendency to puke afterwards which is why I snuck a plastic garbage bag from underneath Thor's sink and put it in my pocket. I figured it would do as a dimension sick bag.

The animals flew for a little bit with Morningdour leading the way. We picked up speed and then the world faded away, replaced by rainbow kaleidoscope lines that passed by us. Then things began to slow and we hovered over the most gigantic and solid looking rainbow I'd ever seen. I had heard of Bifrost, the Rainbow Bridge, but this wasn't exactly what I expected. Each color shone with its own inner light, brighter than neon, yet a man stood atop it without falling.

Damn good trick.

I had a trick of my own, although I'm not sure how good it was, but I made the contents of my stomach disappear by leaning over the side rail. With a quiet heave I lost most of my delicious breakfast, brunch and a cupcake, all of which simply fell off into what seemed like a never ending darkness that surrounded the rainbow.

I knew the watchman, which didn't necessarily make it okay for him to laugh at my weak stomach. His name was Heimdal and he's Mista's significant other. He's spent some time at Bulfinche's Pub as well. Even worked there during prohibition from what I've been told. Had something to do with Thor ticking off his dad and getting a punishment that involved guarding the Rainbow Bridge. It was a task made even more difficult by the fact that he is too dense to stand on it. From what Rudy told me, it was after that her dad began to spend most of his time on Earth.

"Hello to the horse and to the parade float," Heimdal said with a smile.

"Any fool can see it's a chariot," Thor said with a grin.

"Fortunately I'm not just any fool," Heimdal said.

"Any idea why I'm being called home?" Thor said.

Heimdal nodded. "I am forbidden to speak of such matters."

"That bad?" Thor said.

Heimdal made a fist and nodded it up and down. It was American sign language for yes. One of the patrons of Bulfinche's Pub was Judah Maccabee, a mute golem who communicated by sign language. Very few of us were fluent, but we all knew a few signs. I guess he had been forbidden to speak of it, but not to sign about it. Apparently Thor didn't trust Mista's answers so he asked some questions again.

"Is Loki free?" Heimdal placed his index and middle fingers together and made a motion of a snapping alligator with his thumb, the sign for no. "Not Twilight?" Heimdal repeated the sign. "Am I in some sort of trouble?" Heimdal made the yes sign. "Odd, since I haven't done anything of late. Sorry you couldn't tell me anything."

"Me too, but I had to follow my orders. Watch your back on this one," Heimdal said.

Thor simply nodded and snapped the reins on his goats and we flew along the rainbow. The Rainbow Bridge is not exactly like the many different ones that connect Manhattan to other parts of the city and Jersey. For one thing, Bifrost is much longer. At the start you can't see the end. It would probably take the greater part of a day to walk it, if you could figure out some way of managing it. Heimdal let me pass because of who I was with. Otherwise, I might not have gotten by so easily.

Of course not everyone had to walk. I spotted a female adaro, which was basically a mermaid that was able to swim in rainbows. This one was blonde and wearing what looked like a sports bra. She was doing leaps and jumps in and out of Bifrost.

There was a cry that made the hairs on the back of my neck stand up and my blood run cold. I looked up to see a giant bird, larger than a roc, dive bombing us. Or more specifically at Rudy and Morningdour.

"Damn winged monsters! I haven't seen a cornu this near the Rainbow Bridge in ages," Thor said pulling his hammer from his pocket, but it was taking too long to grow and the bird was almost on the Valkyrie and her mount.

The red horse spun in a barrel roll while Rudy pulled her Nemesis & Co. issue gun. It is a very special automatic, filled with hundreds of rounds of magical ammunition. The guns are genetically coded to the users and we're able to switch rounds just by thinking about it. Rudy fired off a flare round followed by an explosive round. The first round froze the bird. As it tried to see again, the second round hit it and knocked it for a loop. It must have had a very thick hide. I didn't see any blood, just a couple of feathers. It flew away from Rudy, but toward the flying parade float. By this time Thor had Mjollnir fully sized and it crackled with lightning. The bird pulled up in mid dive and flew off, wisely deciding not to press its attack.

"Damn vermin," Thor said.

But the cornu hadn't given up yet. It was heading now for the rainbow's swimming mermaid.

"Look out!" I screamed. Apparently it was enough for the adaro to look up and dive beneath the rainbow. The talons of the cornu raked the surface of the Rainbow Bridge but came away empty. "We have to help her!"

"Help an adaro? If a cornu gets them, it's just a predator taking its prey," Thor said. "It's the cycle of nature. Not something to get involved in."

"So you're not going to help her?" I said, shocked. Thor had always struck me as someone who stood up for the little guy. He didn't answer me. "Thor, I'm really disappointed in you." I dropped my coat to the bottom of the flying parade float and started my wings beating. I lifted off into the air. I smiled. Asgard was a magic rich realm, unlike Earth.

Which meant I could fly.

With my gun in hand I flew straight towards the cornu.

Unlike the giant bird of prey, I wasn't about to announce my intentions with a battle cry. In the case of the cornu, its screech was designed to frighten and momentarily immobilize its prey, making them easier to catch. This thing wasn't going to be scared of me. It was hovering above the Rainbow Bridge, waiting. The half woman's head broke the surface of the rainbow long enough for her to check if the creature was gone. It wasn't and that was the reaction it was waiting for as it dove down from behind. The fish woman couldn't see it.

I aimed my gun to shoot it, but hesitated. If I missed, whatever round I used was going to keep going. It might hit the woman and it would definitely hit the Rainbow Bridge. If the thing was fragile enough that Thor couldn't stand on it, I had no idea what an explosive round would do. I was pretty sure cutting off the link between Earth and Asgard, however well intentioned, was probably a hanging offense here.

I reached my arms out in front of me and tucked my wings down in back. The idea was to be as streamlined as possible so I could dive bomb my way into the conflict as fast as possible.

I got between the cornu and the fish woman, having angled my attack so I passed the bird beast under its neck with my wings out all the way to the side. My wings are razor sharp and as hard as steel and I hoped I'd cut its throat so it either died or flew off.

I barely nicked it. The feathers were tough and layered like chain mail armor. I had to flap my wings furiously to pull out of the dive before I hit the bridge. I managed it barely and spun around to face the cornu. Its attention had been successfully diverted from the adaro and was fully focused on me.

I'm a quick study. Always have been. It's helped me survive horrible situations and move up the ranks of Mab's Army to become a Daemor. It's one of the reasons why Nemesis hired me as one of her three agents.

From my observation of the winged monster, I knew it was a stronger flier than I was. It was also faster in the long haul. However, it didn't have my maneuverability. Its wings flapped and caught air currents while mine worked more like that of a hummingbird or a bumble bee. That made it easier for me to hover and change direction. I held my position long enough for it to come at me and I waited until it got close enough that I was sure I wouldn't miss and fired three armor piercing rounds, aiming for its eye, mouth and throat where I cut it. I was pleased to see all three bullets hit their targets. I'm a good markswoman, but even a great markswoman can miss. The blow to its eye made blood spurt out. The one to its mouth was covered up when its beak closed so I couldn't tell if it did any damage, but the bullet that hit the wound did little or nothing except knock loose a couple more feathers.

My assault didn't slow it down, so I had to dive out of its way. Then it stole a trick from my book and lashed its wing out at me as it passed. The blow knocked me for a loop and sent me plummeting straight for the Rainbow Bridge. Unable to get my wings moving in time, I braced for impact.

Instead of hitting hard, I plunged into the rainbow. The adaro was right there. I was guessing whatever part of its magical power allowed it to swim in the rainbow softened it so I went inside instead of landing on top. Unfortunately, swimming in a rainbow was no better for me than swimming in water. My body is so dense I sink.

I had barely entered Bifrost when I started plunging downward. The fish woman swam after me and grabbed hold of my hand that wasn't holding my gun. She pulled me to the surface. I grabbed a quick breath and lifted my gun above my head just in time to see the cornu coming at us talons first. I let off two explosive rounds and pushed us back into the bridge. Even through the multi-colored energy filled liquid, I could still feel the explosions, although they were muffled. I motioned for her to take us to the surface again. Our heads were both above the surface of the bridge. I had a translation spell that I used in Faerie that I never deactivate, but it turns out she spoke English.

"Can you push me up there so I can get it?" I said.

"Are you crazy? It will kill you," she said.

"That's not going to happen," I said with far more confidence than I felt.

She looked at me, then the giant bird of prey. "I can do it. Take a deep breath."

I did and she took me down to the lower level of the bridge and swam incredibly fast until we broke the surface. The adaro tossed me at the height of our arc. It took several seconds of my wings beating to get rid of the remnants of the liquid rainbow I had been swimming in. The cornu was already flying my way. I rushed towards him in an aerial game of chicken. I had no illusions of the cornu breaking off first. If we hit, I'd be the one bouncing off and crashing down again. My goal was far simpler and more dangerous than that. I kept the angle of my approach so I was midway between talons and beak, which was made harder when the bird arched its body so that both of them had moved closer together and were aimed right at me. I braced for impact and tucked my wings in, using my inertia to glide right though the small area where none of its deadly appendages could reach. As I neared the beast's throat, I grabbed hold of some feathers with my left hand and swung so I landed on the back of its neck.

I slid my gun back into my holster and locked it in, then wrapped my right arm around the bird's neck. As big as it was, I still managed to almost reach my arms around it, but almost wasn't enough. I pulled my belt off. I use my Daemor badge as a belt buckle. It had the head of a raven on a silver background and several major magical charms. It was incredibly valuable, both sentimentally and tactically. Because of that, I didn't just use an everyday leather belt. I wore one that Gani had designed for me. It looked leather on the outside, but was incredibly strong. In an emergency, the leather coating could be taken off to expose a razor sharp edge and built in handles. I gripped as hard as I could with my legs and swung the belt around the neck catching the handle with my other hand. I pulled. I slid it back and forth to get rid of the leather. I got the sharpened edge underneath its armor-like feathers and I pulled. The bird shrieked in pain and I pulled some more, as tightly as I could, straining. I even started beating my wings to add to the fun. I felt the cartilage in what passed for its trachea snap, then crumble an instant before the belt blade sliced through its flesh.

With all I had left, I yanked as hard as I could and the belt blade cut a good foot into the neck flesh.

Holding onto the belt with my left hand, I reached for my gun and placed it against the bare flesh. I aimed so I wouldn't end up shooting myself and fired an armor piercing round.

With the dense feathers out of the way and the tissue cut, the bullet penetrated its flesh. I fired a second armor piercing round and then an explosive one. The shockwave made the bird quiver and bulge as it blew up from the inside out. The giant flying predator went limp.

I pulled my belt blade out as the cornu started to fall. I let go of the neck and it plummeted into seemingly endless darkness that lurked far beyond what Bifrost could light up.

Long ago I learned that magic makes monsters hard to kill. I hovered, waiting just in case it managed to somehow survive.

Nothing came up out of the darkness to attack me. Flying over to the Rainbow Bridge, I hovered and placed one foot gently on it. Now it was solid.

I stopped fluttering my wings and stood on the top of a rainbow. It didn't feel like solid ground. It was more akin to standing on a subway car made out of really thick gelatin. The magic poured off Bifrost to the point where it vibrated my teeth. I tried to step, but it was like that subway car was on a roller coaster track. Each step was worse than walking on a boat in rough seas. Probably a defense mechanism to ensure an army couldn't just walk up the bridge and invade Asgard easily.

The adaro came to the surface of the rainbow.

"I owe you my thanks for saving me from the creature. My name is Wanda. What are you called?"

In magical realms, it can be dangerous to give out one's name. My Daemor tag was Razorwing, so I gave her that.

"Well Razorwing, I owe you a debt. Should you ever have need of me whisper my name three times into any rainbow and I will come to your aid." The rainbow mermaid looked over my shoulder before diving down into the Rainbow Bridge and swimming off.

Morningdour and Thor's goats flew down.

"T-Belle, that was intense. Nicely done," Rudy said.

"Thanks and thanks for your help," I said. "Both of you."

In a none too subtle display of my displeasure, I flew up and sat on the back of Morningdour. Now that I could fly, I wasn't quite so afraid of falling off. Also I was strictly a short term flier. Flying longer distances really knocked me out, so I needed to conserve my energy. I was tired after battling with the monster bird, but wasn't about to go near Thor.

"Let's go," I said.

Rudy looked back at her dad, made an apologetic face and shrugged her shoulders. The thunder god simply nodded and we flew toward the Golden City of Asgard where the rainbow bridge and the darkness both ended in fields and sunlight.

"I've always held the belief that you can accomplish more with a kind word and a gun than you can with a kind word alone."
-Terrorbelle, agent of Nemesis & Co. & former Daemor soldier

Most Faerie cities aren't terribly impressive in terms of architecture, at least without using magic to enhance them. Nor are they very big, at least in terms of Earth cities.

Castles and strongholds, are another matter. Those are built to impress. No worries there about the time or the wealth involved. After all, if you can't defend yourself, then someone will take what you have away from you anyway. Impressing the neighbors wasn't just a perk, but the point. If the kingdom next door was convinced they'd have overwhelming losses if they attacked their neighbor, it usually meant they wouldn't.

Cities were for the more common folk to live in, so the ruling elite weren't quite so worried about them. A simple wall and some guards was all they were willing to invest in most cases.

I will always remember the day I came to New York and got my first view of Manhattan. It was breathtaking. To this day, it is still the most beautiful city I've ever seen. The Golden City of Asgard was a close second.

The first thing you notice about the Golden City wasn't the spires that seem to try to reach up to the sky like mini artistic skyscrapers. It was the humongous wall around the place. I've seen walls around cities in Faerie. I have even seen pictures of the Great Wall of China on Earth. None of them held a candle to this wall. It went around the entire length of the city and was easily 100 feet high and 20 feet thick. Having been a soldier, I'd take a look at that wall and the first thing that would come to mind is there is no way that city will ever be taken. Of course, back in Faerie we didn't have fighter jets or flying animals pulling chariots or parade floats. A hundred feet is an immense height to someone on the ground. Even to someone that could fly limited distances it's a long way up. For others, not so much.

We approached at an angle above the wall so we could see inside the city. At this height there was nothing stopping us from just going over the top. Or at least so I thought.

Rudy veered off and flew towards the main gate and then we started to descend.

"Why not fly over the wall?" I said.

"Bad idea. The defenses don't end where the stonework does. There is an invisible dome covering the top of the city," Rudy said.

"A force field?" I asked.

Rudy motioned for Morningdour to land. "I guess, although this pre-dates the term. The invisible dome would make sure anyone trying to get through ended up as a pile of dust. It's a modified half-sphere of woe. Grandfather managed to fold the sphere over on itself, like turning one half of a tennis ball inside out within another half. Normally, they are blood colored, but Grandfather didn't want to block out the sun. The only way in safely is through the gates. Grandfather got tired of frost giants and the like attacking every few years, so he made it not worth their while."

"Still have to watch out for Trojan horses I guess," I said.

"True enough, but I doubt we would take any large gifts without ex-amining them inside and out first. Especially as paranoid as Grandfather is."

The Golden City itself looked like it had been designed by an artist that loved sharp angles. The gates appeared to have been made by a differ-ent artist that lived, breathed, ate and dreamed of intimidation. I had seen fortresses decorated with grotesque faces and shapes meant to frighten. There was none of that on these gates. They were simply big. Massive re-ally. Had a make you feel like a gnat looking at a galaxy kind of insignifi-cant motif going. They were over 100 feet tall, yet appeared to be able to swing open like a normal door. They were built big enough to make giants feel small.

Rudy looked up at them like they were no big deal. Thor didn't even seem to notice them. In fact, he seemed impatient that they weren't already open.

A man with a mace for a hand stood in front of the gates with a frown that undoubtedly took centuries to perfect.

"Hello Tyr," said Thor. "Wotan ..." One of Odin's literally hundreds of names and the more formal of them all. "... has summoned me home. I assume you're not planning on blocking my path."

There seemed to be a drastic personality shift in Thor as he arrived in Asgard. Gone was the easygoing, happy-go-lucky cook and karaoke singer. Replacing him was a somewhat belligerent and angry man.

"You were expected. However your guests were not," Tyr said.

"Mista didn't tell you?" Rudy said.

"I do not take my orders from a Valkyrie," Tyr said.

"Surely you don't expect to bar Odin's own granddaughter from her home? And the warrior with the pink hair is the Daemor known as Terrorbelle, a friend to us both," Thor said.

"My orders did not include allowing her inside the city," Tyr said. "The fairy woman will have to remain outside."

"No," Thor said.

Tyr's entire body tensed up and fell back into a defensive fighting stance, as he brought his mace up. From the look on his face, fighting Thor was the last thing he wanted to do, but he was duty bound and would do what he was told. However, Thor wasn't looking for a fight. He was looking for an excuse.

"Very well. Tell my father that I came in response to his summons, but my guest was refused entry. Unlike some, I refuse to be a poor host, so I'm going home. Tell him if he wants to talk, he can call on me there. Just not between one and two in the afternoon because that's when my favorite cooking show is on," Thor said. He motioned for the goats to turn around and his parade float chariot lifted off to begin the homeward journey. Rudy and I, still sitting on Morningdour, exchanged a look and then took off after him.

"Wait," Tyr shouted. "I will send a message to Odin."

Tyr rapped on a square that looked like a bolt in comparison to the size of the gate. Even though he hit it with his mace, barely any sound was made. The square opened outward revealing a tunnel. The gate was barely five feet thick as compared to the walls. However, it was made of metal, while the walls were made of stone, so it probably didn't need to be as thick. A similar square opened on the inside of the gate. Tyr relayed the message to the inside guard.

"No cell phone service here, huh?" I said. Rudy chuckled as we landed back in front of the gate. Thor and the goats had turned around, but remained hovering in the air. I examined the portal through the door. It was a tactical mistake. True, most of the Norse gods I had met tended to make me look normal sized, but this hole was big enough for a person to fit through if someone on the other side was pushing, although not big enough for someone large to crawl. Maybe it was a way for the outside guard to get pulled inside in a hurry in case of attack.

Regardless, it was dumb. There were plenty of races that would fit. Heck, if I had enough momentum I might be able to make it through if I stretched and tucked. They didn't need something that big for messages. Something the size of a PVC pipe would work just as well, although it would still be vulnerable to pixies. As we sat, I made faces at Tyr. Unlike the guards at Buckingham Palace, he could glare back. I guess it was easier to keep his eyes on us than to look at Thor and be intimidated the whole time.

The guard at the other side of the gate finally returned and gave Tyr the all clear, so he closed the square.

"Please stand behind and inside the lines." Morningdour backed up behind two golden lines that looked like the top of a triangle. Thor and the goats stayed where they were in the sky. The gates opened outward. They did so quickly and in silence. If we stood in front of the lines, we would have risked being crushed into the consistency of meatloaf.

Tyr motioned us to enter. Morningdour walked in. Thor had the goats land and drove them in. On the other side we were greeted by a contingency of Valkyries dressed in a mash-up of modern biker leather and ancient armor. Mista stood at the forefront, looking unhappy. She was having trouble meeting any of our eyes.

In the back of the women warriors stood a man with long white hair and matching long beard, but it wasn't Santa. Although flying reindeer wouldn't be out of the question in Asgard. Nobody would call the man with the eyepatch jolly. From the looks, the only way he'd wear red is if his clothes were covered with someone else's blood. The dour man was dressed in brown pants and matching shirt. The ensemble was topped off with a brown trench coat. A wide brimmed hat sat on his head and two ravens perched, one on each shoulder. The frown on his face only served to confirm that Odin was not a happy man.

My warrior training had already kicked in and I was sizing up our greeters. This was not a welcoming committee. These women were armed warriors and although they were not holding their weapons, their body language made it clear they were prepared to rectify that at any moment. Even the ravens seemed jumpy, nervously looking from one side to the other as if waiting for something to happen.

Rudy and Thor sensed it too. From my perch on the winged horse behind her, I could feel Rudy's body tense up, but could see enough of her face from behind to see she was confused. I looked back to Thor and all I saw there was anger.

"You call home your favorite son, but do not greet him with a welcoming feast, but rather a reception of your battle maidens, ready to fight? What treachery is this, Father?" Thor demanded.

"There has been treachery, Son, but none has been done by me. A warrior in Valhalla is dead," Odin said.

Thor smiled, but it wasn't the genuine article we had seen in his home. It was forced, as the thunder god tried to make heads or tails of the situation.

"Of course there is a dead warrior in Valhalla. They're all dead, Father. That is part of the qualification to earn a spot, to die a hero's or a warrior's death. This way you can train them every day in preparation for the final battle at Twilight."

"That is true. But the warriors in Valhalla can only be wounded. Then they heal and rise again to feast at night. We have a warrior that rises no more," Odin said.

"Although a great tragedy, what has this to do with me?" Thor said.

Odin's frown deepened. "There is a hole through the middle of his chest big enough to have been made by Mjollnir."

"Are you suggesting that I caused the final death of one of those in Valhalla with my hammer?" Thor said, shock momentarily overwhelming his indigence. It didn't last long. "How dare you, Father. Despite all you have done in your manipulations to hold off Ragnorak…"

"How dare you say that name in my presence!" Odin said loud enough to rend both ravens flying from his shoulders. "Even its mention could speed its arrival."

"Mentioning the Twilight of the gods will not hasten its arrival, Father. It is foretold. We will all die in glorious battle." Thor didn't sound like some gung-ho warrior. He spoke the word glorious like it was anything but. "Yet we shall defeat the forces of evil in doing so. Earth and the rest of the nine worlds will be destroyed, but there are those that will survive. And perhaps they will be better off without jealous gods to interfere in their lives. But even with all you have done to me, for you to even think for a moment that I would plot treachery is the deepest insult that you could give. And over the centuries you had given insults aplenty."

"Whether I believe you did it or not, I have been told that the most likely source of the wound is from your hammer," Odin said as the ravens retook their perches.

"Told by whom?" Thor demanded.

A dwarf stepped out from behind the king of the Norse gods.

"Brokk? What would he know of these things? He is no detective," Thor said.

The dwarf smiled with condescension. "I made Mjollnir. I know its power as well as, if not better than you do. I have seen the body. Only your hammer could have made the wound. I stake my reputation on it."

"If you made the first, why couldn't you make a second?" I said. "And then use that one to frame Thor?"

"How dare you speak to me that way! You are not an Asgardian or an

Aesir." Another name for the Norse gods. "Your opinion holds no sway here," Brokk said.

Rudy stepped off of Morningdour, looking down upon the dwarf. "Her opinion holds great sway with me, dwarf." Ignoring the tension between the Valkyries facing off against Thor, Rudy daintily strolled up to Odin, stood up on her tiptoes and kissed him on the cheek. The ravens, whose names were Hugin and Munin, each turned and gave her a dirty look, like they were jealous. "Hello, Grandpa."

Odin's face softened and a slight smile even appeared, but only for an instant. "Hello Granddaughter. I would ask you to stay out of matters that do not concern you."

"How can this not concern me? My grandfather is accusing my father of murder. And then this dwarf, this little creature who tried to marry me when I was but a child, is leading the instigation. And then he insults my friend and partner, Terrorbelle."

Odin's eyebrows shot up. "What!? Partner? Mista failed to mention that relationship."

"I was about to when we were summoned to the gate," Mista said.

"Thrud, why have you brought another member of Nemesis & Co. inside of Asgard? This incursion will not go unpunished."

"Incursion? I was invited for a visit, not an armed insurrection," I said and instantly realized that humor was not the way to go here. Every Valkyrie put their hands on the hilt of their swords or battle axes. "Neither Rudy or I are here on Nemesis' business." Sometimes working for the boss is a good thing, like when the NYPD tries to hold me for something I did trying to help someone or take down a bad guy. The mayor is afraid of her, so as long as what we have done is justifiable, we are let go. But it is a two edged sword. Nemesis is known as a god killer. Not weakened or forgotten gods, but ones in their prime.

As the enforcer for the Council of Thrones, the boss has killed beings that like to think they are untouchable. She has taken down threats both little and large. Odin had good reason to be afraid of her. Part of how Nemesis did as well as she did was by careful choosing of her agents throughout time. However, she might start questioning her choice of me because I got the distinct impression that I had just caused the equivalent of a diplomatic incident between nations.

"We keep our gates closed and monitor who is allowed in and out of our city for a reason, girl. Many things can cause a hastening of the Twilight. I have seen pieces of the future, but even I with all my wisdom cannot see it all. I do not know which pieces might throw off my plans to prevent the Twilight from ever even happening. Thrud, you and your partner will leave."

"Grandpa!" Rudy said exasperated.

"No, they will not. Asgard is Thrud's home. You will not make her leave it against her will, Father. Terrorbelle was invited here as my guest. If you ask her to leave, you will be heaping insult upon insult and you will anger me even more than you already have." Thor reached into his pocket and pulled out the tiny hammer and it grew more quickly than I had seen it before. Probably tied to Thor's emotional state, which at the moment could charitably be described as volatile. The Valkyries started drawing their weapons, but Odin raised a hand stopping them.

"You would raise your hand against your family and your people?" Odin asked.

"According to you, I already have. If you truly wish to make an enemy of me, then continue along this road. I have not forgotten my last punishment, Father. I did nothing to deserve it or the one before it where you had me guarding Bifrost. I will not submit meekly again. And you will be able to experience firsthand what my hammer can do."

"Then I will ask you to leave Asgard as well, forever. You will also turn over Mjollnir to me," Odin said.

"The hammer is mine, Father."

"No, the hammer is Asgard's. I cannot risk not having our most powerful weapon with us when Twilight falls."

"To paraphrase an American actor, you can have my hammer when you pry it from my cold, dead fingers." The hammer began to crackle with energy.

"I am sorry, Thor, then you leave me no choice." Odin turned to the dwarf and nodded. Brokk reached out to touch a gauntlet on his right hand. It had several quarter-sized jewels encrusted along the back of his hand. He hit a white one and Thor's hammer shrunk down to pocket size and fell to the ground.

Thor glared. "More treachery?" The skies over Asgard darkened and lightning bolts began to bounce off of the hidden dome.

The dwarf laughed and threw what looked like a simple chain at the thunder god. As it traveled through the air, it grew and wound around Thor like bandages wrapping a mummy. The chains glowed red and the thunder god screamed as the mystic energy stabbed into him, driving Thor to his knees.

Rudy pulled her gun on the dwarf who smiled evilly. "It makes no matter if you shoot me, Thrud. Your father is trapped and there he will remain for the rest of his murdering days."

Thor struggled against his bonds as the red energy sapped his strength. I leapt off the horse and grabbed hold of the chain to add my strength to the Thunder Gods. I palmed my Daemor badge and placed it against the chain to help cancel the magical charms, then pulled for all I was worth. I felt a link give, but the red energy flared again at the attack and blasted me far away.

"Thor, submit to my authority," Odin said.

"Never again!" Thor said and he strained to the point where his entire face was as red as his hair and the single link that I had pulled apart shattered and with it the rest of the chain. Thor stood and picked up his hammer. Again it grew to its full size.

"So it's war then, Father, is it?" Thor said.

"Valkyries, prepare to kill my granddaughter and her friend if my son takes another step or moves his hammer arm."

"What!?" Thor and Rudy screamed in unison.

"I'm sorry, Granddaughter. I love you, but you're not destined to play a part in the Twilight. Your father is. I cannot have him going rogue. Hopefully he will obey and it will not come to that."

The Valkyries all pointed their weapons at us, but one looked unhappy about it.

"Sire," Mista said. "Rudy is one of our number and Terrorbelle is a friend."

"Are you questioning my order, battle maiden?"

"No, Sire, just asking you to rethink it," Mista said.

"I have spoken."

Mista and the rest of her sisters moved toward us. "Rudy, Terrorbelle, I'm sorry."

"So am I," I said as I pulled my gun and pointed it at Odin's good eye. I returned my Daemor badge to my belt. "Valkyries freeze or Odin One-Eye becomes Odin No-Eye."

One of the ravens flew at my face, but I plucked it out of the air and wrapped my hand around it so it couldn't fly or peck at my fingers.

"You think a mere bullet can harm me?" Odin said.

"This is one of Nemesis's custom made guns. It holds hundreds of rounds of specialty magical ammo, including bullets of purest darkness, forged in the land of night." Nemesis' mother was Nyx, the embodiment of night herself. We had two types of darkshot. The ones we used just had a touch of it in the bullet. We also had ones that were pure darkness. We didn't use those bullets often because there was the danger the darkness could spread. However, now seemed like a really good time to try one out. "Would you like to bet on whether your eye won't go splat? Or be forever covered in darkness, blinding you to the world? However, the lot of you are family. This is not how you should be behaving. I will put down my gun if you give me your word that Thor, Rudy, or I will not be harmed by you or anyone acting on your orders.

"I will extend the protection to my granddaughter and yourself, provided that Thor surrenders himself and hands the hammer over to my custody until such time as this matter is resolved. If Thor should try to escape from my custody or any punishment therein, you and his daughter will pay for it."

"That was a nice speech, but I would like to repeat my original demands …" I said, cocking my hammer back for emphasis.

"Terrorbelle, take the deal," Thor said.

"What?" I said.

"He said until the resolution of this matter. I have not done what I am accused of doing. There is no way it will be shown otherwise. As long as he agrees when this matter is resolved my hammer is returned to me, take the deal."

I repeated everything to Odin, including that he couldn't kick Rudy or me out of the Golden City. "Do you give us your word?"

"I do. You shall be treated the same as my granddaughter."

I uncocked my weapon and returned it to my holster. The Valkyries stood down.

"Now release Memory," Odin said, referring to the bird.

I tossed the bird away so it wouldn't be tempted to turn around and try another attack.

"The hammer," Odin said, holding his hand out toward his son.

"Sure," Thor said, dropping it on the ground. It made a small crater. "Have fun lifting it."

The Valkyries all moved to pick it up, working as a group. Two or three of them were probably half as strong as Rudy, who was stronger than me and able to lift a car well over her head. The twenty of them working in unison weren't able to budge it one millimeter.

"All-Father Odin, may I?" Brokk said, holding up his gauntlet.

Odin nodded. The dwarf walked over to the hammer and hit the white button on his gauntlet. Again the hammer shrunk to pocket size. Brokk bent to pick it up, but Odin raised his hand and the tiny hammer flew into his. There was a look of shock on the dwarf's face.

"I need the hammer to determine if it was indeed the murder weapon," the dwarf said.

"Mjollnir stays with me," Odin said. "Thor, you are now in custody and I expect you to behave that way."

Thor nodded. "Then we best bring this matter to a swift resolution."

"How do you propose we do that?" Odin said.

"Bring us to the scene of the crime," I said.

"If I knew the afterlife was going to be this much fun, I wouldn't have worried so much about dying."
-Vince Argus, Soul For Hire, dead hitman

"Terrorbelle, are you okay?" Rudy said.

The Valkyrie had good reason to ask. We'd arrived at Valhalla and the sight had literally stopped me in my tracks.

"Incredible. This place is massive," I said walking through a door that was easily 1600 feet wide. When I passed through, I stopped short again. The inside wasn't a hall, it was a small country. You could see across Valhalla, but you had to squint. There were equally large doors everywhere I looked.

"How many doors does this place have?" I said.

"Five hundred and forty," Rudy said. "Each one is big enough for eight hundred men in armor to walk through shoulder to shoulder."

Sixteen hundred feet times five hundred and forty. My mind boggled, but I quickly got my head in the game if for no other reason than there was a war going on. Thousands of men were fighting. It didn't look like a normal battle where there were just two sides. For the most part it seemed to be every man for himself. And when I say men, I mean I didn't spy a woman in the crowd other than the Valkyries who stood back supervising the melee.

There seemed to be some alliances between small groups of people against other groups or individuals. Most of the men were dressed in Viking-era garb. There were a few scattered warriors dressed from other times, but they were the exception rather than the rule. And there was one that was more exceptional than most.

The man with black hair, dark sunglasses and black trench coat stood out in the crowd not just because of his modern clothing, but by his weapons. He was running amongst the crowd with an automatic in each hand. And he was shooting everyone and everything. He seemed to be having the time of his life or rather death. He must have thought he was playing pool, because he was calling shots, knocking weapons out of people's hands like he was a sheriff in an old western.

Several groups seemed to be in alliances against him, but none were able to get close enough to do him any harm. The man was shooting arrows out of the air with bullets, using guns that never seemed to run out of bullets.

Rudy saw me staring.

"That's Vince Argus. Used to be called the Soul For Hire back on Earth. He was a hit man that sold his soul to the Devil in return for the power to never miss his target. He was killed saving Paddy Moran's adopted daughter. It was a hero's death, so Mista was able to claim his soul for Valhalla. Ticked off the Devil something fierce."

I recognized the name. Murphy had mentioned it. Argus died of a stab wound in Bulfinche's Pub.

Argus saw me watching and gave me a wink which was just barely noticeable behind the sunglasses.

Rudy was staring too, but not at Argus. She was scanning the scores of warriors.

"Looking for someone special?" I said.

Rudy actually blushed. "Old boyfriend."

"Which one is he?" I said.

"I don't see Adar anywhere, but Valhalla's a big place," Rudy said. "Follow me this way. It is a safe path. The Valkyries use them to get around and the wounded can use them to get off of the field of battle if they don't feel like playing dead for the rest of the day."

"So all these guys fight every day to the last man, killing and butchering each other? Then at the end of the day they get up, eat a feast and start over the next morning?" I said.

"Pretty much. The mead actually helps them heal. Otherwise it would take too much energy to keep replenishing their bodies, but we have two inexhaustible sources of food, a goat's horn that can't run dry of mead and replenishing roasted ox. It's the horn that does the healing. In fact, Grandfather figured a way of having the horn dispense about a day's worth of manna, which saves him power."

"So they'd all die after a day without it?" I said.

"No. If they didn't get seriously hurt, they would live forever so long as they didn't leave Asgard. If they are injured, they'd need to drink the mead by sunrise the next day or die," Rudy said.

"Seems rather pointless," I said. As far as I was concerned fighting was a thing you only did if you had to. Sure there was a certain joy in it, but that only lasted if you won. If you lost, not so much. And in these games only one person could win a day so there was going to be a lot of disappointed souls. Always losing tends to weigh heavily on the psyche.

Thor walked with us, but kept quiet. Apparently Odin, Mista, and the rest of the Valkyries were going to meet us at the crime scene. At least Odin trusted Thor enough to keep his word.

The path led us along the hall. There was all sorts of fighting going on. Ambushes, traps, fist fights, knife and sword fights, and thanks to Argus and a few others, gun battles. Oddly most of the dead seemed to be having a grand old time of it, even the ones that were wounded. In fact, one came up behind us, half his face blown off his head, looking worse than Zombielicious herself.

"Excuse me, coming through. Be careful you don't get any brain on you," the soul said rushing by.

"Is there anything I can help you with?" Rudy said.

"No, nothing to trouble yourself about, battle maiden. As long as I keep my hand up here, I will be fine, but thank you," the man said, as he rushed on ahead of us.

"What would you have done for him?" I asked.

"Tended his wounds to get him ready for the feast later on tonight. I'd do pretty much whatever was needed. That is what a Valkyrie does when she's in Valhalla. That and occasionally training the Valhallan warriors, but they tend to do pretty well on their own these days without our help thanks to all that practice," Rudy said.

Thor frowned as he looked out across the fighting men.

I couldn't quite read what was going through his mind. "Wishing you were out there with them?"

Thor shook his head. "Not at all. Just looking out and trying to figure out why so many valiant men must spend such a large part of eternity fighting each other in preparation for a battle where they will all likely die the final death. It all seems such a waste."

"Dad, don't let anyone hear you talking like that. They already think you killed one of the Valhallans. If they hear you speak ill of Grandfather's master plan, who knows what else will happen," Rudy whispered.

"I'm so sick of all of it. Twilight should have come and gone centuries ago. Now we all just wait to die. It makes a lot of things seem rather pointless," Thor said.

"Like saving innocent merwomen from attacking cornu?" I said.

Thor stopped short and turned around to look at me. "Are you still upset about that?"

I still was. "Yep."

Thor sighed. "I wish I could act in Asgard as I do on Earth, helping everyone that needs it, but I can't. Here I am Thor, the mightiest of the Aesir and heir to the throne. My actions reflect on everyone in this kingdom. If I were to attack that bird, there are a hundred more back at its roost that may seek vengeance. Not against me directly, but against the common folk of Asgard. People I am sworn to protect. People who would have no defense against a single cornu, let alone a hundred of them attacking and carrying off people and livestock. The adaro can usually handle themselves. I couldn't risk what could potentially be hundreds of lives to save one. However, I am happy that you did interfere."

It was like being back working for Mab again. She was a queen of Faerie in her own right and became known as the rebel queen in the war against Thandau. There were times she didn't do what many of us considered the right thing because of politics and how it would affect her allies against the enemy. I didn't like it then, but I learned to accept it as a necessary evil. It was one of the reasons that I left the army once we won the war. I wanted to be able to follow my conscience without worrying about what someone with a higher rank would want me to do.

"I guess I didn't realize that. It doesn't make me like it anymore."

Thor tilted his head sideways. "Terrorbelle, are you truly disappointed in me?"

"I guess I am. I'd only seen you on Earth where you do the right thing, like you did for Isabella against the bikers. I guess I assumed that was who you were. There are too few heroes in any world and I guess I was disappointed to find out that you were only a conditional one."

Rudy's face was a mask of horror at what I had said to her father. Thor however furrowed his brow and seemed deep in thought.

"You know, I've never thought of myself as a hero." He motioned with his arms to the fighting warriors. "These men are heroes. They fought and died for something bigger than themselves. I am just a warrior trying to protect my family and my people. Your words give me inner turmoil, largely because they're true. In my time on Earth I've changed. Mellowed as they say. I've learned to do things my way and I'd like to think I do the right things. Coming back here threw me back into old habits and old ways. I don't know that I'll ever think of myself as a hero. I have been too blessed with strength and weapons. I've been able to overcome most obstacles too easily. But I'll have to give this some thought. I would rather do things because they are right as opposed to what I am told."

Thor put his hands on my shoulders. "Terrorbelle, I am sorry that I disappointed you. I will strive to do better."

I was more than a little surprised that a god would care what I thought, let alone take it to heart. "Then I guess I'll look forward to never being disappointed in you again."

Thor leaned back his head and let out a laugh and then picked me up in a bear hug.

After putting me down, Thor turned to his daughter. "Thrud, I have disappointed you as well?"

"No, Father, I know the way things are the way things are. We are taught not to make waves. That was something your blood brother did."

Thor lifted his daughter up in a hug. "Good, but I think we should both strive to make things better and not settle for the status quo. I must say daughter, you have impressed me over the years and I am much impressed with the quality of your friend."

Rudy looked at me and smiled, and punched me in the arm. "Yeah, Belle's not too bad."

It took an awful long time to get where we were heading. We ended up in a banquet room that could fit tens of thousands. You could probably finish your dinner in less time than it took to cross the room. In the middle of the floor was a twice dead body with a huge gaping hole in the chest. From my understanding, in the afterlives or in magical realms, the dead can be granted new bodies. In some realms, those bodies are eternal and self-repairing. In others, they need help. In Asgard the dead would live forever if they didn't play their little war games.

Odin, Mista, and another Valkyrie were already waiting. She was one of the battle maidens who had met us at the gate. Rudy had said her name was Hladgunner. Like Thrud, many of the Valkyries had unfortunate names.

I remembered Mista mentioning her. She had recently replaced Mista as leader of the Valkyries and it wasn't a smooth transition between them. She was tall and lean like Rudy, but was blonde, her hair cut in almost a crew cut style.

Odin had two wolves who sat on either side of him and his ravens still sat one on each shoulder.

Mista met us part way and gently laid her hand on Rudy's arm. "Thrud, you may not want to see this."

"I've seen dead bodies before," Rudy said.

"But not of someone you loved," Mista replied softly.

Despite the warning, Rudy looked at the twice dead corpse and gasped. "Adar!"

Not the way she expected to see her old boyfriend. Odin frowned at his granddaughter's sadness, but Hladgunner grinned. I wanted to wipe the look off her face.

"You okay?" I said.

Rudy sniffed, holding back tears. "Adar was my first love. Who would do this to him?"

My first answer would have been Hladgunner, but I held my tongue. Just because someone revels in another's misery doesn't mean they caused it. It doesn't mean they're innocent either. I was going to watch my back around her.

"Mind if I take point on this one?" I said. Rudy nodded.

I bent to examine the body. There wasn't much blood for such a huge wound. There was also no sign of a good portion of the twice dead man's ribs, spinal cord, lungs, heart and most of his other organs. There were no fleshy bits lying about.

"This isn't where he died, is it?" I said.

"No, some of the warriors found him unresponsive this morning when they returned to the field of battle," Mista said. "Apparently he never made it to the feast last night."

"No one noticed he was missing?" I said.

Mista looked at her boots. "He was half buried under some sand, but that's no excuse. Every warrior is supposed to be accounted for, which means a Valkyrie screwed up."

"I will find out which Valkyrie and she will pay for her dereliction," Hladgunner said.

"They brought him to the hall, thinking that if he got some mead in him, he would heal. It didn't work," Mista said.

"Where did they find the body?" I said. Mista pointed back toward the battle field. "I suppose it would be too much to hope that the place he was found would remain untouched so we can take a look?"

"Sorry, Terrorbelle. Part of the battlefield's magic is that it is self-cleaning, each morning's ground virgin for that fight," said Mista. "Not even his organs were left."

"Has this ever happened before?" I said.

"No," Mista said. "Even dead, he should have been able to get up and come here under his own power."

Thor and Rudy were bent over and examining the wound. Thor was frowning and Rudy looked torn between trying to find a clue and weeping for her friend.

"It does look like Mjollnir went thought him. The wound is cauterized as if electricity was coming from whatever made the hole," Thor said. "I find that troubling since I know my hammer could not have been used in this. That means that somebody has duplicated my hammer. Could Brokk have made another?"

Now Odin was frowning. "I highly doubt it or he would have done it long before now. Your brother Loki supplied him with sources of power that were fairly unique. Without the deceiver's aid, Mjollnir would still be a mighty weapon, but nowhere near the powerhouse it is."

Rudy stood up. "Then I guess it's time for us to round up the usual suspects. And when something happens in Asgard, there is usually only one suspect."

"Who me?"
  -Loki, imprisoned Norse trickster god

In Asgard, it seems that most of their high points and their low ones were caused by just one god getting them into trouble and getting them back out again. His name's Loki. The Norse trickster had been imprisoned for centuries after causing the death of Asgard's golden child, Balder. Apparently in the Golden City, a jail cell with bread and water isn't considered adequate punishment. Killing Loki outright was also a bad idea as it could trigger the Ragnorak that they were also worried about. So instead they tortured him because there is nothing better than torture to make something evil turn good. Insert sarcastic tone here.

Oddly enough, it may have worked thanks to a brave bartender with bad jokes.

We had to leave the Golden City and head out to the outer reaches of Asgard to a cave where Loki was trapped in eternal torment. I was riding again with Thor on his parade float pulled by the goats. Rudy was flying beside us on Morningdour and we had a pair of winged babysitters, Odin's two ravens. Apparently Odin sends them out into the world to spy for him and report back. The King of the Norse pantheon had no desire to visit his disgraced adopted son.

"That's odd," Rudy said.

"What is?" I said.

"It's quiet. The ground isn't shaking and there is no screaming," Rudy said. "Why is that?"

"Things have changed with your uncle," Thor said. "He has been set free twice a year for the last several. Once in a treaty with Padriac Moran." Paddy is the owner of Bulfinche's Pub. From what I understand the treaty involves him catering Ragnorak. I kid you not. "The other involves… something else." That something was Paddy freeing Loki on April Fools' Day to participate in a trickster contest. It was something that everyone knew, but didn't openly talk about. My fault actually. "Oddly Loki has come back to his confinement each time. That includes a time that he could have gotten far enough away that we wouldn't have been able to find him."

"So Loki willingly returns to his torture?" Rudy said. "Is that why there is no screaming? Did Grandfather get rid of the beast?"

"No," Thor said. "Loki made some friends."

I knew all about this and had some inside information about which one of his friends we would find inside.

There was a small opening to the cave that barely let in any light. There was some sort of self-sustaining illumination that allowed you to see just a short distance in front of you, but not much beyond that other than shadows. More scary that way I guess. However, as the daughter of night, the boss has given her agents the ability to see in the dark, so not so frightening to me.

Not sure why they think they needed mood lighting when they had a gigantic serpent. The five story long snake had his back to us and was spitting venom like a fire hose, although from our angle we couldn't see what at.

The beast's head snapped around as it heard our footsteps. Rudy and I both pulled our guns, but Thor didn't move. The snake came at us, far faster than anything that big should be able to move. Thor's hands lit up with crackles of lightning. The giant snake stopped short. I got the impression that he and Thor had danced this dance before. Thor made like he was reaching toward his pocket and the snake backed away, buying the thunder god's bluff and leaving us alone.

We walked down the depths of the cave toward an occupied ledge. There was a naked man, tall and lean, shackled by his wrists and ankles to the ledge floor by some sort of red metal. I'm told part of it was forged from the intestines of Loki's slain son. Above the trickster was a very large bowl-shaped shield on stilts with a funnel and a tube designed to catch the venom and move it away. Beside the imprisoned god was my favorite bartender.

"Murphy!" I said rushing toward him. I picked him up in a hug not unlike the one Thor gives Rudy, then swung him around and kissed him on the lips. Just a peck really, although we had a real kiss a little while ago after he had saved my life. Murph is still a little hung up on his dead wife, Elsie, which has slowed any romance between us. I'm still waiting and hoping. Although, I'm not against dating other people until he comes around. However, I'm not sure how fair that is to the other people, which is why things with Joe Hannk and I have been going very slowly.

"T-Belle, what are you doing here?" Murphy said.

I brought him up to speed. Thor shook his hand and Rudy gave him a peck on the cheek. Everyone knew Murphy. Not everyone liked him because he tended to be a little bit on the obnoxious side, but most respected him.

He'd accomplished a lot for a human with no special powers.

A voice from the floor rose up. "So something bad has happened and rather than doing any actual detective work, you have all decided to come and see poor old Loki."

"Did you do it Uncle?" Rudy asked. "Did you kill Adar?"

Loki laughed. "Dear niece, you really should work on your interrogation techniques. Most suspects won't simply give an answer up just because you asked nicely."

"Loki, did you do it?" Murphy said.

Loki turned his head with a great look of sadness on his face. "Murph, do you think I would have done something like that?"

"No, not anymore," Murphy said. The look of sadness vanished, replaced by one of pride. The trickster whom all Asgard branded a villain apparently truly cared what a human bartender thought of him. Murphy can have that effect on people. Plus from what Murph told me, he and Loki saved an entire planet of people who weren't able to defend themselves, in no small part to Loki outthinking the enemy. His reward was a chance to get far, far away. And just as Thor said, instead he chose to return to his torment in an effort to prove he had changed.

I would have run.

Then again Loki is a god and a shape changer. Despite the damage that the serpent's acidic venom does to his body, he is able to heal from it. After Murphy and Loki helped save the world of Karma, those involved as well as some tricksters have been taking turns sitting watch with Loki because Odin allows the shield to deflect the serpent's venom as long as someone stays with him.

"However, I think they need to hear you say it in order for them to go on with their investigation and find out who really did it," Murphy said. "And maybe they have come not so much to accuse, but to ask for your help."

We had done no such thing, but all of us saw the wisdom in Murphy's words. Loki was acknowledged even by his foes as being brilliantly devious, able to manipulate people and events on a legendary scale. If he hadn't done this, Loki might be able to give us some insight on who did.

"Very well. I answer only because Murphy asked me and for no other reason. I did not kill Adar, niece. I would never have done so if for no other reason than because of what he once meant to you," Loki said. "Nor did I duplicate Mjollnir."

"Then how do you know about how he was killed?" I said. "We

never mentioned a hammer, duplicate or otherwise."

The trickster smiled at me. "Simple. One-Eye said my name, which alerted me to the discussion and allowed me to listen in." Gods had that power, which is why you didn't mention their names lightly. It was why most people kept referring to Odin as One-Eye, so he didn't know they were talking about him. Mention their names three times and there is no way they don't eavesdrop. And mentioning their names three times is enough to summon them. Name dropping in mystic circles can be dangerous and even deadly. "He knows better, so I can only assume he wanted me to hear what was happening."

"Then tell us –" Rudy said, but was cut off by her uncle.

"However, if you want my help, it will have to be asked for," Loki said.

"Uncle, will you help us find who did this to Adar and clear Father?" Rudy asked.

"For you my niece, I would do most anything. I know your feelings toward poor Adar, but this favor is not yours to ask." Loki turned to his blood brother. "Ask me, brother and do it nicely."

Thor seemed to be fighting an inner battle. Thor wasn't a very good poker player and wore his emotions on his face. It was easy to read that even though there was great animosity between the pair, there was once also great love. Because of that, Loki's betrayal cut that much more deeply. Thor seemed to be debating whether to comply with the simple request or to beat it out of Loki. His hands were balled up into fists, but then he looked up at me and out of the corner of his eye at Rudy. He even took a glance at Murphy.

"Brother, my hammer has been taken from me by our father. I have been framed for a grievous crime against the man my daughter once loved. I have no ideas on how to prove my innocence. I ask you for your help."

"Say please," Loki said.

Thor gritted his teeth. "Please."

Loki grinned, enjoying seeing Thor humble himself. "Make that a pretty please."

"Pretty please," the thunder god repeated.

"With a cherry and sprinkles on top," Loki said. Thor's eyes literally crackled with lightning and for a moment looked like he was going to strike Loki, but he held fast.

"Pretty please with a cherry and sprinkles on top."

"Very well, I will help you," Loki said. There was shock clearly written across the faces of both Thor and Rudy. On Murphy, not so much. "However, I will say that I will be more effective if I were freed from my imprisonment."

"I don't have the authority to free you. If that is what your help costs, I will do without it," Thor said turning to leave. The serpent had been creeping up on us, but as Thor turned, it slithered off to hide in the shadows on the far side of the cave again.

"Maybe you didn't hear me brother; I said I would help. Freeing me was not a condition of that, it was only a suggestion. I can be more effective out and about, but if you choose not to do that, I cannot blame you. You're in enough trouble with old One-Eye as it is," Loki said.

Thor was surprised and suspicious. "Okay then. Assuming what you claim is true, who did it?"

"The obvious suspect is Brokk. He and his brother made the hammer in the first place. The dwarf has always been upset that he was not able to take my head in payment as that was part of his price for making it. Luckily I was able to outsmart him. He's made no secret of the fact that he demanded the hammer back, but didn't have the power to take it. Nor did he have the power to wield it. Or make another without what I had given him. However, he is a master craftsman and could easily make a copy that would mimic Mjollnir. It would have many of the same properties, but not the same power. Unless…"

"Unless what?" I said.

"He found another source of power to use. At the very least he'd have to have added something to the mix to get electric burns to the wound as the lightning in the hammer comes from Thor's power, not from the hammer itself. The hammer merely focuses it much like a magnifying glass would focus a sunbeam."

"He had a glove that he used to shrink the hammer down," Rudy said.

"There you have it. I would not be surprised if that glove allowed him to override Thor's control of the hammer and use it for himself. Probably been working on it for centuries. I wonder how he finally made the breakthrough? I'd bet that it has a charm that would allow the dwarf to lift or throw it. Of course, he can't be your only suspect. Odin and Thor have many enemies. There is no end to the list of giants who still hold much hatred for Asgard. But there are also those within Asgard who would love to see Odin's army of the dead rendered powerless.

Chief among them would be Freyja."

"Freyja? Are you mad?" Thor said.

"Spoken like a true red blooded male," Loki said. He turned to Murphy. "Freyja's beauty is beyond compare. We in Asgard have fought wars over it, which seems appropriate since she wields her beauty and sensuality like weapons. Everyone knows the story that those that die as heroes in battle get to go to Valhalla. Those that die of more natural causes get to go to my daughter Hel's realm. But what about those that die not so heroically in battle? Or are simply wounded and die later? Where do those of our believers get to spend their afterlife? With Freyja in her hall Fólkvangr. She got at least half of those who fell in battle, with One-Eye's approval no less. Even he's not immune to seduction. Sadly, Freyja had no Valkyries to go and claim the souls, so she flew over the battlefields herself in her chariot pulled by two flying cats."

"Seriously?" Murphy said.

Loki nodded. "She has as many dead at her command as Odin does. If something were to start killing those in Valhalla off, the power base would shift in her favor and Odin would need to bargain with her to replenish his mortal soul army for the battle of Twilight."

"Freyja wouldn't do that," Thor said.

"Brother, I am largely immune to emotional charms. That is why Balder could never affect me the way he did the rest of you. And that is why Freyja could not wrap me around her little finger like she did every other male in Asgard, One-Eye and you included. You can't see past what your groin is telling you in order to see her true nature." Personally, I was having trouble seeing past Loki's groin. He was naked and I tried not to stare. The trickster was well endowed, although I understand that's not uncommon for shape shifters. I started to have a little sympathy for the men who stared at my chest, telling me they couldn't help themselves. But only a little. I may have snuck a glance, but I forced my eyes to look elsewhere. "I suggest that the ladies go alone to interrogate her," Loki said.

"Nonsense," Thor said, louder than he needed to. It was obvious that he was denying it with such force because he thought there might be some truth to it.

"I know someone who has it out for One-Eye," Murphy said. Thor and Loki both looked at him. "Nick." Nick was what people called the Devil so he couldn't use the name game to listen in, although his title was used so much in conversation it would take three times in a row to get the evil one's attention. "He came to Bulfinche's in part as revenge over us finding a loophole for the hitman Vince Argus to escape their bargain for his soul. He died a hero by saving Shellie's life, so Mista the Valkyrie was able to take him to Valhalla. From the little I've seen of Nick, he's not one to take such things lightly."

"I hardly think Nick is behind framing me," Thor said. "Or Freyja for that matter. I like Brokk for it though."

"In investigating a crime, you can't simply eliminate most suspects based solely on what you think of them," I said. "However, as Nick is not in Valhalla as far as we know, I suggest we look into Brokk and Freyja and ask around if anyone has heard any rumors of any other plots. Unless you don't want to get to the bottom of who framed you."

Thor sighed. "I suppose." The thunder god looked at the trickster. "I appreciate your insight, Loki."

"My pleasure, brother. Before you leave me, I would like to have a word alone with the lovely Miss Terrorbelle if I may," Loki said.

Rudy glared and pointed at her Uncle. "Terrorbelle is my friend. If you mean her any harm or to use your words to twist her against us, I warn you it will not go well for you, Uncle."

"Thank you for your warning, niece. I will not do anything to harm Terrorbelle or turn her against you. I merely have a few questions that I would like answered in private. I have given you the benefit of my insight for the asking. Is this too much to ask in return?"

"I have no problem with it," I said.

"Very well," Thor said. He and his daughter walked away.

Loki turned to look at Murphy. "By alone, I meant alone, Murphy. Pretty please with a cherry and sprinkles on top."

Murphy looked confused, but not upset. In fact, he was smiling at the way Loki said please. Murphy nodded, winked at me then joined Thor and Rudy.

"I must say it is a pleasure to finally meet you, Terrorbelle. I have heard a great deal about you. Our friend John Murphy thinks very highly of you," Loki said.

"The feeling is mutual," I said, being careful to look only at the trickster's eyes as he shifted his pelvis to what was probably a more comfortable position.

"Is it?" Loki said.

"I don't understand why you are asking."

"Simple really. Murphy is still hurting after the death of his wife, whom he loved dearly and with all of his heart. Murphy does not know how to casually do anything, although his joking manner may make it seem otherwise. From the way he has talked of you, I think there may be a chance for you and him to become romantically involved." I lit up at the trickster's words. "However how far down the road that may be." That took some of the wind out of my sails. "However, if that does happen, Murphy will not do it halfheartedly. He will give all to any woman he loves. I want to determine if you would be worthy of that."

"Excuse me, but why would Murphy's or my love life be any of your business?" I said.

"Normally your love life would be none of my business. However, Murphy's life, in all its aspects, is my business. I don't know how much you know about recent developments in my so-called life. Paddy Moran started me on the road to redemption by believing in me and honoring a promise he made when he thought I had saved his dying wife. He got to her minutes too late for what I had done for him to save her, yet he still honored our bargain to give me a day of freedom every year. Furthermore, he got me an extra day once he learned to trust me. By breaking me out for the trickster competition, he risked the wrath of One-Eye. The man is one of the most powerful gods left and he has an army at his disposal. As powerful as Paddy is, One-Eye could destroy him and Bulfinche's Pub. He risked everything because of his word and belief in me. Paddy Moran may have started me on the road to redemption, but Murphy took me kicking and screaming down the rest of it. Murph didn't trust me at first, but because he trusted Paddy he gave me the benefit of the doubt and believed in me. I saw a mortal accomplish things that a god would be envious of. He helped me change my ways. Murphy means a great deal to me."

"So you say," I said. "You don't exactly have a sterling reputation for telling the truth. Maybe your befriending him is all part of some greater plot."

Rather than be offended, the trickster grinned. "Did you know that Old One-Eye offered me a way to get out of this torment?" I nodded. "It's true. All I had to do was guarantee my good behavior with Murphy's life. If I screwed up, the bartender died. Murphy even agreed to it. I turned it down because I couldn't guarantee my behavior one hundred percent and I was not about to have one of the only two people that has treated me decently pay the price if I messed up. My intentions are good. But, as you point out my track record is not. So I returned to this joyous place when I could have gotten away with the hope that it would prove to old One-Eye and the rest that I have changed and that they will grant me my freedom without me having to steal it. That is why Murphy is important to me—his example and faith in me has made me a better person. That is why I want to know your intentions toward him and if they are sincere or otherwise. I cannot force you to answer. In fact, it would disappoint Murphy if I did, so I wouldn't if I could. I do ask that you answer me honestly, so this is something I don't have to worry about."

The trickster's declaration about Murphy caught me off guard with its emotion and sincerity.

"I care more about Murphy than any man, other than my father, that I have ever known. I would die to protect him. I would take heartache to make him happy. Murphy stepped up on my behalf when Hermes and Hercules were bullying me. Hermes could have made his life miserable and Herc could have broken him into tiny pieces, but Murphy didn't care. He did the right thing just because it was right, even though I had been sexually harassing him all evening prior to that. That moment I first fell in …" I'd never said the L word to Murphy in terms of being in love with him. I wasn't going to say it first to anyone but him. "…cared for him. Then he took me on a date just to spite them. During that we became friends. A friendship that has grown deeper ever since. I would gladly spend the rest of my life with him. I can't imagine not having him in my life. I don't know what else you want me to say."

Loki smiled. "Thank you. That's plenty. I believe you. And what's more, I like you. So I'm going to tell you a few things that will help you understand politics in Asgard a little better. Whether anyone believes it, I have changed, but I'm not the only one. Thor has as well."

Loki creased his brow. "It's funny that you mention Hermes because he did a very great thing for Thor many years ago. After a legendary battle with a giant king who had done a great many bad things, including kidnapping your friend and my niece, there was a huge battle. The giant had a club with power almost as great as Mjollnir. The two met on the field of battle and threw their weapons at each other as hard as they could. The hammer smashed the club, shattering it into a thousand fragments, one of which lodged in Thor's head. None of our surgeons or healers could get it out without risking death or giving Thor brain damage, so it stayed in there for centuries. Gave him the most awful headaches. When he had those headaches, he could be very rash, incredibly unreasonable and quick to rage. You did not want to be on his bad side when that happened. Trust me."

Loki sighed. "Not that many do. After the shard removal, Thor left Asgard to spend most of his time on Earth. My brother has been a much kinder, gentler person ever since. I have always wondered since Odin initiated contact with the giant if those headaches were somehow part of his master plan to postpone Twilight or to keep control of his son. A brutal, angry Thor is much better for defense then Thor the poet. Or these days, Thor the chef. Just something to keep in mind during your investigation."

"Are you implying that One-Eye could be behind the frame job?" I said.

"No, I don't think he would go that far. However, he might let it play out if he thought he could turn it to his own advantage." Loki said. "It has been lovely chatting with you. When the time comes and Murphy sees what is in front of him, provided you stay true to your words, I will grant you my blessing. I would also make another request of you."

"What?" I said.

"My niece has always had some difficulties making friends. She had trouble here as many of the people only wanted to know her because of who her father and grandfather were. At the Valkyrie school, teachers were either lenient or harder on her than the others because of who her grandfather was. She acted spoiled as a defense mechanism. Now that Adar had died the final death, she hasn't any true friends here besides her horse. Did she tell you she demanded a winged horse to match her hair?"

"Many times," I said.

Loki laughed. "That story made me proud."

I frowned at what the god of deception seemed to be implying. "Are you saying it's a lie?"

"Not at all. Entirely true, except that when she tells the story, she lets you think she did it because of vanity. The truth is Morningdour was injured from being too wild and going to be put down because they thought she'd never be fit as a Valkyrie mount. Rudy made her grandfather promise her a red horse and Morningdour was the only unassigned red winged foal. One-Eye couldn't break a promise without losing power, so my niece's supposed vanity saved the animal's life. And then she nursed the horse back to health."

"So you're saying she played him?" I said.

"Like a fiddle. Even had a little help from her Uncle on that one, but it was mostly her. She knew what others thought of her and used it to her advantage. She still uses that aspect of her personality to hide behind.

It's safer. However, you've seen beyond it," Loki said.

My eyes narrowed. "That's true, but how would you know since you've been supposedly bound here?"

Loki chuckled. "I have the ability to look out upon the nine worlds, even when my name isn't mentioned. It helps pass the times while the serpent is turning my body into crispy bits. I have seen my niece's life with Nemesis & Co., even the aftermath of what that bastard Matuku did to her. You have been a true friend to her, even though it was obvious you didn't much like her in the beginning. I ask you to look after her in her time of need and stay her friend. I can speak from experience what a difference a true friend can make in your life. If you do this, I will owe you a boon."

"I'm going to be Rudy's friend whether you ask me to or not."

"Excellent. I also request that you do not tell my niece that we had this conversation," Loki said.

"Why? It's actually a nice gesture," I said.

"Exactly and I am learning that sometimes the nicest gestures are the ones you don't get credit for. If she were to learn of it, she would suspect my motives were less than pure. And rightly so. My reputation is very much based on my actions. It is going to take a while for me to undo that. I'd rather that she changed her opinions of me based on what I do, rather than what I say," Loki said.

"I'll think about it." Then something crossed my mind. "Murphy also thinks highly of you. I would request that you do nothing to hurt him."

"You left off the implied threat," Loki said wiggling his eyebrows.

"Some things don't need to be said, do they?" I said.

Loki laughed. "Murphy would do well with you. If you would be so kind as to send him back after you say goodbye. Old One-Eye only allows the shield when there is somebody to man it. When Murph leaves there is no one in the schedule for a while. I would rather put off the soul wrenching agony of being dissolved alive for as long as I can."

"I can see why," I said. "I hope things work out for you."

"They will. Or I'll make them," Loki said.

And on that note, I walked away to rejoin the others. Rudy and Thor pretended like they hadn't been trying to listen in.

"What did he want?" Rudy said.

"Just had some questions for me. Nothing pertaining to the case," I said. I turned to see Murphy smiling at me and realized just how dangerous he was to me because the rest of the world faded away for a moment. The serpent could have snuck up on me and I'd never have known it. Emotions like that make me uneasy, so I tried to cover it up by acting stupid. I slapped him on the posterior and regretted it instantly.

"You had a little something on your butt," I said, but it sounded lame enough to need a cane.

"Yeah, your hand," Rudy whispered, smirking.

Murphy smiled and gave me a wink. "No worries. Did you get it off?"

"No, but she might get off if you'd just help her…" Rudy had a little trouble finishing her sentence with my elbow in her gut.

"Murphy, we have to go. This was a bust and we still need to figure out who's framing Thor," I said.

"No worries. It's always great to see you, no matter how long it's for," Murphy said.

"And just for curiosity, how long is it?" Rudy said.

Murph had been ignoring Rudy, pretending he didn't hear, but this one he couldn't brush off. "Well, you've heard my old nickname, haven't you?" Rudy shook her head. "Murphy the human tripod." Rudy's jaw dropped as Murph wiggled his eyebrows. "Sadly, it's because I used to have a camera holding fetish."

Rudy rolled her eyes and walked toward the mouth of the cave. "Good-bye Murphy. Good-bye Uncle."

"Fare thee well, Niece," Loki shouted.

Thor shook Murphy's hand and followed his daughter. The pair stood waiting for me by the mouth of the cave. The serpent waited for something else entirely in the darkness at the far side of the cave.

I picked Murphy up in a hug and this time I kissed him on the head. At six feet, I'm only two inches taller than Murphy, but I'm still much broader and stronger than he is. "You be careful. That serpent is nothing to mess around with. And where's the bike?" Paddy had a duplicate made of Mista's flying motorcycle to help him sneak Loki out of his punishment for the annual Fools' Day. Murphy and Loki made use of it during their Karma adventure. In addition to being able to fly and travel between worlds, it had force fields to protect the rider. The serpent and his venom wouldn't be able to get past it.

"One-Eye and Paddy haven't discussed Paddy freeing Loki on Fools' Day." The fact that Odin knew at all is because I opened my big mouth about it while a bunch of us were hunting a chaos stag that could have plunged the entire world into darkness. Mista heard me and was obligated to tell her boss. I still felt bad about it. "They both seem to prefer ignoring the issue. Bringing the bike would be like rubbing his nose in it, so Paddy drops me off in Baby."

Baby was Paddy's 1930 Caddy which the leprechaun loved more than almost anything in the world. Like the bike, it was magically modified and could travel between worlds and fly. Had shields too.

Murphy held up his wrist. "My watch controls the bike. I push this button and the bike is here in less than a second."

"Good. I don't want anything bad to happen to you," I said.

"Ditto," he said.

"When we both get back to New York, how about a movie night?" I said. I loved movie night. We curl up on my couch and usually ended up falling asleep. Yes, not exactly a steamy time, but I'm never happier than when I wake up next to him. Although I'm pretty sure if I could figure out a way for us both to be naked when that happened, that it would make me way happier.

"Sounds good," Murphy said.

"How about Anaconda? Be like you were still here," Loki shouted.

"Hello, private moment here," Murphy said.

"Hey, you were there when I was with Rilga," Loki said.

"You watched Loki with a woman?" I said. "I didn't know you were into that."

"I'm not. He was with a dragon while shaped as a dragon and they wrecked the landscape. I had to watch or risk getting crushed," Murphy said.

"Bet you learned a lot," Loki said. "Might help you in the bedroom."

"Not unless I was playing dodge ball," Murphy said.

"I'll leave you two boys to get back to your play date," I said.

"Play date? Do I get milk and cookies?" Loki said.

"I have some in the provisions," Murphy said. "I'll get them out."

"I thought we had eaten them all," Loki said.

Murphy smiled. "You almost did, but knowing how much you like them, I put some aside so there would be more later."

"You think of everything." The trickster frowned, then shouted. "But I didn't! Curse me for being a fool and not thinking this through. Brother, listen to me. If someone was able to give the final death to a warrior in Valhalla, there is something more important than simply solving the murder."

"What's that?" Thor shouted back.

"If this person or persons did it once, why couldn't they put aside more of what they used for later? Adar may just have been a test run to see if they pull it off. And they probably chose him to cloud the judgment of the family because of his connection to Rudy. Much less chance of rational thought when emotion is involved. Since no one has figured out how it was done yet, what's to stop them from doing it again? And on a larger scale. Perhaps you will figure it out soon, so the best time to strike again is now, before anyone can stop them. Any of our enemies would love to wipe out Odin's hero army. If they can somehow cut off the power that revives one, why not do it with all of them the next time? And if it was me, I'd take the horn out of the mix, maybe poison it. Think about it – at the end of the day there would only be one hero left and nothing to revive the rest. Brother, you need to halt the fighting before more heroes die the final death."

Thor muttered something about excrement and ran out of the cave. A raven, Hugin I think, suddenly burst into flight from where he had been hiding behind a rock and spying on us. We ignored the black bird and raced after the thunder god.

"Valhalla gives the phrase never-ending battle all new meaning."
-Vince Argus, Soul For Hire, dead hitman

Thor put the goats into overdrive and they actually outpaced Morning-dour, but Rudy caught up when we stopped to get in the gate. Hugin flew right by us and Tyr simply opened the little message door for the raven to fly through. I guess now I knew why they had the door in the door – to allow Odin's feathered spies an easy way in and out. I assumed he was on his way to let One-Eye know what we were doing.

There was no drama this time as Tyr was expecting us. Thor didn't bother to get out of his flying parade float and just rode it all the way to Valhalla and through one of the huge doors until he was flying over the eternal battle of heroes.

It looked as if almost half the warriors were already wounded or taken out. Vince Argus seemed to be winning. Of course, he had a huge advantage in that his guns were longer distance weapons than spears, swords, and bows. Not to mention his Hell given power to never miss.

Thor raised his hand above his head and threw a lightning bolt across the sky that was easily as wide as the length of the goats and the chariot. The resulting boom of thunder got everyone's attention.

"Stop! Cease all fighting," Thor said.

Most of the Valhallans obeyed, but one with a sword who was sneaking up on Argus didn't listen. Argus spun around and shot the man between the eyes.

"The man said stop," Argus said.

The other raven, Munin, was in the hall and flapped his wings, flying far faster than a raven should be able to. He was a black blur as he left the hall.

"I fear that eternal battle itself may be victim of a dastardly attack. Cease all hostilities for now and take the wounded into the banquet room so everyone can feed early today," Thor said.

The warriors moved to obey the thunder god. However, a half dozen Valkyries met us in the air above the battlefield on their own winged horses. Three stragglers on flying motorcycles with side cars joined them a moment later. None of them looked happy.

"By whose authority do you do this?" Hladgunner demanded.

"By my own," Thor said.

"This is your father's hall. We do not have to obey your orders here,"

Hladgunner said.

"There may be a problem with the healing magic. There is a chance that the Valhallans will not be revived," Thor said.

"What?!" Hladgunner said.

"I will explain it all to Father when he gets here."

It turned out Thor didn't have too long to wait thanks to the tattling ravens. Odin came through what would be considered the main doors to Valhalla, slamming the football field size door open. It made a sound almost as loud as thunder. He was on a flying eight legged horse. The sheer number of airborne animals in this realm was amazing. One of these days I was going to have to figure out what kind of magic they used to fly and to see if it would work for me on Earth.

"Thor, talk to me now," Odin said, the missing ravens on his shoulders. Thor motioned for the goats to land by his father and his octo-legged horse.

Thor told him Loki's theory about the Valhallans not rising again.

"Nonsense," Odin said. "He is just playing another one of his games."

"I am loath to trust him again too, Father, but I have to admit that something about him has changed. I think he is actually trying to help without ulterior motives, as odd as that may seem," Thor said. "Some of these warriors have been fighting every day for a thousand years, so would one day do them that much harm?"

"Yes. We do not know on what date Twilight will fall. Not even one minute can be wasted. And you know my orders regarding Valhalla. You broke them and even for you, that means punishment," Odin said.

"Fine, but don't you think that since I have already stopped everything that it would be prudent to check and make sure that all your Valhallans are okay?" Thor said. "And check the horn?"

Even Odin saw the logic in those words, so off we went to the feasting hall.

It seems the Valkyries doubled as waitresses, bringing the warriors their food. One of them met us as we walked in. "My Lord, the heroes are not healing, which is especially bad for those that have suffered mortal wounds or worse."

Odin cursed and his words shook the very foundations of Valhalla as if an earthquake had rocked the place.

"How can this be?" Odin demanded.

Vince Argus came up to us with a flagon of mead in his hand. "Sir, the mead doesn't taste right. I think it has been switched out."

"What?" Odin said, taking the flagon from the former hit man and sniffing it. "This is not the right mead. Bring me the horn."

They had a giant ram's horn that acted like a never-empting keg. Mista brought it to the King of the Norse gods, examining it along the way.

"It looks like it, but it doesn't feel the same. It looks newer, as if it was just taken from the beast. It doesn't empty, but the mead seems just to be alcohol. I'd say it was a clever forgery," Mista said.

Odin took the horn and examined it. He didn't speak, but his body trembled with barely contained fury. The hall vibrated in sync with him.

"Mista, summon all my Valkyries to me," Odin said, much to the chagrin of Hladgunner who was standing nearby. "We will search through all of Asgard until we find where the true horn is." Odin looked down at the fallen warriors with a look I recognized. Odin was summoning his mystic sight. "They have been poisoned. All of them have been cut off from the power of Valhalla. Without the magic of the horn…" His silence hung in the air for a moment, unable to finish the sentence. "We need to have it found before the dawn." I gathered that the Valhallans that had died in battle would be in major trouble without it by that point.

Looked like Loki was right. Didn't mean I was entirely convinced he wasn't behind it, but it seemed like someone else was to blame. Although without the horn, finding who was to blame wasn't going to do the heroes of Valhalla much good.

"From the mouths of children can come some of the cruelest things you will ever hear."
-Rudy, Norse storm demigoddess, Valkyrie, agent of Nemesis & Co.

"All right, we're going to have to go hall to hall on this one people," Mista shouted. "I want every Valkyrie on hall duty to report to me anything unusual or anyone who's been in the hall. We'll check with Tyr to see if anyone left the city and make sure he locks everything down."

Rudy raised her hand. "We've been in the hall and we left the city to interrogate Loki."

"You might as well admit your guilt now," Hladgunner said. "Bad enough to be conspiring with your father, but the great deceiver? And now you've managed to prevent our warriors from reviving? Death would be too good for you and your ilk."

"I'm not ilk. I'm much better looking and more charming than ilk. And we're the ones who figured out enough to stop the battle," I said.

"It only makes sense that you would have knowledge of your own crimes," Hladgunner said.

"We've committed no crime, Jerkgunner," Rudy said.

"I am your leader," she yelled.

"You are a bitch and a bully who still lives up to her nickname," Rudy said.

"Enough infighting," Mista said. "Good men are going to die forever unless we find that horn."

"Exactly, so here is what we are going to do," Hladgunner said.

"Odin put me in charge of finding the horn," Mista said.

"And he put me in command of the Valkyries," Hladgunner said with a smirk that it was obvious that Mista wanted to knock off her face.

"You cheated," Mista said. "Odin said capture the beast, not trap it."

Hladgunner shrugged. "I beat you. The how doesn't matter. Same as now. Finding the horn is what matters, not how we do it."

"I hate to agree with Jerkgunner, but she's right. We have to find the real horn before it's too late," Rudy said.

"The last thing I need is the Sipill to take my side," Jerkgunner said.

"Sipill?" I said.

"Literally pot licker. Jerkgunner and her friends made my childhood miserable. She thinks I was only made a Valkyrie because of Grandfather, not on my own merits, which is a load of ox crap," Rudy said.

"Is it? Then why were you exempted from hōra when none of the rest of us were?" Jerkgunner said.

"Hōra?" I said.

"In addition to training and feeding the warriors of Valhalla, part of a Valkyrie's duties include taking care of their more manly needs," Mista said. "The winner of the daily tournament gets his pick of the Valkyries for his bed for the night."

"Glad to see you remember since you have been exempted since you and Heimdal have been together," Jerkgunner said. "But at least you were on the front lines with the rest of us. The Sipill never was."

"That was Grandfather's decision, not mine," Rudy said. "And I have participated in hōra."

I tried not to do a double take at my friend.

"With Adar, a man you loved. Bah. There is no duty in that. There is no sacrifice in that. You are not a true Valkyrie and I ban you from helping with the search," Jerkgunner said. "Whore."

Rudy's face was a dark pink and her hands made into fists. As much as she might despise the woman, Hladgunner was her commanding officer and Rudy had to obey.

Fortunately she wasn't mine. "Okay, that's it. I've had enough of you badmouthing my friend. Mista, what's the rite of challenge you lost called?"

"A vigr," Mista said, narrowing her eyes at me.

"Very well, I challenge you to a vigr," I said.

Jerkgunner laughed. "You are no Valkyrie, so you cannot challenge me for anything."

"Really? Odin said I would be treated as his granddaughter. Rudy could make this challenge?" I said.

"She could," Jerkgunner agreed.

"But Grandfather asked me not to so long as I was part of Nemesis & Co.," Rudy said.

"But you still could," I said.

"Of course," Rudy said.

"And so it follows that I can too," I said. "Unless you wish to make a mockery of your king's words."

"You don't stand a chance against me, fairy," Jerkgunner said, getting up in my face. She was even taller than Rudy, easily six-eight.

Tall doesn't intimidate me. Growing up at Ogre Rock, I was always the smallest and nobody there took it easy on me.

Of course, it didn't take much for me to even things up. My wings started buzzing and I lifted off the ground until I could look her in the eye.

"Wrong. I was a Daemor. I am an agent of Nemesis. I am Terrorbelle –" Who sometimes finds herself referring to herself in the third person when I'm dealing with pompous jerks. "– and I am royally ticked off. You will let us help and you will stop insulting my friend…"

Hladgunner leaned into my face so closely that our noses practically touched. "Or what?"

"I'll show you how we do things downtown," I said.

"For a proper vigr, you need a female second." Jerkgunner grinned. "But I hereby forbid any Valkyrie from helping you."

"But I can pick anyone else?" I said.

"Of course. Any woman your little heart desires who will agree to help you who is not a Valkyrie. Wait, you do not know anyone else in Asgard, now do you?" Jerkgunner said.

"You said I could pick anyone else I wanted. You never mentioned anything about them being in Asgard. Although I know someone who can shadow step her way here in an instant," I said.

Mista and Rudy gasped in unison and almost in two part harmony.

"Who are you speaking about?" Jerkgunner said.

"Her boss, dumbass," Mista said.

"But the daughter of Nyx is forbidden in Asgard," Jerkgunner said.

"But you just invited her in," I said.

"I did no such thing," Jerkgunner said.

"Actually, you did when you said she could pick anyone she wanted," Mista said smirking.

"But the All-Father has forbidden her presence," Jerkgunner said nervously.

"I guess you'll just have to explain to him why you overruled his decree," I said.

"You cannot prove this," she said.

"I heard it and will have to tell the All-Father the truth if asked," Mista said, sporting an evil grin of her own.

I could practically see the wheels in the Valkyrie leader's mind turning to figure out a solution.

"Fairy, you have no desire to lead the Valkyries," she said,

"I don't, but I do have the desire for a little respect for me and Rudy, not to mention being allowed to help in the search," I said.

Hladgunner nodded. "Fine. I apologize to you both. You may help in the search. Any place in particular you would like to be assigned?"

Rudy and I exchanged a look.

"Folkvang," she said.

Jerkgunner laughed. "You want the sex witch's hall, it's yours. Now if you will excuse me, some of us have real work to do."

Hladgunner rushed off, while Mista started dividing up the Golden City into grids and handing out assignments to the other Valkyries and some of the Valhallans who were fit for duty.

One in particular had been watching the scene with amusement.

"I never liked her much," Argus said.

"It seems you have good taste," I said.

"Since everything here is at a standstill, would you two mind if I tagged along?" Argus said. "You never know, I might come in handy."

"What's your real reason?" Rudy said.

"I've been cooped up in here a long time. Be nice to get out." Rudy folded her arms over her chest. "And I want to see if the stories about Freyja are true."

Rudy looked at me. I shrugged. "Your call."

"You willing to do what you're told?" Rudy said.

"Mostly. At least until I'm not," Argus said.

The pair glared at each other. Argus smiled, Rudy sighed.

"Fine, you can come," Rudy said.

"If what they say is true, that's a very real possibility," he said.

"Enough about you. Let's talk about me."
-Freyja, Norse lust goddess

For such a large place, the Golden City was largely empty. It seemed to consist of mainly huge, impressive architecture and few people. Or maybe I was just so used to Manhattan where you would be hard pressed to find a deserted street even at three in the morning. Here we walked for a long time and saw no one.

"Why is this place such a ghost town?" I asked Rudy.

"Grandfather has become very paranoid and does not allow many people into the city anymore. Too worried about the effects they will have on the end of our world. The villages and towns outside are where most people live these days," Rudy said. "Plus after the way Grandfather cursed and the land quaked, most are probably hiding. Grandfather is never more unreasonable than when he's angry."

"I like it," Argus said. "Then again, I've spent months in a tournament with thousands of other people who are trying to kill me. Don't get me wrong – it's the most fun I have ever had, but I could do with a spot of solitude every now and then," Argus said. "Almost makes me sentimental for home. I tended to spend a lot of time by myself."

"Lone gunman kind of thing," I said. Argus seemed like a nice guy, but I couldn't forget that he made a living killing people before he got to Valhalla.

"I sold my soul to the embodiment of evil. I knew things weren't going to end well, so I didn't see the point of getting anyone else mixed up in the mess with me," Argus said.

"So what was so valuable about getting flawless marksmanship that was worth your soul?" Rudy asked.

"It was all in Nick's timing. At any other point in my life I would have turned his offer down, but he asked at the right moment. My parents and the rest of my family had just been gunned down while we were having dinner in a restaurant. Nick offered me the chance to avenge my family and enough time to do it with. If I didn't take what he offered I would have died and the people who killed my family would have gone unpunished," Argus said.

I started to revise my opinion of the Soul For Hire. Back in Faerie before I became a soldier, in fact the very the reason I became a soldier was because graycoats from Thandau's army had raped my mother and me, then killed my mama. I went through a bit of a dark period. I avenged myself on those soldiers. It took a long time and it is not exactly something I'm proud of. Then again, it's not something I'm ashamed of as I ought to be.

"Did you get your family's killers?" I asked.

Argus nodded. "Every last one of them. But killing people, even for vengeance changes you."

"Yes, it does," I agreed. Argus met my gaze, his eyes behind his dark sunglasses. We each saw something of the other in that meeting of the eyes. When Argus was done, he seemed to be looking at me differently. With more respect and empathy.

"I wasn't the same person as I was before. That guy died with my family. When they were all taken care of, I was at a loss for what to do with my life. I couldn't see myself getting a job at a burger joint. I was the greatest marksman alive and I turned out to be very good at killing. What else was I going to do but shoot people for a living?"

He smiled when he said the word living as if he had made a joke. Back in the Daemor we had our own assassin. Her name was Daye. She had the same sarcastic smile whenever she made that comment. Assassin humor.

"Turns out that there were a lot of people who were in the same boat I was, but without any magical powers to help them get vengeance or justice. I realized I had found my calling. I killed people, but only those I felt deserved it. Other killers mainly. But I had rules. There was no collateral damage. No innocents got caught in any of my crossfire or at least not by any bullets that I fired. I didn't go after family and I never went after children."

"You were already damned. It wasn't going to get you out of Hell. Why make the effort?" I said.

"Why not?" Argus replied.

I nodded. It was a good answer. We continued our walk down the long deserted streets.

"It's a nice city. They don't really let us leave Valhalla, so this is my first time being out and about. So what do you know about this Freyja? I have heard some of the Valkyries and other dead talk. She's supposed to be a real looker," Argus said.

Rudy snorted. "That is an understatement. Freyja is the most beautiful woman in all of Asgard. Loki wasn't wrong when he said men would do anything for her. Most tend to get very stupid in her presence."

The Valkyrie looked at Argus. "Hey I sold my soul. I think that already qualifies me to sit in the stupid section."

"She wields her sexuality as a weapon. She's probably the second most powerful person in all of Asgard because of it," Rudy said.

"I figured your Pops was the number two guy," Argus said.

"In pure physical power, he is probably number one, but I'm talking political power. You'll see when we get to her hall," Rudy said.

"So you two ladies are really part of Nemesis & Co.?" Argus asked.

"Yup," Rudy said.

"Your boss has got one badass rep. We crossed paths with each other on occasion back in the day. We even went up against each other once," Argus said.

"And you survived?" I said.

Argus shrugged. "I'm pretty sure she let me. Underneath all that dark and awe, I think your boss is pretty okay."

We turned the corner and the two non-natives stopped short and our jaws dropped. Most of the buildings in the Golden City went for beauty and geometric designs. Freyja's hall looked like it belonged in Vegas. The whole building seemed to be made out of solid gold and the front of it was basically a giant statue of a woman sitting spread eagle, whom I could only assume was based on Freyja. On the building behind the sculpture, there were smaller sculptures of the same woman's face and body. There was a large amount of tacky in the overall scheme, but it was just as huge as Valhalla which still gave it quite an expensive – and tacky – air. There seemed to only be one gate and it too was designed after Freyja or at least one specific body part.

Don't get me wrong. I'm a woman and I have said part, but it's not one that I am likely to go showing off in public, let alone having a twenty foot gate designed after. The sidewalls were modeled after her thighs. At the corner, the knees bent and the walls were the calf and foot. Looking up the rest of the front face of the hundred foot statue, I marveled at the woman who was so confident that she would have herself portrayed as naked as she wanted to be, which was entirely.

"So I take it Freyja is very shy and reserved, huh?" I said.

Rudy giggled. "Hardly."

Argus was still staring. Rudy and I both looked back at him.

"Hey, I'm a guy. For a statue it looks amazingly lifelike. And gigantic. It's not actual size is it?" Rudy didn't answer. Argus raised his eyebrows and his jaw dropped even further. "Is it?"

Rudy shook her head. "Freyja is typical size for an Aesir, although her abilities allow her to become the right size for whatever partner she is with, whether it be a dwarf or a giant."

"I guess that's convenient. Although I am a bit more interested in the eye candy watching the door," I said. The front of the gate didn't just have a single guard or even a few. There were a hundred well-muscled men with spears standing shoulder to shoulder across the front of the hall. I know – I counted. Who could blame me? They all wore thongs and were oiled up, like if Buckingham Palace had let Chippendale's redesign their guard uniforms. "I might not have appreciated her taste in décor, but I certainly can't fault her with her choice in personnel. I would hate to try and storm her hall. It would be a tragedy to damage those works of art she has guarding the place." Rudy gave me a confused look. "Not the sculptures, the guys."

"I'm more a fan of the sculptures. But to each her own," Argus said.

We stepped up to the gate. As one, the hundred men shouted out "Halt, who goes there?" lifting up one hand in front of them as if they were doing karaoke for "Stop In The Name of Love." I have to admit the effect of that many well-muscled guys moving in sync was damned sexy and I would have had no complaints about karaoke at Snake's if they were participating.

"Thrud of the Valkyries and Nemesis & Co. By order of All-Father Wotan, we have come to search the premises."

In unison they spoke again. "None will pass without the mistress' leave."

"Then why don't you just send her a message and let her know that we are here?" I said.

The looks on the faces of the guards became confused and perturbed. Apparently they were simply supposed to stand there and let no one in. And since they were trained to work as a unit - my mind boggled at the implications of that for when they were off duty - they couldn't let one break off of the group to go get her. And all of them going would leave the highly narcissistically shaped gate unguarded.

"Mistress!" the hundreds shouted in unison. I sensed movement above us - as a flyer, I tend to think in three dimensions and, unlike ground-locked people, always tend to check above me. I saw two shapes drop out of the nostrils of the golden goddess and dive down toward us. I started to pull my gun, but Rudy put her hand on my arm.

"It's okay. The cats are her familiars, much like Grandfather has his ravens and wolves." A pair of cats, significantly larger than the household variety, flew down and hovered in front of us.

"Please tell your mistress we are here and require entry on the order of Odin," Rudy said.

The cats flew up and back inside the nostrils. A moment later the anatomically shaped gates slid open and the soldiers parted fifty on each side to let us in.

"Modest? What exactly do I have to be modest about?"
-Freyja, Norse lust goddess

We followed Rudy through the anatomically shaped gate and I was pleased to note that the anatomical theme didn't extend to the inside of the building. I wasn't looking forward to the idea of trying to find my way through the bowels of the place, especially if it was literal.

I must say Freyja impressed me even before I met her. The entire hallway leading to her throne room was lined on both sides by more well-muscled and greased men in thongs with large spears. That wasn't a euphemism, but as I glanced south I realized it could be. The woman really knew how to accessorize.

The throne room wasn't hard to find. We just followed the stationary parade of half-naked guys until we emerged into a stadium that the Giants would have been pleased to play in. For all I know, maybe the Asgardian giants played here, but the game probably wasn't football. The place had stadium seating although no one sat. The place was lined wall to wall and floor to ceiling with more of her spear carriers.

Despite myself I whispered, "Damn!" Argus and I followed a step behind Rudy to either side of her as she walked up to the podium. Freyja's throne was equal parts chair and lounge. She was surrounded by men who had forgone the thong loin cloths and were feeding, massaging and fanning her. I would have been like a kid in a candy store, but the goddess seemed bored by it all, which seemed kind of sad.

Rudy bowed her head and beat her fist on her chest. "Lady Freyja, Lord Odin has sent us to search your hall for something that is missing."

Freyja kind of reclined on her throne and rolled her eyes. "What's Od...in lost this time?"

She made it sound as if his name was Od, which was odd.

"I am really not at liberty to say," Rudy said.

"Then I'm really not at liberty to let you search," Freyja said.

"We have our orders," Rudy said.

"Dear, you may be his granddaughter, but who do you think he will side with in this or any dispute?" the goddess said.

Rudy later told me that it was an ill kept secret that Freyja's missing husband Od was Odin in another shape. He couldn't bear the thought of another man having her as his wife, so he married her and then disappeared. This prevented her from marrying again, although it didn't do much to deter her from taking more lovers than an entire small country.

"However I see you brought something to bargain with," Freyja said looking at Argus. "A little too many clothes for my taste, but I can fix that soon enough."

The Soul For Hire didn't look happy. "Listen lady, Vince Argus isn't anyone's play toy."

At the mention of his name, Freyja was no longer bored. In fact, she jumped up from her throne and rushed over to the hitman. "You really brought me Vince Argus? The newest champion of Valhalla? Nothing would anger Odin more than me having his champion. Thank you girls so much. You can have whatever you like." Argus stood ramrod still as the lust goddess rubbed herself up and down him and ran her fingers down his chest. When she approached one of his holsters he grabbed hold of her hand, pulling it off and pushing her away. There was shock on every face in the stadium room, not the least of which was Freyja.

"You … reject me? That has never happened before. Not even with men that prefer other men." Freyja looked down at Argus' pants that were much larger than when we had walked in, so it was obvious that her powers were working. I had seen lust magic before and she was right about it working on any man. It tapped into the primal centers of the brain bypassing everything else, so it made no difference what the target's sexual preference was. All that mattered was the sex. Some vampyres tapped into the same parts of the brain.

"I don't do anything I don't want to do, sister. So back off," Argus said.

I expected anger on Freyja's face, but there was only a huge smile. She jumped up and down and clapped. The eyes of all the men in the room ascended and descended as certain attributes of hers did the same, much like a vertical tennis match. She wore a golden gown that couldn't seem to decide if it was formal or slinky, but showed plenty of flesh and a necklace with five jewels, four red and the center one yellow.

"A challenge. I have not had a challenge in ages. Very well, Vince Argus, I shall have you. Maybe not today or tomorrow, but you will be mine." Freyja turned to Rudy and me. "If either of you can help me in this endeavor to bed Vince Argus, anything I can grant you will be yours, this I promise you and give you my word."

"Thank you, but as a sign of goodwill to have us consider your offer, will you allow us to search your hall?" Rudy said. Freyja was circling Argus like a cat around a mouse. A horny, perverted cat who was thinking of going trans-species.

She waved her hand in such a way I almost expected her to say pish posh, but instead she went with, "Yes, yes. Whatever you wish. So long as Vince Argus stays here to keep me entertained during your search."

Rudy looked at the Soul For Hire who rolled his eyes. "Go on. What we're looking for is more important."

"Thanks," Rudy said. She motioned for me to follow her, but that didn't stop me from hearing their conversation as we exited.

"So it said that you could hit any target you're aiming for. Is that true?" Freyja said.

"It is," Argus replied.

"Can you do it repeatedly?" she said.

"For as long as I need to."

"And you realize there are parts of a woman that can be considered targets?" she said.

"I learned that years ago and I've only gotten better with practice," Vince said grinning.

Freyja let loose an orgasmic sigh that made the wall of men weak in the knees. As we exited her throne stadium, I wondered if Argus would have the fortitude to not give in before we returned.

"Hide and seek is much easier to win if the other side doesn't know that you're hiding or that they should be looking for you."
* -Rudy, Norse storm demigoddess, Valkyrie, agent of Nemesis & Co.*

It's easier to search a New York apartment than it is a hall in Asgard. For one thing, there is the matter of size. Basically, we were looking for something you could stick in a microwave that was in a place bigger than Yankee Stadium. Still we did our due diligence and hit every place that we could, including Freyja's bedroom. Although, from the looks of the place, I doubt she got much sleep. There were a huge number of contraptions that had functions that were beyond my keen. There is a trend in New York these days for women to install stripper poles in their homes both as a form of recreation and exercise. Freyja's bedroom went far beyond that. There were things I can only describe as indoor rock climbing with trapezes and ropes and harnesses that would put acrobats to shame. We went floor to ceiling in there and the only thing we had afterwards that we didn't have before was the need to disinfect our hands.

"We're never going to find this horn," I said.

"Don't despair, T-Belle. We haven't searched everywhere," Rudy said. The Valkyrie went to a far corner of the room where there was a chair that was carved so that part of it resembled a huge male phallus.

"You're not going to sit on that thing are you?" I said.

"Yup," Rudy said, straddling it like it was a saddle instead of the way it was probably meant to be used. She then grabbed hold of the top, twisted and leaned forward. The seat tilted at a 45 degree angle and the wall behind it slid open.

"Do I even want to know why you knew to do that?" I said.

Rudy stood and wiped her hands on her jeans. "It is nothing like that. I grew up in Asgard and I was curious. Grandfather banned me from ever coming into Freyja's hall, so of course I had to figure out how to do just that. It was quite an education, let me tell you. I also found out that several of her gentlemen callers didn't want to be seen entering or leaving her hall for one reason or another. For some, it was jealous wives or fear of angering Grandfather or one of her other multitude of lovers. It also allowed her to sneak out when she wanted to."

"Or maybe little Valkyries to sneak in?" I said.

Rudy smiled a devilish grin. "Maybe. If she was going to hide any-thing, it's likely going to be in a hidden passage."

"But if it's such a well-traveled hidden passage, wouldn't that defeat the purpose?" I said.

"It would, except where would the best place to hide a real hidden passage be? In another hidden passage, of course."

"And you, of course, know where this secret-secret passage is?" I said.

"I might, as long as she hasn't moved it or changed it," said Rudy. "We've got to go through the door together because as soon as one person enters, it closes. That is unless you want to have a go at opening it?" The red-haired Valkyrie wiggled her eyebrows.

"I think I'll pass," I said.

"Suit yourself," Rudy said.

We stepped through the door together and it snapped closed behind us. Rudy pulled out a glow stick and snapped it in half, lighting up the passageway. For half an instant, I thought we weren't alone and were being invaded by an army of naked women before I realized Freyja had just lined the walls of the passageway with more statues of herself, except these were flesh colored instead of golden.

"This woman has some serious narcissistic issues," I said.

"No argument there. Sometimes she would wait for her lovers in the hallway, pretending to be one of the statues. Her lovers would have to try to figure out which one was the real her. All of them can be moved to make the game more challenging. All of them except one." Rudy moved a decent way down the tunnel and stopped in front of one particular statue. They were easy to tell apart as each had the image of the goddess in a different position. The writer of the karma sutra might have been able to learn a couple things just from walking down this tunnel.

"The secret passage is behind this one," Rudy said.

"How do we open it?" I asked.

"A very simple combination lock. Of course one needs a key." Rudy wiggled her eyebrows again and gave me a wink.

"You've got to be kidding me. That's disgusting."

Rudy shrugged. "It is. But it has to be done to get us in." The Valkyrie held up her glow stick. "Would you like to do the honors?"

"Hell, no. I am not committing statutory rape for you or anybody."

"It's official. With that joke you've proven you are spending too much time with Murphy," Rudy said, taking her makeshift key and thrusting it into the lock repeatedly. It gave a weird strobe affect, but other than that nothing happened.

"Must not be big enough," Rudy said. I rolled my eyes as the Valkyrie took out a collapsible baton, similar to what the police use in addition to billy clubs these days. Rudy's was a little thicker and more dense. She swung out her hand and there was a noise as the baton expanded to its full size. It may have looked like a thin weapon, but I have seen humans break kneecaps with the regular version. In Rudy's hand it could smash through one side of a lamppost and out the other.

"Do you want to make the joke about size mattering or should I?" Rudy said.

"Just get it over with," I said.

"Trust me, if you ever get lucky enough with Murphy or Joe, never say that."

Rudy reapplied the new key and this time it worked. The statue's legs moved from the ground to over the statue's neck, leaving a small passageway to crawl through. Rudy went in first and I followed.

This passageway seemed empty, but we searched it anyway.

"Maybe yet another secret passage?" I said.

"Could be. Guess we'll have to do this old school," Rudy said.

The two of us began knocking on the walls, floors and ceiling. It was the floor which came up with an echo. The pair of us grabbed hold of either side of that tile and lifted. It was heavy enough that it took both of us to move it.

And underneath we did find something, but it wasn't the horn.

"That looks like Mjollnir. But it can't be. Grandfather still has it," Rudy said.

"Then I guess someone did create a duplicate hammer and hid it here," I said. "But why?"

"Easy. No male would have done this thorough of a search. The lady of this house enjoys special protection."

"She'd have to in order to not get a venereal disease," I said.

Rudy laughed and looked at the hammer more closely. "Beside it's obvious that this is not Dad's hammer. There was a defect in making the handle too short. Uncle was involved and tried to use that as an excuse to get out of paying Brokk with his head. This one's handle is slightly longer."

"We need to bring this back to clear your father. But how are we going to lift it?"

"My uncle had a hand in the making of the original. He supplied the dwarves with magic that could not be gotten again, so this hammer couldn't be as powerful. Maybe that means it's not as heavy." Rudy bent down to try to lift it up. She got the handle off the ground and managed to get the hammer itself up a few inches before dropping it. "See? Not as heavy. I'd never be able to lift Father's hammer that high." The sound of clapping filled the tunnel. Both Rudy and I drew our guns so fast that anyone watching would probably have to go to a video replay to see us actually do it. There was a man standing there, dressed in what looked to be an expensive Italian made suit, putting his hands together for us.

"Very impressive. You are, of course, right in that it is not as powerful as your father's. I helped supply a substitute for the missing ingredient, but with hammers, like horseshoes, hand grenades and hydrogen bombs, almost is good enough. Still, it is no easy task for anyone to pick it up. Truly impressive. I have put a lot of work into what is going on here and I must insist that you leave the hammer right where it is. Perhaps forget that you even saw it."

"Why would we do that?" I asked.

"I could give you any number of reasons. It is within my powers to give you a great many things. Perhaps arrange for Murphy to finally fall fully in love with you, Miss Terrorbelle. Or you Miss Thrud could finally lead the Valkyries like you were born to do. All you would have to do is grant me this one small favor."

"At the expense of my Father? No way," Rudy said. "Who are you anyway?"

The man grinned. "In another form you might recognize me, but since I'm not really supposed to be in Asgard, I'd prefer you'd not even guess my name."

At the guess his name crack, my mind flashed to Murphy's number one suspect and was suddenly glad we had left Argus upstairs. Still, the Devil did not have a reputation for being shy, so it could be anyone.

Whoever he was, I had no idea if this joker had anywhere near the power he claimed he did, but I had a way to find out and maybe get him off our backs.

"Does Nemesis know you're here?" He obviously knew who we were, which meant he knew who we worked for. "It seems to me that you might be in violation of an agreement."

Many of the powers that be had treaties or other agreements with the boss to keep on her good side. It wasn't too farfetched to assume this guy might be one of them. She had one with the Devil.

"So you do recognize me, even disguised as I am. Very impressive, Terrorbelle. And no, your boss does not know I'm here. Unfortunately, communicating with two of her agents without her present is a violation.

Since I do not want to involve the daughter of night at this juncture, I'll concede this round to you. I trust you will not hold it against me if I continue to hope that you fail in this endeavor."

And with that, the man simply vanished, as if he was never there.

"Who was that?" Rudy said.

"I think it may be Murphy's suspect," I said.

Rudy cocked her gun and pointed it at shadows.

I'm just lucky he bought my bluff. "Now we just have to figure out how to get the hammer out of here."

Rudy pulled a knife out of her boot with her gun hand and sliced it across her palm, careful not to damage anything but the skin. A whole lot of blood poured out. She reached down, placed her palm on the hammer, then wrapped her fingers around the handle which made it glow and crackle with energy. When Rudy stood up, the hammer came with her and the bleeding had stopped.

"How did you know blood magic would work on the hammer?" I said.

"My father told me long ago that in order to bond the hammer to him, blood was required, not unlike the genetic encoding Nemesis does with our guns."

I noticed with amusement that neither of us had put our guns away just yet. The clapping man might still be nearby, just unseen.

We headed back up to confront Freyja about what we found.

"What Freyja wants, Freyja gets."
-Freyja, Norse lust goddess

The lust goddess paid us no mind as we re-entered her arena of men. She was still hanging all over Argus. I had to give the guy credit – very few men would have managed to not succumb to her charms at this point. If anything the tent pole in his pants looked larger than when we left.

"Freyja, we need to talk," Rudy said.

"Yes, yes. You didn't find the horn. I could have told you that, but at least it gave me some quality time with my new man here."

"We may not have found the horn, but we found something even more interesting," Rudy said.

Freyja turned and saw the hammer in Rudy's left hand.

"You found it? And were able to move it? How dare you intrude into my secret places."

"I don't know about how secret they are. It seems like everyone can get into them," I said. "So how do you take care of the crowd here? Does everyone get a set time or do you do a raffle every night?"

"How dare you speak to me that way. I will have both of you destroyed."

"Not going to happen," Rudy said.

Freyja turned and stepped toward Rudy. The goddess lifted her hand up as if to slap the Valkyrie.

Rudy only smiled. "We had your permission to search your entire hall. It's not my fault you can't hide things well. But keep coming if you want a piece of me. This may not be the original, but I'm sure it packs a wallop and I'm itching to try it out. Please give me an excuse."

Freyja backed away and put her hand to the necklace she wore. Her fingers resting on the center of five jewels. The outer four were red, but the inner one yellow.

I have no idea how to describe what happened next. Suddenly, I was overcome with the most intense feelings I ever experienced. As if my entire body was suddenly tingling with electricity, especially the parts that Freyja had monuments to all around her hall.

The lust goddess snapped her fingers and instantly I was surrounded by more men than I could count, especially since I now seemed incapable of higher thought. I'm not embarrassed to say that I've never been one for casual sex. Not surprising considering my fate at the hands of the graycoats that killed my mother, but suddenly I was different. All my inhibitions and emotional wounds seemed to vanish in a puff of lust. As the men approached me, they held up their hands to touch or embrace me. My normal reaction would be to stop them with a joke or a punch. Instead, I reached out, grabbing hold of one behind the neck, bringing him in for a lip lock. I moved my head and realized there was another to the side of him trying to kiss me. I smooched him next. There were hands all over me and instead of being upset, I was thrilled. I was grabbing and touching parts like it was an all you can grope buffet and it was going both ways. Men had their hands underneath not only my shirt, but under my bra and had even managed to get inside my pants. Not an easy task under normal conditions. I was about to rip off my clothes when suddenly there was a jolt from my Daemor badge belt buckle that brought me back to reality for the merest instant and I realized I had been the victim of a lust spell. I shoved the men away from me and saw that Rudy had also succumbed to the same magic. If it wasn't for my Daemor badge, I would still be bespelled. Happy, but for all the wrong reasons.

Freyja was still far away from me, so I picked up two men by the fronts of their loin clothes and tossed them like I was going to jump on top of them. I just made sure that they landed at their mistress' feet. And as I jumped, I ripped the necklace off of her before I could succumb to the spell again. It worked. I no longer felt supernatural urges. Nor apparently did Rudy, judging by the men flying through the air. Rudy survived being raped and tortured by a mad demigod several months ago. No woman goes through that without being affected. Trust me on this.

Without the magic, it felt like she was going through it again. If the men had been alive, they would have been crippled. In fact, they were crippled, but since they were dead, I was sure Freyja's magic would heal them again.

"Give me back my necklace, you treacherous whore," Freyja screamed, coming at me. I kicked her in the gut and she doubled over. The goddess may have actually been stronger than me, but she had never had to fight for anything in her life. Men just tripped over themselves trying to give things to her.

"Not going to happen. And considering your recreational activities, should you really be insulting any other woman's virtue? I mean sluts in glass castles shouldn't really throw sex toys," I said. "Now you are going to answer some questions."

"I'm not going to tell you anything," she said.

"Then I'm going to start smashing some jewels," I said.

"Even Thor wouldn't be able to smash those jewels barehanded," she said.

Rudy stormed up and lifted the hammer. She had figured out how to tap into the magical properties, because it was crackling with electricity. "Of course my father wouldn't have to use his hands and now neither do I. Terrorbelle, put the jewels all on the floor and I'll smash them all."

I bent down with the necklace in my fingers.

"No! I will tell you anything you want. Just don't hurt the necklace," Freyja pleaded, falling to her knees, which seemed to be well callused. No judgment from me. Aw, hell who am I kidding? Being a goddess of lust doesn't make her any less of a slut than the normal variety.

"Why did we find this hammer here?" Rudy said.

"I was keeping it for a friend," Freyja said.

"Don't you mean hiding?" I said.

"Semantics," she said.

"Who is the friend?" Rudy said.

"I can't tell you that." Rudy lifted the hammer up and Freyja put her hand up. "He is too powerful. You have to swear to me that you will not say I told you."

"You are not in the position to ask any favors. Who is it?" I said.

"Brokk."

"Where is the horn?" Rudy asked.

"I have no idea." Rudy raised the hammer again. "It is the truth."

"You have some form of magic to heal your dead, don't you?" I said.

"Of course."

"How does it work? I want you to pack it up so we can take it with us," I said.

"I can't do that. It is tied specifically to my hall. I can store up the energies during sex and use them to heal. Since I don't use my warriors to fight, I have a lot of energy stored up. But I can only use it here."

So much for an easy fix. "So who was the guy we saw in your tunnel?" I said.

Freyja looked confused. "I don't know of any guy that would have been there other than Brokk."

"What is Brokk's plan?" Rudy said.

"I don't know. He didn't tell me. All I know is that he had a partner," Freyja said.

"Maybe it was him in the tunnel," I said.

"There shouldn't be anyone there," she said. "I would have sensed it."

"Not necessarily," Rudy said, speaking from past experience. "So why did you do it? Why did you betray Asgard?"

Freyja bowed her head. "Brokk managed to steal my necklace. It amplifies my natural powers. I have been using it for centuries. I would be nothing without it."

"So you did it to get a piece of jewelry back?" I said.

"She slept with four dwarves to get it in the first place," Rudy said. "What's one more?"

"Actually, Brokk's partner helped him enhance it with the yellow gem. The red gem works on men, but the yellow one works on woman. I answered all your questions, now give me my necklace back," Freyja said.

I smiled, holding the jewels up in my hand. "I only said I wouldn't smash them if you answered our questions. I never said anything about giving them back." I put the necklace around my own neck. My intent was to heighten my negotiation stance with Freyja, but when I put it on the entire world seemed to shift slightly. I looked up and every man in the stadium suddenly turned their head to stare at me. Worse, they moved toward me with military precision and lust clear on their faces. And even if I couldn't see their faces, other parts were changing the shape of what little clothing they wore.

"Oh ckuf," I said.

Freyja saw what was happening and her eyes narrowed and her face turned a dark shade of red. "You have no idea the power you are wielding. You can't control it. Give the necklace back to me and I will stop them."

"Terrorbelle, I've got a little bit of an idea of what those guys are feeling, cause you are looking pretty good to me and you're not my type at all," Rudy said. "I'm barely keeping myself from groping you and they're feeling four times what I am."

My body's first reaction was panic as I flashed back to what Thandau's soldiers had done to me. So many men moving like soldiers totally freaked me out. My first instinct was to start shooting. My second was that the men were acting under a spell and weren't responsible for their actions. My third was to run for the exit, but men chased after me, while others beat me to the exit, cutting off my escape.

I was so flustered I forgot I wasn't on Earth until I was almost to the blocked door. I leapt and flew high up into the stadium.

I hovered as I tried to get myself under control. Men were leaping off the upper rows in an attempt to reach me, but didn't have the leg power to pull it off. Instead, they plummeted to the ground, each landing more painfully than the next.

I took a deep breath. I wasn't a child anymore. I still have nightmares about what happened, but I stopped letting those soldiers hurt me years ago. I wasn't a mage, but I'd been trained in using basic magic. A large component of any magic was will. I focused on the jewels and I felt a warm hum, almost a vibration course though me. Another part of many magics was the spoken word. It was time to put that to the test.

"All of you, stop where you are," I said.

The acoustics in the stadium were incredible. Every last one of Freyja's dead soldiers stopped and halted exactly where they were, with the exception of one that was mid-leapt. Amazingly he didn't even put his arms up to protect his face from the impact of landing.

One soldier dropped to his knee and slammed his fist against his chest. Almost as one, the other several thousand did the same.

"Mistress, we live only to serve you," said the one who went to his knee first.

Cautiously I landed in the center of the arena. Freyja was screaming all manner of obscenities at me.

"Shut up," I said.

"The necklace doesn't work on me," she whispered, but I didn't believe her, mainly because of the way she was staring hungrily at me and rubbing her hands along her body, one hand above the waist, the other below. "This is my place of power and you will obey me. Take off all your clothes and come to me – no, I mean take that necklace off and give it to me, harlot."

"Not a chance," I said.

The obscenities started again, but when she started insulting my dead mama I had all I could take.

I pointed to one side of the room. "Shut her up."

The men moved toward the goddess.

"Halt. Stop. I command you to listen to me. I am your mistress, you will…" That was the last thing she said as her former sex slaves dragged her to the ground and covered her mouth.

Rudy moved up next to me and whispered in my ear. "Several thousand men willing to be your sex slaves. Not too shabby."

"The sex part is not too bad. It's the slave part I have issue with. I was a slave for a time back in Faerie and I won't put anyone else through it."

"So are you going to give the necklace back?" Rudy said.

"Hell no. They'll still be slaves then, only to somebody that will take advantage of that." I turned and saw Argus was still standing there, still a statue. He was looking at me the same way the men were, only he somehow had the strength to resist the magic and stay in place.

"Release her," I said and the men back away from their former mistress. "We will be taking our leave of you Freyja, but rest assured we will be telling Odin what we have found here."

"But what about my necklace?" Freyja asked.

"You mean my necklace," I said. "You're from Asgard. Look at these men all around you. I know you are familiar with the concept of spoils of war. You attacked us and we won. The spoils are ours."

"You have made a powerful enemy of me," Freyja said.

I patted the jewels on my chest. "Not so powerful anymore. Don't leave town as we might have some more questions," I teased and we turned and walked out. Argus and Rudy followed, but so did all of the thong soldiers. I let them at least until we got to the door then I turned. "I command you to live with honor and integrity. To do what is right and to be a slave to no one."

"You know that will only work until someone else uses the necklace on them, right?" Rudy whispered in my ear.

I nodded. "Then I guess I'll have to make sure no one else gets a hold of the necklace."

We exited through the gate, but this time the hundred guards got on one knee as I walked by. It was a little disconcerting, especially when I realized that I wasn't sure if I had willed them to bow down to me or if they had done it on their own.

"It's hammer time!"
    -Rudy, Norse storm demigoddess, Valkyrie, agent of Nemesis & Co.

We were back on the streets of Asgard again. "I just have to try this out," Rudy said, tossing the hammer in front of her. It shot down the length of the long street then turned around and returned to her hand. "Sweet!"

Out of the corner of my eye, I could see Argus still staring at me, particularly two prominent parts that many men stared at because of their unusual size. I had given Argus credit because I hadn't caught him staring before, then realized it was probably the necklace at work. I took it off and put it in my pocket, breaking the spell. Argus' eyes returned to look at my face.

"So how did you resist Freyja's charms, especially when she was wearing the necklace?" I said.

"I have had to deal with mind control magics before. They only tend to work so long as you are not focused. The key is to get something else to focus on," Argus said. True enough. Part of the Daemor badge's magic broke certain spells by sending a painful shock through the wearer, temporarily breaking the magic's effect. As far as I knew, Argus didn't have any such charm or amulet on him.

"So how did you distract yourself?" I asked, as Rudy ran up and down the street playing with her new hammer.

Argus turned and spat on the road. His spittle was red. "Simple. I kept biting my tongue. The pain helped me focus past the mind control magic."

"That's got to hurt," I said.

"That's the idea. I doubt it hurt as much as knowing your mind was controlled by someone else," the Soul For Hire said.

I couldn't argue with him there.

"Hey T-Belle, you want to ride the lightning?" Rudy said.

"Sure."

Rudy threw the hammer and this time I managed to hop on first time around.

"Nice," Argus said. "Me next."

"If I had a hammer…"
    -Rudy, Norse storm demigoddess, Valkyrie, agent of Nemesis & Co.

Rudy shrunk the hammer so it fit in the palm of her hand and ran in to Valhalla, thrilled to be able to show her grandfather what she had found.

When we entered the dining and throne room, Brokk was down on one knee in front of his throne. Thor sat beside his father, watching the dwarf warily.

"My Lord Odin, I know for years you have been handicapped in your quest for wisdom by the loss of your eye. I believe I have come up with the solution for that," Brokk said. He held out a golden eyepatch. "I have crafted this myself. It will replace your lost eye, allowing you to see again. In fact, it will allow you to do far more than that. You will be able to see through objects and view into many different spectrums. It will reveal to you hidden things and you will be able to tell if something is bespelled with a simple glance. All-Father, it will not replace your lost eye, but perhaps it can help make up for your loss in some small way," Brokk said. "Maybe let you find the missing horn."

"It sounds marvelous, but what is the price of such a wondrous gift?" Odin said.

"I wish to become an advisor in your court. Like all in Asgard, I fear the coming Twilight. With all due humility, I am the greatest craftsman in the realm. I feel that by putting my services exclusively at your command, that together we may yet win the coming battle. This is simply a token of good faith to help me get into your good graces, my lord," Brokk said.

Odin held up the eyepatch. "If it does even half of what you claim, this patch would help me greatly. I shall take your request under advisement."

"That is all I ask," Brokk said. "That and you doing me the honor of trying on my gift. Once you do, I am certain you will see I speak only truth."

Before the king of the Aesir could try on his new accessory, Rudy ran in front of the dwarf and onto her knee.

"Grandfather, do not accept that gift. I have something to tell and show you," Rudy said, holding out her closed hand.

"But it cannot be as important as what I have found," Hladgunner said, rushing in behind Rudy and holding the missing ram's horn above her head.

Odin's eyes got wide and he and stood, walking past his granddaughter and the dwarf. "Excellent work, battle maiden. Where was it found?"

Hladgunner hung her head, but did not answer.

"I said where?" Odin yelled.

"In Bilskirnir, the Lord Thor's hall…"

"That's preposterous!" Thor shouted, leaping to his feet.

Odin turned and stared at his son. "Is it?"

"Father, why would I steal it and then come here to warn everyone to stop? If I had truly wanted all of the Valhallans dead, wouldn't I have waited until there was only one victor left standing?" Thor said.

The dwarf Brokk practically skipped up to Odin's side, giddy at Thor's predicament. "Perhaps that is exactly what you wanted us to think in order to give you an alibi. How do you explain the horn being found in your hall?"

"I haven't even lived there in ages," Thor said. "Obviously it was planted in a further attempt to frame me."

"Nonsense. Who would ever do such a thing?" Brokk said.

"Maybe you, dwarf. You have hated us all even since we got Mjollnir from you and your brother," Thor said.

"Through trickery and deceit. And I never received my full payment. But that does not mean I would or could orchestrate your troubles," Brokk said.

"Bilskirnir has been closed since I left Asgard, but it is still tremendous. How did a single Valkyrie manage to search the entire hall and just happen to find the horn?" Thor said. Rudy has said his hall was the biggest in Asgard, so he had a point. "This stinks of frame job."

"A pity there is no way to tell who handled the horn and who hadn't, thereby proving your innocence or guilt," Brokk said.

"That isn't necessarily true," I said. The dwarf turned to glare daggers at me. "On Earth they use forensics to determine what's happened in a crime. They can do things like fingerprinting and DNA testing among others."

"Are you suggesting that we call in an Earth detective to perform these tests?" Odin said. "Science does not always perform well in a realm of magic."

"True enough, so what if we brought in an expert that could handle both?" I said.

"Who do you have in mind?" Odin said, eyeing me suspiciously.

"Ganieda," Rudy said having figured out where I was going.

"The sister of Merlin? And the third agent of Nemesis & Co.?" Odin asked, frowning.

"One and the same. She has been studying magic and science for centuries. In fact, she has made magic a science. She may be able to give us more insight and prevent the railroading of someone I believe to be an innocent man," I said. "A feeling I believe you share."

"This is beginning to feel more and more like an invasion by your employer," Odin said.

"Grandfather, I personally vouch for Gani. She is beyond brilliant and her honor is above reproach. She once served the Round Table of Camelot," Rudy said.

"Arthur's deeds of valor and honor are well known to us. Very well, if you give me your word that you will guarantee her behavior and honor, she may come to perform an investigation. However Nemesis is still forbidden in my realm," Odin said.

"I think we can work with that," I said.

"Grandfather, I have something to tell you about Brokk," Rudy said.

"Thrud, your dislike of the dwarf is well known to me. Whatever it is can wait until we figure out what has happened here," Odin said.

"But Grandfather, it cannot…"

"Enough. Do not bring the matter up again, Thrud," Odin said. "When can the Lady Ganieda be here?"

"That depends. Do you have someplace I can make a call?" I said.

"Some calls always come collect,"
  -Terrorbelle, agent of Nemesis & Co. and former Daemor soldier

My cell phone has some magical properties, although that doesn't always mean it gets service. Especially in a city of paranoid gods. The modified half sphere of woe apparently blocked most known forms of communication, magical or otherwise. However, by going outside the gates of the city toward the Rainbow Bridge, I was able to get reception on its mystic circuits.

Gani was number three on my speed dial. She was thrilled with the prospect of visiting a realm of gods.

"I'll be there shortly," Gani said.

"Should I send Rudy to come and get you?" I said. Shortly to Gani could translate as hours, especially if she was involved with some research project. Better to have someone collect her than stand around waiting.

"No need. However, the boss wants to talk to you," Gani said, handing her phone off to Nemesis.

"Terrorbelle, explain to me what is going on," Nemesis ordered in her dark and spooky voice. I was glad I couldn't see her. When the boss gets upset, you can see things peeking out from the darkness in her eyes that can make your bladder forget to do its job.

I brought her up to speed.

"So you think someone is framing Thor?" she said.

"Yes," I said.

I heard the boss sigh. "I don't like this at all. I don't like having my team in another world whose ruler has forbidden me to visit. You all need to be careful. However, if you're in trouble, just send a gun back." Nemesis' guns were very dangerous, considering the types of ammo they held. They could do major damage in the wrong hands. Because of that, Gani built in a charm that allows us to make the guns teleport back to the office in New York City if we're captured. It was also a way to call for help.

"Will do, boss." I turned at movement behind me on Bifrost, then relaxed as I saw a familar face.

"Good, because no edict is going to stop me if my people need help," Nemesis said.

I knew she meant it too, which would cause no end of political problems between her, the Council of Thrones and the realm of Asgard. We said our goodbyes and I turned toward my visitor.

"You have cell service in Asgard? Impressive," Wanda said. The rainbow swimming mermaid had her arms up against the end of the bridge like she was leaning on the edge of a pool. "I can't get any reception outside of Earth and even then it's meager at best."

"Magically enhanced," I said, wiggling the cell phone.

"Any chance of me getting a plan like that?" the adaro said.

"Not without working for Nemesis & Co."

"Oh well. I've heard rumblings of what is going on in Asgard. Not pretty," she said.

"Not at all." Then something occurred to me. "You haven't heard any rumors about who or what might be behind it?"

The mermaid shook her head. "The only name being mentioned is Thor's and bets on whether he is being framed or not. Still I owe you for your help with the cornu, so I'll ask around. In fact, I'd be happy to hang around here until you leave. Asgard can be a violent and deadly place. You might need a quick escape route out of here and I'd be happy to give you a ride."

I thought about it. It was a good idea. "Thanks, I appreciate it. I might have friends with me though. I'll make sure to tell you when I'm leaving so you don't have to wait around any longer than you have to."

"Don't worry about me. This is one of the best rainbows for swimming anywhere and Bifrost is permanent. Usually I have to jump off a rainbow onto another one before they disappear or I can actually fall out onto land. Very painful. Also since Heimdal and I got to know each other in the hot tub at Bulfinche's Pub a few May Days back, he has been a little bit more tolerant of my presence. Hasn't called me a gopher in months," she said. "So who are you waiting for?"

"A friend, but she's always late, so it will likely be a long while," I said.

As if trying to prove me wrong, a flying carpet appeared over the crest of the Rainbow Bridge, with Gani riding atop it. It was her alternate means of getting around when she couldn't use the elevator, but that only worked to go places she's already been and made an invisible magic sigil to allow the elevator to link on.

"Or maybe not so long," I said to the white-haired beauty. "I'm in shock. I always end up having to wait for you."

"Nemesis was worried about Rudy and pushed me out the door," Gani said.

That explained it. "Good. Now that we have you to examine the crime scene, this frame job should be exposed within the hour."

"What do you think this is, a TV show?" Gani said. "Although I am sometimes just that good."

"Maybe they'll give you your own show," I said.

"We could call it MCSI for Mystic Crime Scene Investigation. After all, the original put Murphy's books on the set. You think maybe he can put in a good word for me?"

Murphy's books were indeed used as props on the show. "I'll ask him, but I don't think he has that kind of pull."

"Who's your adaro friend?" Gani asked. I made introductions. "We better get moving. Nemesis wants this solved so all of us can get out of Asgard before One-Eye starts causing trouble for her with the Council of Thrones."

"Okay." I turned to the rainbow swimming mermaid. "Wanda, thanks for your offer."

"Happy to do it. Take care, Razorwing. Remember, say my name three times near any rainbow to call me," she said and dived back into Bifrost.

Gani went over to a tree that had a diameter of at least ten feet. She stopped and put an elevator summoning sigil on it.

I smiled.

"What? It'll make leaving easier. And coming back," Gani said, climbing on her flying carpet. "You want a ride?"

I started beating my wings and rose up into the air. "Are you kidding? I'm in a place with enough magic for me to fly. Besides, it's not that far. It does me good to brush up on the old flying skills. Race you to the gate."

"You're on. You want a head start?" Gani asked.

I could maneuver better than Gani's carpet and probably beat her in a sprint and definitely in an obstacle course, but over the long haul the carpet was going to win.

Problem is, I'm not one to turn down a challenge. "I don't need it. Let's go," I said shooting up into the sky to give myself a little more speed by using gravity on the downslide.

Gani held back a little and didn't pull ahead of me until we were almost at the gate.

We had to go through the same security process all over again. A half dozen Valkyries escorted us to Valhalla.

"It doesn't look like they trust us," Gani said. "Do they think I'm going to steal the silverware?"

"More worried about wild cards moving up the end of the world," I said.

"Fair enough. One-Eye has bought the world centuries with his maneuvering. In exchange for that, I can deal with the indignity of an escort," Gani said.

Along the way, Gani stopped to tie her designer boots. She managed to put a sigil on a wall by leaning against it as she got up. I was worried she'd get caught, but she didn't.

When we arrived, we were lead into the dining hall. Odin sat on the throne on the far end with Hladgunner on his right and the dwarf Brokk on his left. Thor was standing in a corner. For lack of a better word, he looked like he was sulking.

We were marched before Odin's throne.

Gani was in academic mode today. Her snow white hair was French braided down the back of her head and she was wearing a pair of glasses. To complete the ensemble, she had even gone so far as to keep on the white lab coat that she wears when she does her experiments. The rest of the outfit was white as well. She tends to like the color, even after Labor Day.

She used the lab coat as if it were a skirt and did a combination curtsy-bow. Most people would have looked ridiculous, but Gani made it look regal. I guess she had enough experience in her days in Camelot alone.

"Odin, I am humbled by your request to have me and my talents to assist you in this matter. I assure you I will do everything I can to help find the culprit or culprits," Gani said. "I also bring you greetings from Nemesis and her assurances that both she and her people have only the truest of intentions and are here to help you in exchange for your hospitality."

The message was double edged – trying to relax Odin's paranoia, but also letting him know subtly that Nemesis' good graces are dependent on his.

Odin nodded. "What has happened is a grave insult and a danger not only to myself but to all of the nine worlds. I want to find out who did this and then make sure they are punished for it."

"To that end I would like to examine the body first and then both the false horn and the true horn," Gani said.

"Proceed," Odin said.

The entire time Gani and the head of the Norse pantheon had been playing diplomacy 101, Brokk and Hladgunner both had been eyeing Ganeida with a mix of hostility and suspicion as well as exchanging looks with each other. From the ones the Valkyrie was giving, I'd say she had a thing for the short guy.

Gani examined Adar and the gaping hole in his chest. Rudy and I stood by her side. Rudy struggled to keep her game face on. At some point I was going to have to ask her about what happened with the two of them.

She prodded, sniffed and touched. "Interesting."

Rudy and I both knew better than to interrupt Gani while she was working. It only distracted her.

"You tell him yet?" I whispered.

"I couldn't. Grandfather just sat there since you left. He didn't allow anyone to speak," Rudy said. "I tried three times, but he just kept hushing me."

Gani moved to the horns. She took some dust out of a designer handbag – not that I could tell you which one – and put it on both. She waved her hands and was rewarded with mystic glowing. She then took a pair of flagons and poured from each horn. She sniffed the mead and then put different powders in each. Both turned red and then black. She walked back toward One-Eye.

"Lord Odin, I have learned many things," Gani said.

Brokk stepped forth from the side. "All-Father, I do apologize for my interruption, but this would be the perfect time for you to try my humble gift. Perhaps you using it will aid the mortal witch in her investigations."

Gani made a face at the term witch.

Odin took the patch and held it up.

"It is possible that by wearing the patch you will be able to examine the body and the horn and know what happened without any outside aid," Brokk said.

Odin nodded. "It is a fine gift." Odin took off his black eyepatch, revealing an empty socket. No glass eye for him.

"Grandfather, don't trust him," Rudy said, but was ignored.

Odin put on the golden eyepatch. The moment the gift touched his socket, the gold moved as if alive, seeming to flow into the socket as if it had little wires or tentacles. Odin stiffened and Brokk smiled.

"I see so differently now," Odin said.

Gani looked nervously between dwarf and one-eyed god. She picked up on something the rest of us didn't. "I'd like to share my findings. First and foremost, at no point should your warriors drink from either horn."

"But most of the wounded and many of the others have already drank from the false horn," Mista said.

"That is bad. They have both been tainted with crux. Instead of reviving their soul bodies, drinking will only serve to destroy them by blocking their ability to heal by processing manna. Adar had also been poisoned with crux which is why he could not get himself to the hall after the battle."

Odin jumped out of his throne. "What?! Who did this dastardly deed?"

"Crux is not easy to come by. It is used in the Pit to further torment the damned whose bodies heal from almost any damage. However, I hope to be able to find out. First, I would like to point out that the hole in the dead man's body was not made by Mjollnir," Gani said.

"How would you know such a thing?" Brokk said. "You have never even examined Mjollnir."

"Actually I have," Gani said.

"How is this possible?" Odin said, reaching in his pocket and pulling out the tiny hammer. "It has been with me the entire time you have been in Asgard."

Thor had let Gani examine his hammer as she has a curiosity that would knock off an entire herd of cats. However, she wasn't about to get Thor in trouble.

"I have seen your son use his hammer previously and examined it at a distance. It has a fairly unique energy signature. The original properties of the hammer have been altered by Thor having used it to channel his powers for so long. The energy signature in the chest wound simply mimics that of the hammer with a mild electric discharge thrown in. I'm not picking up any Thor signature, only hammer. Whoever did this wanted it to look like your son did it. Can you see with your patch what I'm talking about?"

Odin looked at the wound, then the tiny Mjollnir and then Thor himself. "Yes. Are you suggesting that there is a second hammer in play?"

"I'm not only suggesting it, I am outright saying it," Gani said.

"Grandfather, that's what I've been trying to tell you. I have proof not only of a second hammer, but that Brokk is the one who made it," Rudy said.

Brokk's entire body began to tremble and shake. We had no way of knowing if Freyja had warned him or not.

"Nonsense. I am a loyal subject of Lord Odin. One thing is clear," Brokk said, twisting the thumb on his gauntlet. Odin's eyepatch seemed to grow thicker. "All-Father, whoever did this is obviously trying to undermine your authority. If I might make a suggestion – issue an edict that anyone found with this false hammer shall be exiled from Asgard. Now would I suggest such a thing if I had anything to do with it?"

Rudy raised her hand. "Grandfather, if you would only let me finish…"

"Hush, Thrud. The dwarf is willing to put his head on the chopping block, so very well. I hereby make an oath on my authority as King of the Aesir and give my solemn word that anyone found with this imitation shall henceforth be exiled from Asgard," Odin said.

Rudy's pupils got as wide as quarters as Brokk gave her an evil grin.

Gani saw the exchange, then looked from Rudy to me and realized that one of us must have the hammer. She stepped in to redirect matters.

"Lord Odin, those who handled the horn were very careful and extremely thorough."

Brokk struggled to hide a smile. "So you were unable to find anything?"

"Not at all. Those that did it were good and would have fooled most people. However I'm not, nor have I ever been, most people. I take great pride in that." Gani motioned to the horns with her right hand and they began to glow. Silver translucent tendrils rose off each horn and stretched outward until one from each horn was going into the chest of both the dwarf and the head Valkyrie.

"This is an outrage," Hladgunner said. "For this witch to even imply that the leader of the Valkyries would ever betray Valhalla or Odin is a grave offense."

"How do we even know you cast the spell you say you did? You could have simply put on a light show and geared the tendrils specifically toward us," Brokk said.

"Not only that, but I was the one who found the horn. I am also the one to set up the horn for the warriors. Of course I would have touched them," said Hladgunner.

"I assure you the spell is what I said. I also geared it merely for the last battle cycle. You will see that Thor's essence does not show up on either of them. However, I will let the spell expand going back in time."

Gani waved her hand again and several more tendrils came off the true horn pointing to every Valkyrie in the room, including Rudy. Several of them left the hall. One even went to Odin himself. However, the false horn still only had two tendrils coming off it. "As you can see many of the Valkyries and you Odin have handled the true horn. Yet only these two have touched the false," Gani said.

"Not true," the dwarf said. "We all saw you touch them. Why is there no tendril going to you?"

"Very simple. The one casting the spell does not become part of the finding unless there was a touch prior to that," Gani said.

Odin looked from Hladgunner to Brokk to Gani, his patch and its strap now a half inch thick.

"I thank you Lady of Camelot and representative of Night's Daughter. You have saved us much time and trouble. And you have saved my son's good name," Odin said.

The dwarf did not look happy, nor did he look nervous any longer, which was troubling. Odin was not known for being easygoing on offenders.

"Odin, I love the new eyepatch. It really does *shimmer*," Brokk said into the twisted thumb on his gauntlet. And I swear the patch reacted by glowing.

Gani put her hands behind her back and finger signaled us.

"Ckuf," I whispered. It translated as the crap was hitting the fan so hard that the fan would be destroyed.

The dwarf moved next to Odin and whispered something that I couldn't hear. The one-eyed god stiffened.

Gani's eyes went wide. She is able to see magic that is invisible to the rest of us. "Lord Odin, remove your eyepatch quickly."

"Don't do that," Brokk said. "In fact, now you can see clearly that the human witch is lying to you. You know that Hladgunner and I had nothing to do with this crime and that the real criminal is your son Thor."

Odin nodded and spoke in very stilted tones. "Yes, Brokk. I can see that now. Thor, you are guilty of trying to destroy the warriors of Valhalla and you shall be punished for it."

Thor stood frozen, too shocked to move.

"He should share the same fate as his blood brother beneath the deadly serpent," Brokk said.

Odin nodded again. "That is exactly what will happen. Thor, I sentence you to a lifetime of torture, sharing your fate with that of your blood brother Loki."

Thor fell into a fighting stance. "Even without my hammer, there is no one in the kingdom or this realm that can defeat me, so how do you plan to enforce that rule?"

Brokk smiled. "Lord Odin, did you not strike a deal with Thor for his continued good behavior? And if he breaks that deal, doesn't your order of protection for your granddaughter and her winged friend end? Wouldn't it be scrumptious to punish them all together? Don't you think that is a grand idea?"

One-Eye nodded stiffly. "Very grand indeed. Which shall it be Thor? You might very well get your own freedom, but would you be able to do it before these two …"

Brokk pointed to Gani. "Three, my Lord."

"Three women pay the price?"

The three of us were anything but defenseless and we had already pulled our guns, even Gani who rarely drew hers. She was quickly making motions with her free hand, preparing offensive magic.

"Thor, we are Nemesis & Co. We can take care of ourselves," I said.

"Father, don't do it," Rudy said.

"Perhaps I can help matters along even further," Brokk said, holding out his hand that had the jeweled gauntlet to the Norse All-Father. "Give me Mjollnir."

Without hesitation, Odin put the small hammer in the dwarf's outstretched hand. The dwarf used his other hand to fiddle with the jeweled controls and it grew to normal size. He threw it directly at Rudy's head so fast that she was not able to get out of the way. He pressed a red jewel and the hammer stopped a hair's breadth from her head. I could see her hand on her pocket where she had stashed her hammer on the sly and I hoped she kept it there. If Brokk had figured out a way to control Mjollnir, there was no way he didn't work in the same or better controls on the second hammer.

"Impressive, no? Not even you Thor have such control of Mjollnir." He turned his hand and the hammer flew back to it. I shot the red jewel.

"Damn you, fairy," Brokk said, hitting a silver stud on the glove. I fired again, but a huge red glowing shield shimmered into existence in front of the glove. The dwarf motioned to throw the hammer at me. There would be no stopping it this time.

"Stay your hand, Brokk. I surrender," Thor said. "However, in doing so, our agreement of protection for the women of Nemesis & Co., including Ganieda, remains. They have unrestricted access to the Golden City and may go anywhere in Asgard without interference."

The dwarf shrugged. "Fine. Odin, don't you think we better get your son chained down in the cave of torments?"

Odin stiffened for a second. The gold eyepatch glowed and the white bearded god's entire body twitched before he nodded. "Yes, we should."

"Kind word? I've found that a gun alone is usually more than enough on its own. Although a hard, cold stare never hurts."
-Vince Argus, Soul For Hire, dead hitman

Thor asked us not to go with him to Loki's cave. He didn't want Rudy to have to watch what was going to happen.

I heard all about it much later.

Odin was obviously under Brokk's control, but the Aesir of Asgard were loath to disobey their king. In fact, rather than face him, many of them simply went into hiding. Odin sent an escort of Valkyries and Valhallans to chain Thor, including Argus. By one heck of an alleged coincidence, Brokk had custom-made chains for this purpose just lying around.

Hladgunner led the group and arrived first. She saw Murphy standing watch over Loki with the shield on its tripod. She tossed her spear, collapsing one of the legs, causing the shield to falter and fall.

Murphy scrambled to get the shield and put it back up without being scolded by acid.

The head Valkyrie had a pouch on her belt that held a dozen spears that collapsed much like a law enforcement baton. She shook another one out and prepared to aim it at Murphy.

The Soul For Hire recognized the bartender and pulled one of his guns then placed it against the Valkyrie's temple.

"That man is a friend of mine. Tried to help me out of a predicament once, so he is partly responsible for my being here. You're not going to hurt him are you?" Vince said, cocking the hammer back on his automatic. "You also remember the rules – Valkyries may never harm any of the warriors in Valhalla. It is one of the first things we are taught when we get here. Oddly that doesn't seem to be a rule going the other way. So let me ask again – you are not going to hurt my friend Murphy, now are you?"

"Impudent mortal. How dare you …" started Brokk, but without even looking, Argus lifted up his other gun and shot off half of the dwarf's moustache without drawing a single drop of blood.

"Excuse me, little man, but I am talking to the lady." The dwarf hit his silver stud and his glowing shield extended in front of his glove, blocking him from head to toe. "That's cute."

"Cute? What's cute about a shield strong enough to deflect any attack?"

"That you think I couldn't nail you from behind or the side with a ricochet," Argus said with a grin.

Brokk twisted the stud so the shield became a dome around him.

"Smart, but that thinned out the shield, didn't it? Means it ain't as tough. Even has a couple of weak points now, don't it? I can see them and just how many shots it will take me to shut it down, not to mention exactly where to put them," Argus said.

"How about you just go back to Valhalla, human?" Brokk said, twisting the stud back so that the energy went back in the traditional shield shape, then vanished.

"I didn't take any guff from the head of Hell or mob bosses, so I'm not going to take any from you. We both know I can kill you now or later. Killing is what I do and I'm very good at it. Even better now with all the practice I've had in Valhalla. In fact, I've won most of the daily battles. No other warrior has ever achieved that, have they?"

The dwarf pushed another jewel and Mjollnir appeared full sized in his hand. Brokk raised the hammer. Argus cocked the one in his gun.

"If you think a hammer can beat a bullet, then by all means, let's throw down. We both know you ain't a fighter. You go against me and you'll get the Asgardian equivalent of a body bag. But let's say you get lucky and take me down, how are you going to explain Valhalla's number one guy getting hurt, Brokk? People'll start to figure out that you pulled a fast one with the eyepatch. The people in this town are gods. One of them will just yank it off Odin's head and when that happens, you'll be the next dead man. Even with that hammer. Plus, One-Eye stiffens every time you give him an order. He's fighting you. That means you have to be careful what you tell him to do. If it is something he doesn't like, he fights you more. The more distasteful it is, the more he fights the mind control. From what I've seen, nothing means more to the man than winning Ragnarok. What do you think his reaction will be if he finds out you killed his best Valhallan warrior and maybe ruined his chance at victory? Think the mind control will hold up to the fury of that reaction?"

The dwarf grumbled, but turned away and put the hammer down. "Let's bind Thor over there across from his treacherous brother."

Brokk stood over Loki, hammer in hand. The serpent recognized it and backed off.

"Hello, Loki. My how things have changed," Brokk said.

"Not really. You are still as ugly as ever."

The dwarf kicked the trickster in the mouth. "Still don't know when to shut up do you? Last time you messed with me, I sewed your mouth shut."

"Yeah, but I got the hammer without paying. You were supposed to get my head. That didn't work out so good for you, now did it?" Loki said.

"But I have the hammer now. And you're subjected to torture, although how you got a mortal to do your bidding, I am not sure. I rather enjoyed hearing the screams once your wife left you after all of your constant abuse. Maybe I'll just take that head I am owed now."

Murphy turned the shield so the acid spilled out toward the dwarf, who barely backed away in time.

"That ain't going to happen," Murphy said.

The dwarf pulled the hammer back as if to throw it and another gunshot rang out. The other half of his moustache was gone.

"Man's under my protection, short stuff," Argus said. "There won't be a third warning."

The dwarf moved away from Loki and reached for the silver stud, but saw Argus was still aiming at him and put his hands by his side.

"Lay down there, thunderer," Brokk ordered.

Thor listened and the dwarf bound him, the chains moving like living things as they wrapping themselves around the thunder god's wrists and ankles, then melting into the stone itself.

"You can struggle all you want, but these chains will never let you go," Brokk said. "I made some improvements over the last batch."

Argus sat down on the stone beside Thor, next to Loki and Murphy.

"Will you not be returning to Valhalla?" Hladgunner said, looking at Argus.

"I'll be back. Valhalla is my home now. But I owe this man a debt of honor. I'm going to stay here to make sure nothing happens to him. When I'm certain he's safe, then I'll return."

"Very well," Hladgunner said. She leaned over to whisper into the dwarf's ear. "That one is too smart and too dangerous. He could cause a lot of trouble. It is probably best that he stay here."

"Leave me one of them winged horses and I'll rejoin you shortly," Argus said.

"You dare to order…" Brokk said, but Hladgunner raised her hand.

"As the winner of the last tournament, it is within his rights to ask. I will leave Wynterbale," Hladgunner said, then leaned into the dwarf's ear. "Don't worry, my love. Wynterbale is one of the foulest tempered mounts we have ever had. No mortal soul would be able to tame her, let alone survive riding her. And with the crux in his system, he won't be getting up from any falls."

Brokk smiled and nodded. He had the hammer behind his back, then motioned to the serpent. It looked at the warriors and Valkyries with their weapons and the seemingly unarmed dwarf who was calling to him.

Convinced the vision of the hammer was a trick of the light, the beast lunged at the dwarf who pulled Mjollnir from behind his back and threw it. The controlled hammer-shaped missile knocked the serpent down. The dwarf pulled a dagger from his gauntlet that was the same shade of gold as the eyepatch he had given Odin. Brokk made sure his body blocked what he was doing from the view of the prisoners and those foolish enough to help them before he threw the blade at the beast's head. Instead of cutting the serpent, it seemed to melt through to the inside of its skull, the hilt forming a circle on its forehead, where it could work its mind control magic.

The serpent rose up, swaying side to side as if drunk. The dwarf motioned again and spoke.

"*Shimmer*," Brokk whispered into his thumb. The metal glowed and thickened. "To me, my new pet,"

The serpent slithered to the dwarf and bowed its head like a puppy, waiting to be scratched. Brokk resisted the urge to pet it.

"You will wait for my call," Brokk whispered and the serpent nodded its giant head and the gold medallion glowed.

Brokk exited the cave, the rest of the imprisonment party following in his wake.

The serpent turned towards his new victim. The shield still protected Loki, but Thor, who taunted and threatened him, was bound and helpless. He slithered and took position over the thunder god. The serpent opened his mouth and his venom began to flow like a waterfall.

It hit Thor and the first thing to go was his clothes, then his skin, followed by his muscles. Loki's screams would shake the mountains. Thor's screams shook not only the land, but the sky.

"Murphy, protect Thor," Loki said.

"If I do, then the serpent will come for you," Murphy said.

"That's okay. I'm used to it. I can take it. Thor's not as tough as I am. Not inside anyway. Besides, I did things that make me even deserve it. Thor hasn't. Protect him, please," Loki said.

"Argus, give me a hand moving this," Murphy said.

The Soul For Hire picked up one side of the tremendous shield tripod and helped the bartender carry it over in front of Thor, both of them being careful so that the acid didn't spill on them. It would kill Murphy and for the time being Argus had no way to regenerate. A mortal wound would ensure the hitman would die the final death. Thor started to heal, but not being a shape shifter, it was nowhere near as fast as Loki.

"My thanks Murphy and Argus for choosing me over Loki," Thor said, having not heard the trickster's words over his own screams of pain.

"Your brother told us to save you over him. This was his choice, not ours," Argus said. "He's not quite the nasty guy you all made him out to be, now is he?"

By this point the serpent had reached Loki and his screams had started anew. Thor turned his head to look at his brother, who was willingly taking the worst agony imaginable to protect Thor from it.

"Maybe he isn't."

Argus took shots at the serpent, blinding it in its right eye, but it only turned its attack toward the humans and the shield, battering its giant head against it and knocking them to the ground. Loki mocked the serpent until it came back after him.

"Don't try that again," Loki said. "There is no need for the two of you to end up dead on my account. I can take it." But the screams that followed made them all doubt the truth of those words.

"Kids today."
-Ganieda, twin of Merlin, mage of Camelot, agent of Nemesis & Co.

"Let me get this straight," Gani said.

"Actually that's what the lust goddess said," Rudy giggled.

"You think the fact that your grandfather will exile you once he finds out you have the mock-Mjollnir is funny? Not to mention that an angry dwarf appears to have taken over the mind of one of the most powerful gods still around and has death and destruction on his agenda. And that doesn't even take into account that thousands of men are going to die the final death and leave the forces of good minus one army for an impending armageddon."

"Not funny, but I had to say something. It's not like I'm Murphy or anything," Rudy said.

"True. With this much trouble happening, we'd never get the bartender to shut up," Gani said.

"Yeah, he'd say we wouldn't have to worry until we had an impending arm and legageddon," I said and got a couple of stares for my trouble. "Well, he would."

Gani turned her stare on me. "And you stole a goddess' source of power?"

"She ticked me off," I said.

"Oh, that makes it okay then. I'm sure she won't be planning to rain down death and destruction on you and those around you at all. Heaven help us if she complains to the Thrones," Gani said, then turned to Rudy. "Where is the hammer now?"

"In my pocket," Rudy said.

"Seriously? You didn't even have the good sense to hide it and give yourself plausible deniability?" Gani said.

"Hide it where? And that would risk Brokk getting his hands on it," Rudy said.

"He likely made the thing and probably has a control charm in his gauntlet for it," Gani said.

"Then maybe we should take the corresponding charm out of the hammer to neutralize it," I said.

Gani nodded and grinned. "And by we you mean —"

I sighed. Gani was easygoing, but every so often she liked to remind us just how indispensable she was. "You."

"Where are the bathrooms?" Gani asked.

"Follow me," Rudy said and we did.

Once we were inside, Gani opened a stall door and held out her hand. "Give it to me."

Rudy pulled the tiny hammer out of her pocket. "It's small, but it's still very heavy."

"I know. I'll use the same spell I used on your father's hammer when I examined it," Gani said, wiggling her fingers. The hammer floated into her hand.

Gani sat on the toilet without adjusting her clothes.

"Anyone besides me find it odd that Valhalla has modern plumbing?" I said.

"Why wouldn't it? Grandfather never lost contact with any of the nine worlds and has no problem adopting any tech or magic for use here at home," Rudy said. "And let me tell you no one was happier about the situation than Tulla."

"Tulla?" I said.

"The goddess in charge of Queen Frigga's toilet," Rudy said.

"So even bathroom attendants here became goddesses?" I said.

"Tulla's a sweetheart. She really helped me the first time I got my period..."

That unfortunate line of conversation was cut mercifully short by the bathroom door opening and Jerkgunner walking in. Apparently she was back from imprisoning Thor.

Gani dropped the hammer and it fell between her legs and into the toilet. The Valkyrie leader saw the three of us in one open stall and made a V with her index and middle fingers, then pointed from her eyes to us and repeated the motion.

"I'm watching you. All of you," she said.

"And it's a little creepy. We're in the bathroom," I said. "A little privacy, please."

"Your father screamed like an infant when the serpent went for him. My how the protector of Asgard has fallen," Jerkgunner said. "Can his daughter and her friends be far behind?"

Jerkgunner left the room laughing.

"Bitch," Rudy said, then looked in the bowl. "And I can't believe you dropped my hammer in the toilet. Ick."

"It won't hurt it," Gani said, standing and sticking her hand in and pulling it out. "This is almost an exact replica of Mjollnir – excellent craftsmanship. But I found the control charm – oddly enough the water made it show up easier."

"Can you remove it?" Rudy said.

Gani gripped either side of the miniature hammer with her thumb and index finger. Silver energy jumped from each finger into the hammer and what looked like the offspring of a diamond and a computer chip came out the top.

"Done," Gani said, handing Rudy back the hammer. Without touching it, she dropped the jewel chip into the toilet and flushed, but it didn't go down. Instead it adhered to the porcelain surface. "Impressive cohesive charm. Glad I didn't take my time removing it or I never would have got it off. It's going to be stuck there for a long time. Now if you'll excuse me," Gani said, pushing us out of the stall.

"What?" Rudy said.

"I really have to use the facilities," Gani said, shutting the door.

I did too. Apparently so did Rudy.

We finished, washed our hands and exited, only to be faced again with the dying Valhallans.

"Here's what I don't understand. They're all dead. How can they die again? What's the difference between death and final death?" I said.

"Death separates the soul from the mortal body. A soul can still be damaged, but generally can be repaired. In this case, the Valhallans were poisoned with crux, destroying the souls' ability to self-heal. Since One-Eye had tied up all his healing manna in the ram's horn and someone has rendered it useless, he simply doesn't have the spare manna left to heal them from the poison or the wounds. The soul often mimics the body, since it is the person's perceptions that control their shape. The dead could appear as almost anything they want, but most still appear as themselves because that's what they think they should look like," Gani said. "And because they still picture themselves as human, they can still be killed."

"So if we can convince them otherwise, we can save them?" I said.

"It's not that easy. It would take a master shrink or con artist to convince them otherwise. And with the poison in their systems, they are likely too weak to try," Gani said.

"Uncle is a master con artist," Rudy said.

"Who we are unlikely to get loose in time to help us," I said. "So what happens to the souls who die the final death?"

"Well, energy is neither created nor destroyed and neither are souls. They likely move on to another plane of existence, not unlike Oblivion where forgotten gods go," Gani said.

The wounded men were moaning loudly. Being an afterlife, they had no anesthesia or pain medicine to help them. There was no need for it before today.

"Now let me take another stab at figuring out a way to counteract the poison. Maybe even fix the horn if One-Eye will let me near it again. If I can talk to him without the dwarf around, I might even figure out a way to get the patch off," Gani said, wading into the wounded.

"You think Dad's okay?" Rudy asked.

I had no idea, but that's not what my friend needed to hear. "Thor's as tough as they come. I'm sure he's fine."

"I hope so," Rudy said, picking up a tray of mead tankards from a different source. I did the same as we brought the wounded the only means we had available to try to ease their pain.

"I don't know nothing about looking a gift horse in the mouth or anywhere else. I mean, who gives a horse as a gift anyhow? Unless it's just the head of course."

    -Vince Argus, Soul For Hire, dead hitman

"Are you sure?" Argus said.

"Go!" Loki screamed as the flesh dissolved off his bones yet again. The serpent would back off just long enough for some of the flesh to grow back before unleashing the next barrage of venomous acid on the chained trickster.

"We got this," Murphy said.

"I'm willing to stay," Argus said. "Like I told the dwarf, I owe you. Without you and the others, I never would have beat Nick."

"I appreciate it, but we're okay. Vulcan designed the shield well enough to protect whoever is behind it," Murphy said. "And the serpent has strict orders not to harm those who man the shields."

"Could have fooled me earlier," Argus said. "I'm just worried about the others. Hell, I'm the one who wounded a lot of them, but it was just supposed to be for fun. I've got enough blood on my hands without adding any more."

"Then go and see what you can do to help them," Murphy said.

"Thanks. Any idea how to ride a flying horse?" Argus said.

"Not really, but I'd imagine it would be along the lines of get in the saddle and don't fall off," Murphy said.

"You're a big help," Argus said, walking across the cave. The serpent glared warily at the hitman. "You still have one eye. Come after me and I'll take the other."

The snake watched until Argus left the cave. To his surprise, there was indeed a winged horse waiting for him. Never having learned to trust anything is as it seemed, he checked the saddle to make sure it was secure and hadn't been tampered with. Then he checked it again.

Argus went to the front of the horse. "Listen, I understand animals here are smart, so let's get a few things straight. I need to get back to Valhalla ASAP. I'd appreciate a ride. No funny business and nobody gets hurt. We understand each other?"

The horse nodded.

"Good," Argus said and climbed into the saddle. "Giddy up!"

Wynterbale flapped her wings and took off into the sky so fast, Argus had to grab hold of the saddle's pommel so he didn't fall off.

"I told you no funny business. You fly right or I'll shoot you," Argus said.

The winged horse shook her head no, then barrel rolled five times. Wynterbale knew something the hitman hadn't taken into account. Sure, Argus could shoot the horse, but then the horse couldn't fly. Since neither could Argus, that meant the two of them would plummet to their doom. The horse rightly figured that even a dead hitman didn't want to deal with the injuries caused by a fall from the altitudes they were traveling at.

So Argus didn't shoot the horse, instead holding on for all he was worth and trying not to scream.

One of Odin's ravens was watching the Soul For Hire's struggles and his caws sounded like laughter, as did the whinnying of the horse.

"You never know what you can truly do until your back is against the wall or those you care about are in danger."
-Daemor saying

Argus stumbled back into Valhalla like a drunken bum, cursing at the raven that followed him in. It took him a few moments to get his legs steady, then he looked around at the dying Valhallans. "Damn."

"They're dying the final death and there is nothing we can do to stop it," Mista said, tears streaming down her face.

I looked at the Soul For Hire. "I heard you were watching out for Murphy."

"I was, but the bartender seemed to have things under control and told me to come back to see if I could help," Argus said.

"How's my father?" Rudy said, unable to hide her worry.

"Your old man is fine. Murphy's got the shield over him," Argus said.

"What about my uncle?" Rudy asked.

"His call. Loki jumped on the grenade for Thor and is taking the full brunt of the serpent's venom."

"Why would he do that?" Rudy asked.

"He wanted to keep his brother safe. His screams shake the entire cave. Damn brave man, that Loki," Argus said. "Any luck figuring out a solution?"

"None of it good," Mista said. "Nobody's figured how the horn was tainted yet. Brokk won't let Gani near it and he's kept One-Eye distracted."

"Gani, there has got to be something you can do to get the crux out of the horn so it can revive them again," Rudy said.

"Given enough time and actual access to it, probably, but we don't have that luxury. Sunrise will be in less than three hours," Gani said.

"Is there any way we can shift some manna from the unwounded to the others?" I said.

"It's One-Eye's manna. The only way is with his consent and Brokk's not likely to let him give it. Sad thing is Thor has enough manna to spare. If he were here, I could use some of his to burn out the crux and start the healing. As it is, he's going to be spending a lot of his to stay alive," Gani said. "We'll need a source of manna to fix this. A big one."

"How is the horn able to make new manna?" I said.

"It isn't, any more than it is making mead. The ram's horn is a variation on a horn of plenty. Neither is infinite, but has the power to continuously duplicate what was put in it when the spell is cast. One-Eye had a brilliant idea by filling it with mead and manna when he triggered the spell. One-Eye worked out the perfect cycle, allowing the Valhallans to get wounded with their soul bodies having just enough manna to make it through about a day, then get replenished by the horn if they got wounded," Gani said. "Of course, who ever came up with this plot is even more brilliant. Once the dawn has come, the injured will start dropping and if the others get injured, they will die within a day."

"Then we need to find a supply of manna we can use to heal them," I said.

"Manna is rarer and more valuable than uranium. There is no deposit of it just lying around. There are too many gods vying for the stuff for any of it to stay hidden or unspoken for," Gani said.

"Well, don't magí make new manna?" I said. "Couldn't you tap into some of your brother's the same way you tap into his magic?"

"Merlin allows me to use his powers while he waits for England's darkest hour, but he is saving that manna for Arthur and his new vision of Camelot. Even imprisoned, there is no way he'd let me tap it," Gani said.

"Then we are up a creek without a boat," Mista said.

Rudy stroked her chin and stared out into space before her eyes lit up. "No, there is a way. We can take them to Freyja and she can heal them. She has enough sexual manna saved up to heal a hundred times this number."

"Freyja would never help the competition," Mista said. "And Old One-Eye would never allow it"

"Probably, but he is not exactly in his right mind. If he were, Grandfather probably would have found a solution. We know he is under Brokk's mind control, so we will have to do what he would want rather than what he says," Rudy said.

"You're talking treason," Mista said. The very word carried and caused a hush to fall over the hall as all eyes turned toward Rudy.

"You are a Valkyrie, the same as I am. We took a vow to protect these men at all costs. Maybe the rest of you didn't take that oath seriously, but I did. Grandfather needs these warriors to fight Twilight. Without them to help beat back the darkness, we will not hold the line. We will fall and with us, billions of others. We all know the Ragnarok was supposed to be a losing battle for the forces of good. Thanks to Grandfather, we are going to be able to pull at least a draw. So we're not just talking about what will happen to us. We are talking to what will happen to everyone that lives in all the nine worlds. I don't know about you, but I am a soldier. A soldier's job is to fight, regardless of the danger. And that danger is great. We may all be put to death for our actions in saving these men, but they will be alive and the forces of good will have their army at the final battle. If I have to give up my life or my freedom to accomplish this, so be it. I know I can't be the only one. Who is with me?" Rudy asked.

I looked around at the crowd. The other Valkyries who had viewed her as some spoiled brat who was only one of their number because of her lineage were shocked. While they cowered with no plan, Rudy had come up with a solution.

Mista gritted her teeth. "Damn it to Hel, if you're not right. I'm with you. But how will you get Freyja to help?"

"She promised us anything we wished in exchange for something she wanted," I said.

"What's that? Her necklace back?" Mista asked.

"No." I turned to look at the Soul For Hire. "Argus."

"So let me get this straight – you want to pimp me out?" Argus said, trying to hide a grin.

"Yep," I said. "Unless you have a better idea."

Argus looked around at the wounded, his gaze lingering on the ones with bullet holes. "Valhalla's been great. A chance to kill without anyone dying. Whoever did this took that away and hurt a lot of good men in the process. I'm in. Besides what other guy can claim that sex with him could save the entire universe? How could I turn that down? Whatever you need from me, just say the word."

"Consider it said," Rudy replied. "What about the rest of you?"

One by one, the other Valkyries and unwounded Valhallans warriors shouted. "We're with you!" I think it shocked as much as thrilled Rudy. The raven that had been following Argus took off.

"So what is the plan, Thrud?" Mista said.

"And whatever it is, we have to get it done fast. That raven flew away to tattle on us," I said.

"We have to get all of the wounded to Freyja's hall," Rudy said. "Then we make her keep her word and pimp out the hitman. She lost a lot of power when Terrorbelle took her necklace. She probably hates us, but she made a vow. Breaking it would cause her to lose even more power and I doubt she can afford that right now, especially as it would be far greater than the sexual manna that would be needed to heal our warriors."

"I see one big flaw with the plan. Souls are wealth and power here. This would more than double her power. Are we going to assume Freyja's just going to give the heroes back to One-Eye after she's healed them? The gain in souls might well offset the loss from breaking her vow," Mista said.

"Her vow said anything and I will make it clear that the return is part of the deal. We'll worry about enforcing it once we're sure they won't die," Rudy said. "I need everyone who is uninjured to pick up one of the wounded. Get them on the horses and the bikes. Those we cannot fit will have to be carried. We need to get moving now," Rudy said. The Valkyries and the Valhallans obeyed without hesitation. Rudy may not have been a natural born leader, but she was on her way to becoming one.

I grabbed a warrior under each arm and flew. The Valkyries managed to get two plus themselves on their winged horses and three on each motorcycle–two on the sidecars and one on the back. Gani got seven on her flying carpet. Argus and the rest of the dead warriors carried their comrades who could limp and the great escape party headed toward the main door of Valhalla.

Of course nothing can ever be easy. Odin, Brokk, and Hladgunner were waiting for us and blocking the exit, the tattletale raven perched on Odin's shoulder.

"What treachery is this? That my Valkyries and my warriors should steal souls from me like thieves in the night," Odin bellowed.

"Grandfather, you are not in your right mind. The dwarf has clouded your thinking with that patch. Almost half of your warriors will be dead when the sun rises. I am just trying to save them," Rudy said.

"My own granddaughter leads the rebellion against me? This is too much to bear." Odin's hands began to glow.

Rudy got off Morningdour, pulling her shrunken hammer from her pocket. It grew to full size in her hand.

"And it was you who killed the warrior with that false hammer! I swore that whoever hid it would be exiled from all of Asgard. Granddaughter, the Golden City is your home no more. For your treason you are exiled from Asgard on my word as All-Father of the Aesir. The rest of you bring those warriors back into the hall."

Rudy stepped between Odin and the escape party, her hammer at the ready. "No, Grandfather. We are going to save them with or without your consent. You are the one who made us swear the oath to protect the warriors of Valhalla at all costs. There was no stipulation in that oath about you changing your mind and letting them die."

"Strong words, Thrud, but you will have to get by me to get them out and we both know that will not happen. Even your father could not defeat me and you have barely a fraction of his power," Odin said.

"I've tried to tell you that Brokk made the hammer and Freyja hid it for him, but you wouldn't listen. After all, I'm only a girl. Well, I not only was good enough to find the hammer, but I was smart enough to bind it too me."

"What?!" Brokk shouted.

"Yes, dwarf, I know you hadn't because if it was found, the blood used could be traced back to you," Rudy said.

"As if that would trouble me," Brokk said, pushing a white gem on his gauntlet. His grin was soon replaced by a frown. "Why is it not shrinking?" He hit another gem and held out his hand as if expecting the hammer to fly into it. Instead, there was a crash in the bathroom and a shrunken toilet flew through the wall and to the dwarf's hand, shattering and soaking him on impact.

Gani smiled from her flying carpet. "Oh, your controller charm? I removed it. And bonded it to that toilet."

"Thrud, you will stand down or I will be forced to harm you," Odin said, his arms and knees ramrod straight.

"You underestimate me, Grandfather." Rudy pulled back her hand as if she was going to throw the hammer at the god king's head. Not knowing the power level of the new hammer, Odin flinched, which allowed Rudy to make the throw she actually had intended – at the far wall. The hammer flew at the far wall and burst through to the outside of Valhalla, crumbling a large portion of the stone to rubble. Thanks to her trajectory, the hammer's path curved and did as much damage on the way back. By the time the hammer smacked back into her palm, there was enough room for our escape party to make a getaway. That is if they had enough time.

I was going to make sure they got it.

"Rudy, go. I'll hold them off," I said.

"I'm not going to leave you, T-Belle. We'll fight them together," Rudy said.

"Yes, we will," Gani said, a glow surrounding her.

"At the cost of these soldiers? Not going to happen. I got this. Freyja made that vow to Rudy and me. One of us has to be there for this to work. Rudy, this is all you. They don't see me as their leader. The Valkyries and warriors will follow you. Only you can pull this off. Get on your horse and fly. Save those men. Gani, Freyja will do anything she can to screw Rudy, so do whatever you can to make sure that doesn't happen. I'll cover you."

Gani didn't look happy, but nodded.

Rudy was not so easily convinced. "But…"

"Rudy, I was a soldier too. If one soldier has to die to save thousands, that is a damn good trade. Soldiers have died for far less." I reached inside my pocket and put on the love charm necklace. "Besides I have a trick up my sleeve or rather in my cleavage. Now get."

Rudy nodded, but tossed me her gun. We could use each other's weapons, even if almost nobody else could. Normally I wouldn't have taken it, because it would leave her defenseless. However, her new hammer was a great big equalizer.

I turned, a gun in each hand, to face the king of the Norse gods, an evil dwarf, and a treacherous Valkyrie. Odin was already building energy in the palm of one of his hands. I shot an explosive round into it. It didn't do much harm, but it did tick him off big time. Which was good for the mission as it distracted him from the great big escape party we were throwing. Bad for me, because One-Eye was now focused entirely on me. Since Nemesis used me as bait for the monsters most of the time, you'd think I'd be used to this kind of thing by now. I wasn't.

"You have both broken the covenant I had with my son, so it no longer protects you. Now you will both die," Odin said.

I unloaded three more explosive rounds. They might as well have been water balloons. "I doubt it, but mind if I start the party anyway?"

Now it was time for something completely different, not to mention difficult. I played at being a flirt sometimes, but it was just that. I talked a good game, but no man was getting in my pants unless I loved him. However, a lot of afterlives depended on me being able to convince Odin otherwise.

Not letting go of either gun, I reached up and tore open the top of my t-shirt which exposed my specially reinforced bra and rather excessive amounts of cleavage.

All three enemies were staring at me now. Odin looked like he could see right through my clothes. Then I remembered the dwarf saying the eyepatch let him see through things, which apparently included my outfit. I pushed aside the creeped out feeling and focused on making the charms on the gems kick into overdrive. They radiated lust, so I figured I needed to feel lust to do it.

I searched my memory for the sexiest man I could think of. Of course Murphy popped into my mind. The problem was he was still fully clothed. A little tweak of my imagination fixed that. Still it was a little hard getting myself horny while fighting for my life, so I doubled the stake and added a shirtless Joe Hannk to the picture. It felt wrong, but it didn't mean they weren't fun thoughts. I felt the necklace hum and tingle. Both Odin and Hladgunner stopped short to drool at me. It was working.

"Now Odin-poo, are you sure you want to hurt little old me when we could come up with much more pleasant things to do," I said taking a few steps with a wiggle that the succubus Ryth would have been envious of.

"I want in on this," Hladgunner said, the yellow jewel doing its work.

"Perhaps I was too rash. What could I offer you for a taste of your virtue?" Odin said, stroking his white beard.

Before I could answer, Brokk slapped Odin across the face with his jeweled gauntlet. "Stop it!" The dwarf smacked Hladgunner's cheek. "She is using mind control on the both of you."

"Takes one to know one I guess," I said. "I assume since you had a hand in the creation of the necklace, you are immune to it?"

"I only made the yellow gem. But the other four were created by dwarf magic and I know my way around that enough to not be affected. Odin, I think it is time to follow through on the part where you said the fairy should die," Brokk said.

"Is that just because I wouldn't have sex with you, even to save my life? Not that I would have before, but after talking to Freyja, I definitely wouldn't," I said.

"What'd that bitch say?" Brokk growled.

Honestly she didn't say a thing, but I needed Brokk to get angry enough to focus on me instead of controlling Odin.

I held up my pinky in a limp fashion. "Only that most dwarfs weren't proportional, but you were less than that. She said it was like doing a pixie." Although that honestly wasn't necessarily an insult, at least for anyone that knew my father. He was named Thunderrod at birth and he had no lack of women of any race, including my mama the ogre.

"That's a lie!"

I smiled, looked at his crotch and smirked. "According to her you were done and she didn't even know you had started."

Brokk turned to Hladgunner. "Tell her that's not true!"

The Valkyrie started to open her mouth, but I cut her off. I could feel the magic of the necklace pouring off of me. The Valkyrie and god hadn't taken their eyes off my cleavage. Which had kept them from realizing that the rest of the escape party was now clear of Valhalla. "If you want some of this –" I said doing my best Zombielicious impersonation. "–you better back my story."

"Okay, Brokk is really teeny tiny. Can we get naked now?" the Valkyrie said like some kind of idiot child focused on a present dangling before her that she desperately wanted to unwrap.

"That's it." Brokk pulled Mjollnir out of his pocket and it grew to full size.

"If only the rest of you could grow so easily and large," I mocked.

Brokk hit a golden stud on his metal glove. The gold eyepatch lit up like a magnesium flare and the one-eyed god fell to his knees screaming, his wide brimmed hat falling off to the side. It was a harsher version of what my Daemor badge did for me. As pain trumps lust control, Odin wasn't quite so interested in me anymore. I guessed the patch used direct contact to control, so the pain didn't break Brokk's control.

"Odin, ignore your loins or you will get more of the same. Go after your granddaughter and the rest of them. Stop whatever they are planning and imprison the lot. I'll deal with them later. Hladgunner, you help him." He hit a jewel on his glove and hit Jerkgunner with some sort of ray. Seemed to cool her down a bit. Brokk touched another jewel and a hologram of a drooling serpent appeared above it. The scaly beast looked up as if he could see the dwarf and acted like he too was under a mind control spell. "My pet, kill all of them."

Sweet heavens, it was going to kill Murphy. And Thor and Loki too. The hologram expanded to show everyone. Murphy was pressing his watch, but no magic motorcycle was appearing. Brokk had probably mystically jammed the signal. Murphy started running and the serpent chased after him.

I hit the away button on Rudy's gun. At least that way the boss would know something was wrong and get to Asgard on the double. I couldn't leave this fight to save Murphy or thousands would die forever. Maybe billions more later on. As much as I loved him, I couldn't save him and sacrifice them. And I knew that if he was told the choices, Murphy wouldn't want me to. It wouldn't make me hate myself any less if he died though.

Maybe I could beat Brokk and get help for Murphy at the same time, since he was helping me by getting rid of Odin and Jerkgunner.

I rapid fired three more explosive rounds – the first in Brokk's face, the second in his groin and the third in his knee. The hammer blocked the face shot, and his armor stopped the other two from doing lethal damage.

He fiddled with his glove again and his red shield shot out in front of him. I took a few more shots, but the shield stopped them. Still, it had to distribute the energy from the explosions somewhere, maybe even weakening the field in the process. I hoped the shots at least annoyed and maybe even hurt him.

Before the smoke cleared, I was already flying out the exit Rudy created.

"Catch me if you can, little man. Unless you're scared," I said hovering. I looked the opposite direction from Freyja's hall and shouted, "Run Rudy, they're coming!" Maybe in his controlled state Odin would fall for it. Then I saw Jerkgunner, still with her eyes practically glued to my cleavage. I guess the ray only helped a little. "They went that way. Don't follow them."

Odin ran out in the wrong direction. Jerkgunner followed, but stopped beneath me.

"You complete me," she said. Brokk yelled and threw the hammer at his Valkyrie accomplice. It looked like it went high on purpose, but the shock was enough to make Jerkgunner run after One-Eye. He hit her again with the ray as she fled.

Mjollnir returned to his gloved hand and he tossed it a second time, but now I was the target.

As I was already airborne, I was able to dodge the hammer's forward and backward path.

I flew like a pixie out of a dragon's mouth toward Bifrost, trying to figure out how to get past the gate and get out of the Golden City. Over the wall would turn me to dust, so there was only the one way. I figured Brokk had no chance of keeping up with me on foot. Then he changed the rules and pulled a small disc out of a pouch on his belt and shook it until it was the size of a manhole cover.

The dwarf set it down and stepped on it. Then the disc floated up into the air and after me.

Ckuf me.

"There is nowhere to hide, Daemor. You can run, but you will not be able to escape me."

I ignored him and raced ahead. When I reached the gate I saw that the Fates were smiling on me. It had to happen occasionally. After all, they sit on the Council of Thrones.

Tyr and his inside guard must have gotten bored during guard duty and had the porthole open to chat. I fired a full clip of stun bullets at the inside guard and flew for all I was worth at the porthole. I bet everything on being able to make it through to the other side of the gate. I prayed my aim was good as I pulled my wings back, put my head straight with my arms in front of me.

An instant later, I was surrounded by metal as I slid into the porthole.

"One thing I learned from my time in court watching kings – if you can act like you know what you're doing, most people will follow you, especially in times of crisis."
    -Ganieda, twin of Merlin, mage of Camelot, agent of Nemesis & Co.

Rudy led the great escape party to Freyja's hall. The hundred guards fell into defense mode, their spears in front of them.

"We outnumber them. We can take the hall," Mista said.

"Which won't help convince the temptress to help us," Rudy said. "Let's try it a different way."

Rudy landed Morningdour in front of the anatomically correct gate.

"You shall not pass," the hundred said as one.

"We are here on behalf of Terrorbelle," Rudy said. The hundred men sighed as one, remembering me as the sexual avatar of the necklace. Rudy figured Freyja had used the magic of the necklace to control the men for so long that their loyalty might have been transferred to the new owner. "When she joins us, what shall I tell her – that you let us pass or made us fight? Fighting would upset her."

"The pink haired beauty would be pleased if we let you pass?" they again said in unison.

"Absolutely," Rudy said.

"Then you shall pass," said the hundred, as two cats flew into the giant nostrils to warn their mistress.

The Valkyries left their winged horses outside and the great escape party brought the wounded and dying souls inside.

When they got to the stadium, the assembled men were not standing around looking pretty, but were armored up and ready for war.

"Good, it looks like some of you are all ready to die. That will make this much easier," Freyja said. "Any last words before I kill you, granddaughter of Odin?"

"Only that we claim safe passage in fulfillment of your sworn oath," Rudy said.

"I never swore you safe anything," Freyja said.

"But you swore to me by your word that anything you can grant me will be mine if I helped you bed Vince Argus," Rudy said.

"Well, I have not bedded him. Too bad. Now die," Freyja said, a sword in her own hand pointed at the Valkyrie.

Argus stepped up and pointed his gun at her. "That's not nice. I heard you make that vow. So did all of your followers here. You break this vow and you will lose your sway over all of them. And a significant part of your power. Can you afford that loss, given your current situation?"

"If I raise the souls here back to health, they become mine. That will give me a new source of power," Freyja said.

"Won't do you any good if you are dead and in Hel," Argus said.

"I cannot be killed in my place of power. And I will never go to the realm of Loki's daughter," Freyja said.

"You already know how my power works. That I can hit any target. That includes kill spots on gods," Argus said.

"You're bluffing," Freyja said.

Argus took off his sunglasses and looked the lust goddess in the eyes. Argus hid his eyes except when he was going to kill someone who was close enough to see him. It was a final courtesy to the soon dead.

"Goodbye," was his only reply.

"Wait!" Freyja said, holding up her hand. "Thrud, what do you wish from me?"

"For you to heal all the wounded Valhallans back to health and allow them to return to Valhalla," Rudy said.

"And in exchange for this, Vince Argus agrees to freely come to my bed?" Freyja said.

"He does," Rudy said.

"Fine," said Freyja, reaching out for Argus' hand. He tucked his gun under his black trench coat as she led him to her throne.

"Wait. Heal first. Nookie second," Rudy said.

"Not how I interpret our agreement," Freyja said.

"We have less than two hours," Mista whispered.

Gani smiled and floated over to Argus.

"Who are you?" Freyja demanded at the show of power. Although their animals could fly all over the place, very few Aesir could. Freyja supposedly had a falcon cape that let her transform into the bird and fly, but without it she was grounded. For Gani to float here was a huge display of mystic muscle.

"Lady Ganieda, twin of Merlin. I am a former mage to the Round Table of Camelot and currently the mage for Nemesis & Co.," she said. "I just have a few words of wisdom for Vince Argus. And a charm."

"What kind of charm?" Freyja asked, her brows narrowing.

"Something to help with his staying power, which would be a challenge for any man in the presence of a woman as beautiful as you. We wouldn't want him to be done too soon, now would we?" Gani said.

"What?" Mista whispered. "We want him to be as premature as Hel so this can be over and she can heal the men."

"Easy. Gani is brilliant. She has her reasons and I trust her implicitly," Rudy said, putting her hand on the other Valkyrie's arm.

Gani whispered in the Soul For Hire's ear. The hitman nodded and she reached out to touch his bare chest where his shirt was unbuttoned. A glow passed from her hand to him.

Gani turned and did a courtly bow to the lust goddess of Asgard. "May I offer you a charm as well?"

"What will this one do?" Freyja asked.

"Enhance your pleasure, among other things," Gani said.

"And what do you get out of it?" Freyja said.

"I merely get to tap into your union," Gani said.

Freyja smiled. "You wish to feel what sex with the goddess of love is like vicariously."

Gani pretended to blush. "Something like that. Do I have your permission?"

"It will truly enhance my pleasure?" Freyja said.

"Tenfold," Gani said.

"Then you may," Freyja said.

Gani placed one hand on Freyja's face and the other on the part that her gate was sculpted after. Energy shot between her hands and through the goddess, who reacted with a moan.

Freyja tore the clothes off of Argus, then herself before placing the hitman on her throne and herself on him.

"They could at least get a room," Mista grumbled.

"She likes an audience," Rudy said, which was an understatement. With the tens of thousands of dead in the arena, she had more eyes on her than anything shy of pay-per-view.

Gani floated backwards to Rudy, never taking her eyes off the couple.

"Why did you help this take longer?" Mista demanded of the white haired mage.

"Simple. Freyja's too pissed about the necklace. She's not planning to go through with her end of the bargain. She'll take the power hit and try to keep the souls," Gani said.

"How do you know? Magic?" Mista asked.

"No. I'm an excellent judge of character," Gani said.

"Then why prolong it?" Mista said.

Gani smiled. "Because for a few extra orgasms, she just gave me the ability to tap into her manna."

"The charm is a fake?" Mista said.

"Oh, no. It's real. Nimue used a variant of it on my brother when she trapped him. It heightened his pleasure until it was off the charts, but let her steal some of his power. Enough to weaken him so he could be imprisoned. I tweaked it a bit so I don't have to be the one having the sex so long as I had both parties' permission. I can heal the heroes without her and burn the poison out of all of their systems. Fortunately, the endurance charm I gave Argus is real too. But she's a lust goddess, so he's got to focus on lasting, because once he stops she will notice the power drain and then it's all over. So quickly, start bringing the men to me."

Gani convulsed and shot into the air as Freyja let out a scream of passion. "Of course, I have to do this while feeling everything she does, so I'll leave the logistics of getting the men to the rest of you. I'll be throwing the healing manna in that direction. Just make sure the wounded are in front of me and keep them moving."

There was a pounding that shook the entire hall. Most assumed it was the couple locked in passion's embrace, but another Valkyrie ran in to report to Rudy.

"It's our lord at the gate and he's not happy. Apparently the lady locked down her hall, so we couldn't escape, but it is also keeping him out and he's very angry about it."

The hall rumbled from a combination of Freyja's pleasure and Odin's pounding, making most of those who were standing, lose their footing.

"I thought things were going too smoothly," Rudy said, rushing out of the stadium.

"Sometimes the smartest thing to do in a fight is run away. Sometimes it's also the hardest."
      -Terrorbelle, agent of Nemesis & Co. and former Daemor soldier

I got partway through the gate peephole by the skin of my teeth, but the skin on my arms wasn't so lucky. I lost a bunch of it to the walls of the metal tunnel.

I was bloody and I didn't even make it all the way through. Luckily, my arms and shoulders did, so I was able to pull and wiggle myself out further. As soon as my wings were free, I was able to fly myself the rest of the way out past a startled Tyr, who was too busy looking at me to think to close the porthole. The magic of the necklace at work again.

Brokk was screaming for them to get the gate open. I had the tiniest bit of a head start and I intended to make full use of it, so I sucker punched the one handed god and took off.

I hate to admit it, but I was out of practice when it came to flying. Luckily my hovering workouts on Earth had made my flying muscles stronger. I could fly faster and farther than I could before by practicing where physics, not magic, holds sway. Made just hovering a lot harder. Kind of like a swimmer who switches from training in a pool to going against ocean currents.

But there was still a difference. And flying all out didn't feel as natural as it should. I turned my head and saw the gates open. I flew faster, but a moment later Brokk was coming through the sky after me on his flying disc.

Damn it. It was faster than me. Brokk was closing the distance between us fast.

I wasn't going to be able to fly my way out of this one. My gun was a great weapon, but Mjollnir had it beat. The last thing I wanted to do was stand and fight the dwarf when he had the hammer, especially in its native magical realm.

My plan might still work, if Wanda was true to her word and still waiting in the rainbow bridge.

I got to Bifrost and kept flying, not daring to stop.

"Wanda! Wanda! Wanda!" I said, screaming her name three times. "Where are you?"

A blonde head and an incandescent fishtail popped above the Rainbow Bridge.

"An evil dwarf has Thor's hammer and is chasing me. I need to get out of here fast," I said, breathless.

The mermaid looked behind me and smiled. "I never liked Brokk. Real slime ball." Wanda looked at me, her glance going up and down my body. "And damn, you look hot." The magic necklace at work. "Hop on and hold on."

I sat on the adaro's back at the point where her pelvis became a tail and wrapped my legs around her waist. I barely had taken a deep breath when she dove beneath the multi-colored surface of Bifrost. We were off like a shot out of a gun.

Wanda swam faster than a jet ski, diving above or below the incandescent waves of colors at random intervals so I could catch a breath. Each time we broke the surface, I looked behind us and the dwarf on the disc was still there. And closing.

To slow him down, each time we came up for air, I took shots with different types of ammo, but he had his energy shield up, so all my bullets did nothing more than slow him down.

Wanda started to swim along the surface and looked back at me. "We're almost to the halfway point. That means we have to decide where we want this rainbow to end. It tends to be limited to places it's been raining."

"What about Bulfinche's Pub?" Paddy Moran had used his leprechaun pot of gold to buy the place, so now rainbows lead people who needed help to the bar. The magic there doesn't always need rain to work if the people were in enough trouble. And I couldn't imagine anyone in more trouble than we were right now.

"I can do that," Wanda said with a smile, diving beneath the incandescent waves again. She did some fancy twists and turns as we approached Heimdal where he stood guard.

I tapped the mermaid on the shoulder and motioned for her to go up. The look on her face made it clear that she thought it was a bad idea, but she listened anyway. We popped up in front of Heimdal, his sword already drawn.

"Heimdal, Brokk has taken over One-Eye's mind with a magic eyepatch. He has already made sure that Thor is being punished next to Loki and One-Eye can't think straight enough to let Rudy save the Valhalla heroes. I'm hoping Brokk will follow me to Bulfinche's and I can get some backup to take him out. Any chance of a little help?"

The big god smiled. "I heard the whole thing." Apparently among his god powers was magic hearing and sight. "Luckily, Odin never ordered me to obey the punk. If he is dumb enough to fly low, I'll take care of him for you," Heimdal said and winked at me. "And I have to say Terrorbelle that necklace looks better on you than it ever did on Freyja. Forgive my staring, but it's hard to take my eyes off you. I've got your backs. You two get going."

"Thanks, cutie," Wanda said, with a wink for Bifrost's guardian. He smiled and winked back. I was thinking Mista might have something to worry about with these two.

It was back into the rainbow for us. The mermaid continued swimming, making sure she twisted and turned to avoid Brokk targeting us with the hammer.

Suddenly, the rainbow trembled like it had been hit by a train. Brokk must have thrown the hammer at Heimdal. I hoped the god was okay.

Up ahead it looked like the rainbow ended, dropping off into nothingness. If I wasn't afraid of drowning, I would have screamed. The pair of us shot out into darkness, our momentum making it seem like we were flying. Then suddenly, we were surrounded again by a rainbow, but this one was nowhere near as solid as Bifrost. It was easy to see through and I could breathe.

We picked up speed as we headed almost straight down toward the nighttime New York City skyline. I almost wet myself. Being back on Earth meant I couldn't fly. And we weren't simply falling. The adaro was using gravity to help her swim the rainbow even faster.

I had no clue about how she was planning on stopping. As we neared the concrete canyons, I almost stopped being afraid as I was struck by the beauty of the Manhattan skyline at night, which was followed by the thought about how even a magic rainbow could appear without sunlight. I looked behind us and there was a full moon. Maybe that helped. My eyes were again drawn down to the beauty of the city lit up. Then I stopped acting like a tourist and recognized the building Bulfinche's Pub was in and the cross on top of the Our Lady of the Lake Church that was just up the block. Wanda flipped herself so that her tail was in front of us, using a back and forth movement to slow our descent. That change in speed saved our lives as there was no warning as Mjollnir flew through the rainbow right where we would have been if we were still moving at full speed.

The mermaid came to a stop in the air twenty feet above the fire hydrant in front of the bar, treading rainbow with her tail. She motioned with her thumb for me to get off, but I knew the dwarf wasn't the type to just let her go. I shook my head and grabbed hold of her and used my wings to propel us out of the rainbow. Unfortunately, we came out sideways. I used my wings to right us, but she weighed a few hundred pounds with that tail of hers, which is way over the weight I could hover with on Earth.

I managed to flip her around bride style and used my wings to slow our fall, but it didn't do much. My legs took the brunt of the impact with the sidewalk. It cracked under us. I knew Hercules or one of the patrons was going to use that to make fun of my weight.

Brokk rode the rainbow like a surfer on his disc, dive bombing toward us. I sprinted toward the door of Bulfinche's Pub. From the looks of the street it was probably three or four in the morning local time, which meant chances were there was nobody in the pub. Luckily, Paddy never locked the doors in case someone in trouble needed to get in.

I made it to the door and got it open just as I spotted Mjollnir coming at us out of the corner of my eye. I threw the adaro across the barroom floor to get her out of the strike zone, but tripped in the process. I rolled around and tried to dodge the hammer, but it wasn't enough. I wanted to close my eyes, but I wasn't going to give the dwarf the satisfaction of seeing me flinch as he killed me.

But I didn't die. Instead, something strange happened. As I lay on all fours looking out the door and watching the head of the hammer coming to pulverize my face, it stopped and not due to the dwarf playing with his control glove. Halfway through the doorway, it simply hung in the air for an instant, then dropped down to the floor.

I remembered Murphy explaining to me that the doorway acted oddly where magic and other things were concerned. Outside magic worked. Inside it didn't. The entry was a couple feet long, with a wall on one side and a window on the other. It was a transition zone. Part of the magic Paddy used in the bar made sure no weapons could be fired into the pub, be it bullets, arrows and apparently magic hammers.

Brokk hovered on the city street, moving his glove frantically back and forth, hitting gems, and trying to make the hammer do something. It didn't respond and the dwarf was furious. I was safe for the moment.

Then I saw a couple dressed in their finest club wear, walking arm and arm, so enamored with each other that the rest of the world didn't exist. They didn't even notice the little man on the floating disk or the nighttime rainbow.

The dwarf pointed his index finger and placed his other hand above a dark crimson gem. He pressed it and the entire glove started to glow with arcane energy. Brokk make his hand into the universal sign for gun and pointed at the couple, then motioned for me to come out. It was clear that if I didn't, those two people would pay the price. I looked around the bar for backup. There were a few lights on, but the only ones in the place were me and the rainbow mermaid who was crawling on the floor.

"Wanda, start banging on the door behind the bar. Wake Paddy up. Tell him to go get Murphy before the serpent kills him and to call Nemesis and let her know that Gani and Rudy are under fire in Asgard," I said, just in case the gun's escape hadn't gone as planned. It's possible the half sphere of woe was able to disintegrate it, but I doubted it. Gani was too good at what she did to not have planned for something like that.

"What are you going to do?" she asked. The dwarf's finger started to crackle with arcane energy. I bent and lifted for all I was worth and got the hammer off the floor. The magical charms that made it super heavy were also nullified in the door, but it was still damn hard to lift.

"I am going to end this once and for all," I said.

I lifted the hammer to chest height and walked out the doorway where the charms and magics of Mjollnir kicked back in.

Mjollnir flew towards Brokk, with me still holding it.

Shielding is nice, but I had faced enough in my time in the Daemor to know one thing. They were not able to simply let one object pass through without making a hole in the field. I was hoping that it would work the same here. Or if he kept the field up, that the hammer would crush it. Either way, Brokk was in for some hurt.

I raced through the air on the end of the hammer like the tail of a kite that had been strapped to a missile. As I got near, the shield dropped and I swung around so that my boot connected with Brokk's jaw. It made him stagger and fall back off of the disc and onto the pavement. I landed on him, making like his face was a piñata with a winning lotto ticket inside and my fists were twin baseball bats.

I got in about six shots before his index finger exploded with light, knocking me back about twenty feet. I hit the ground numb, feeling like I had been cooked from the inside out. I was barely able to breathe. My Daemor badge had deflected some of the energy, otherwise I would have been a crispy critter. I forced myself to take a breath, then another and got to my feet just in time to see the dwarf throw the hammer my way again.

It had taken me the better part of an hour to master riding the lightning back at Thor's farm. I did okay on Rudy's hammer, but I was only going to get one shot at this.

Turns out, one was all I needed. The dwarf didn't know what to make of me, leaping on and riding the hammer, but managed to bring up his ungloved hand to block his face.

Good. That's what I was hoping he'd think I was up to. When I got close enough, I spun so my back was to him and resorted to a classic Terrorbelle attack. Lashing out with my wing, I sliced his forearm right below where his magic glove was. The dwarf screamed as my wing went through flesh and bone, severing his hand from the rest of his body.

Luckily, his armor stopped at the deltoids. Pretty stupid. Then again, I go out all the time without my body armor trench coat – including during this fight – so I should hardly talk.

Brokk surprised me by not collapsing from the pain. Instead he ripped part of his sleeve to use as a tourniquet. The dwarf pulled it tight, tying a one handed knot to stop the bleeding. Brokk didn't stop there, reaching down with his remaining hand for the magic glove. He pulled his severed hand from inside it and was about to put it on his remaining hand upsidedown. I spun and cut off that hand too.

"You bitch! Do you think you can beat me! I still control Wotan, king of the gods!" Brokk said.

"Yeah, about that. One-Eye don't seem to be here, now does he?" I said, picking up the gauntlet and putting it on. "A little small for my hand, but it fits."

I reached down and picked up Mjollnir using the metal glove. This time there was hardly any effort involved.

"You do nice work. Fortunately, so do I," I said, pulling back the hammer as if I was going to smash his head in with it. Brokk did more than flinch – he curled up into a fetal position with his bloody arm stubs covering his face.

When nothing happened, Brokk looked out from behind his hand which is when I slugged him. Of course, that's when backup finally arrived.

"What the blazes?" said Paddy, stepping out on the street. The leprechaun actually wore a nightshirt.

"Nice legs," I said. "Wanda gave you my message?"

Paddy nodded. "Just came out to see if ye needed any help. I'm guessing that you don't."

I nodded. "One-Eye's mind has been taken over by this guy. Can you keep Brokk inside the bar so he can't affect One-Eye anymore?" I said, figuring the magic nullifying field of the bar would prevent him from giving any new commands to the All-Father of the Norse Pantheon.

"Yes."

Behind Paddy came Hercules who apparently slept in just a pair of boxers. The Greek demi-god was a sight to see and it took me half a second to take my eyes off of him, especially since it was obvious he was happy to see me too. That or he had a flashlight in his shorts. I've learned to respect Herc, but I've never really gotten past the way he made fun of my size the first time we met, so there's never really been a serious attraction. Now there was, which made me realize the lust that the jewels in the necklace produced was a two-way street. "Terrorbelle, you look different. Amazing really, the way your pink hair catches the street lights. Would you like to go out sometime?"

I realized looking at Herc in his undies was setting off the necklace, so I tried to think bland thoughts. I was completely ignoring his six-pack abs and well-rounded butt. Not to mention those massive arms and chest.

Paddy seemed to have a sense of what was going on. "Herc, take care of him. Make sure he doesn't bleed all over me bar floor. I'll go get Murph. I already called Nemesis—she said she'd gotten your message and was on her way. She's probably already shadow stepped to Asgard."

Just then Baby, Paddy's 1930 Cadillac, pulled out of the garage with a satyr at the wheel. It was Fred, the son of Pan, who worked as a busboy and bartender at Bulfinche's.

The satyr waved to me as he got out of the car and Paddy hopped in. Fred was openly staring as well and I started realizing how creepy having this power really was.

The Caddy lifted itself a few feet off the ground and the leprechaun opened the window. "Terrorbelle, do ye need a lift back to Asgard? Or should we get Wanda?"

I looked at the glove on my right hand and the hammer I held in it. I grabbed onto it with my left hand as well.

"No thanks." I looked up and the rainbow was still there. "I think I have a quicker way to get back."

"Okay, ye go take care of business and as soon as I have Murphy, I'll be joining ye at Valhalla," Paddy said.

"Hurry, please," I said, but the car had already simmered and left using its transworld drive.

With the slightest flick of my wrist, I just barely tossed the hammer behind me and put the gloved hand in front of me. As soon as it flipped, I used my left hand to grab onto the shaft and pulled it to my chest. It lifted me off the ground, trying to get to the gauntlet. I positioned my gloved hand so it was pointed up along the rainbow. I flew with the speed of a rocket. As long as my arm was able to hold on, I could make the hammer fly where I wanted by moving my right hand. I'd be back in Asgard in moments, although thanks to the wonders of quantum geography, I had no idea how much time had passed there since I left.

"I've always heard that you should walk a mile in a man's shoes before you judged him. Whoever said that was an idiot."
-Thor, Norse god of thunder

"Murphy, hit the button!" Loki shouted, the muscles starting to grow back around his skull in the time since the serpent had stopped torturing the trickster to instead try to kill the bartender.

"Gee, why didn't I think of that?" Murphy said, leaping behind a boulder, barely dodging the lunging serpent's head. "It's not working. Why is it not working?"

"Brokk probably figured a way to jam the signal," Loki said, fat forming over the muscle around his head as he wore away the flesh from his wrists and ankles in a struggle to get free.

Murphy threw a rock with surprisingly good aim, nailing the serpent's wounded eye. The pain got it to back away for the moment.

"How do I unjam it?" Murphy said.

"I don't know," Loki said, his wrists now open to the bone as flakes of skin appeared on his face.

"I'll settle for how to beat the serpent," Murphy said, climbing toward higher ground. "Or a snake charmer's flute. Or a really big stick, but all I've got is shtick."

"Don't worry about beating him. Get out of here!" Loki ordered.

"Could this thing kill you two?" Murphy said.

"No," Loki said at the same time Thor said, "Yes."

"I'm not going to let it kill you," Murphy said. "Hey scaly, I'm going to make a boa tie out of you. You know why? Because boa ties are cool."

The serpent had a low level intelligence and was swaying its head side to side warily, trying to figure out why the mortal was taunting it instead of fleeing.

"Too bad your mother didn't have a hissterectomy before you were hatched. Stop making passes at me – there's no way you're getting a good-night hiss. You're just making an asp of yourself," Murphy said, wedging himself between a boulder and the cave wall, his legs on the rock.

"Murphy is insane," Thor said. "He's joking when he should be running."

"Murphy don't run away if someone's in trouble. He's dumb that way. And when he's scared the puns come out faster. It's how he copes," said Loki. "We have to save him."

"You're the genius in this family. How do we get out of the chains?"

Thor said.

"Hey, if we shared women's underwear, it would be a co-bra," Murphy said. "Or maybe a pythong. Or a pair of water moccasins."

The snake had had enough and figured Thor was right. The human was insane. And probably tasty, so he moved forward to flush him out.

"Time to snake, rattle, and roll," Murphy said as the serpent's head came up toward him. The bartender pushed his legs as hard as he could and the boulder rolled down onto the beast's scaly head, stunning it.

Murphy moved to even higher ground in hope of dropping more rocks, but the serpent recovered its wits quickly and darted at him. The bartender dodged, but the scaly head hit him on his side, knocking him off the wall.

Murphy managed to land on the serpent's neck on the serpent's blind side. The beast began to shake its head to try and knock him off.

"Thor, you need to do something!" Loki shouted.

"I'm trying," Thor replied, struggling against his restraints – they stretched, but held.

"Damn it, you are supposed to be the strongest SOB in the universe. Are you going to let a few measly links of chain hold you?" Loki said.

Thor was turning crimson with the effort. "They are not budging."

Murphy was finally thrown off and crashed down onto the rocky floor, too stunned from the impact to move.

"Murphy! Get up!" Loki screamed, trying desperately to break the magic on the chains that prevented him from shape shifting. His wrists were bare down to the bone from his trying to pull free.

Murphy didn't stir and the serpent was closing in.

"Thor, I swear to you if you don't do something to save my best friend, I will figure out a way to cause Ragnorak by tomorrow," Loki said.

"You think I want to deal with Terrorbelle or Paddy if I let Murphy die?" Thor said, straining so hard, veins were popping out all over his body. "I'm trying."

"Try harder!" Loki said.

Thor saw the serpent posing to swallow the bartender and realized he'd never get loose in time. His eyes narrowed and he called to the storm that was building inside of him. His chains were designed to block his control of the weather and lightning by causing him untold pain if he tried to summon either.

Thor ignored the pain and the lightning came to his fingers. He let it build as long as he could stand before releasing the thunderbolt from his hand straight at the serpent.

The beast convulsed and twitched as the electricity coursed through it, before finally collapsing.

The vibration from the snake's impact with the ground stirred Murphy from his stupor. He crawled across the cave, climbing up to where the two Norse gods were chained.

"Nice shot," Murphy gasped, breathless.

"Thanks," Thor said, in between gasping for breath.

"I should have known with you here we'd win it in the lightning round," Murphy said.

"Glad it worked, because these chains drained everything else out of me. I don't think I could do it again."

Which is when the serpent's head rose up behind Murphy.

"Despite claims to the contrary, it is not always good to be king."
 -Odin, King of the Norse gods

Rudy looked down Freyja's golden nostrils at her grandfather, or at least the giant carved ones on the woman-shaped building.

The hundred guards lay battered and broken where the god in the wide brimmed hat had thrown them when they tried to stop him.

The one-eyed god motioned for his raven to fly up into the nostril opening to gain access to the hall. Munin obeyed, fortunately picking the nostril on the right, leaving Rudy's position undiscovered for the moment.

Odin banged on the doors, shaking the entire building. "Let me in!"

"Not by the white hair on your chinny, chin, chin, Grandfather," Rudy said.

Odin's head snapped up and he saw the red-haired Valkyrie looking down at him.

The one-eyed god started to float upwards, but Rudy waved her hand and a strong wind blew him back to the ground. She may not have had her father's level of control over weather, but she was damn good with wind.

"You think you can keep me out? I know what Freyja is doing in there. I can feel it." Not that it was that impressive a claim. Anyone in the neighborhood could feel as the hall shivered and shook along with its mistresses' pleasure. "She must stop!"

"Why Grandfather? We're using her power to heal your heroes back to health and burn the crux out of their systems. How can that be a bad thing?" Rudy asked.

"She is my wife!"

"Won't Frigga be surprised to hear that? She thinks she's your wife," Rudy said.

"Don't mock me child. I have a thousand names and a hundred lives. No one single aspect can contain me," Odin said.

"Yet you let a dwarf's tiny creation control your mind," Rudy said.

"No one controls Odin!"

"Prove it. Take off the eyepatch," Rudy said.

The one-eyed god reached for his eye covering, but his hand stopped short. "Brokk said…"

"That you're his bitch now?" Rudy finished.

"Not even your father would dare talk to me like that," Odin said.

"And look where that got him."

"Open these gates!"

"Maybe if you bought them a couple of drinks and tried some romantic poetry, they might spread for you," Rudy said.

Odin turned toward the doors and placed his fingers at the point where they joined in an attempt to open them.

A hammer hit him in the back, knocking him to one knee.

"You dare!?" Odin raised a hand and pointed it at Rudy.

"I can't let you in until the heroes are all healed or…" but Rudy was cut off by the beam of energy that shot from her grandfather's hand.

The angle of the nostril didn't allow her the cover to be able to back up far enough to avoid the mystic bolt, so Rudy did the next best thing. She jumped out of the building's opening, a hundred feet up. She used her control over wind to create an updraft, but that only slowed her fall. She let out a shrill whistle and suddenly Morningdour was flying toward her. Odin took another shot, but his hand jerked at the last second, which caused him to miss. It was almost as if he were fighting two battles, one on the outside and the other within.

The winged horse caught the Valkyrie, who landed in the saddle just like a cowboy in an old western, if the movies had used flying horses. Odin's entire body was glowing, energy leaking out from his eyes. Where the light met the patch, the metal sizzled. "I will destroy you," Odin said, then stumbled as the lights surrounding him went out. "Flee, my Thrud before I lose control again."

The white-bearded god stiffened as the golden patch shone so brightly it looked like it was on fire. The glow was back, but confined to Odin's hands this time. The one-eyed god looked up in fury, suddenly firing a third mystic bolt. Again, it did not hit his granddaughter, narrowly missing her shoulder. However, it did hit a Valkyrie. Hladgunner had been sneaking up behind Rudy, spear in hand on her own winged horse. The head Valkyrie was poised to deliver a deathblow, but the stray bolt took her out, knocking her unconscious. Her winged horse flew off into the sky with her unconscious in the saddle.

Odin stood immobile, forces battling within him. Finally, he turned and raised his hands. The streets began to tremble and shake. A scarlet energy rose up in a bubble around Freyja's hall, trapping Rudy and Morningdour inside of it.

"This hall may be Freyja's place of power, but all of Asgard is mine. If she wants to keep me out, then I shall keep her and the rest of you traitors trapped inside until such time as I see fit to deal with you. And before you get any bright ideas, know that my barrier extends below the hall, cutting off access to her tunnels. The lot of you are my prisoners. When I return granddaughter, your punishment and exile shall begin."

Odin stormed off toward Valhalla, the Golden City itself shaking with each angry step.

Morningdour landed next to the hall, whinnying nervously at the deadly energy barrier that had trapped them inside.

"Don't touch it," Rudy told the horse. "It's a full sphere of woe. I saw Grandfather use it once on an army of giants. It turned the ones that tried to go through it to ash. Fly me up to the nose and I'll go back in to check on how the healing is coming along." The horse whinnied like it was laughing. "No, I wasn't making a joke. Just wait for me out here. And be careful. I couldn't bear the thought of losing you."

The horse nodded and pressed her head alongside that of the red-haired Valkyrie and her whinny sounded amazingly as if she said, "Me too."

"How do I keep getting myself into these situations?"
-John Murphy, bartender at Bulfinche's Pub

The enormous serpent opened its jaws and thrust its head down to swallow Murphy whole.

"Look out!" Loki screamed. Thor whistled so loud it shook the cave. Murphy turned and put his arms out in front of him as if that alone would somehow ward off the beast, but the snake apparently never got that memo.

The fanged jaws snapped shut. The instant before they closed, two flying goats dove in front of it and scooped up the bartender, one of his arms wrapped around each of their necks.

"Good Nasher and Grinder," Thor said. "Get the mortal out of here!"

The goats nodded and made for the cave exit, but the huge reptile slithered quicker than they could fly and blocked their path.

Murphy shifted onto Nasher's back and Grinder flew at the creature, his horns cutting into the serpent's neck as he soared past. Grinder repeated the maneuver twice more. The beast reared back and venom shot out of its fangs, disintegrating the goat's flesh as it made its next pass. Grinder's bones fell to the ground.

Nasher put Murphy back on the landing next to the chained gods and made his own attacks on the serpent. The goat got five slashes on the reptile's scaly hide before the acid took him out.

Murphy was spending that time helping Thor pull at his chains to no avail. The serpent lunged toward the bartender and he took off running, but he wasn't fleeing, just looking for more rocks to throw. He threw some fist-sized stones which did nothing but annoy the beast and keep his attention focused away from Loki and Thor.

Then Murphy ran out of rocks and the serpent knew he had the bartender trapped. Rearing up, the serpent seemed to smile as it posed for the fatal strike.

"C'mon, I still need that boa tie, you scaly monstrosity," Murphy shouted defiantly.

The serpent moved to end things when the sound of a car horn playing the Cavalry charge made the huge head turn just in time to be hit by the front fender of a flying 1930 Cadillac.

"When storming an enemy stronghold it is always polite to knock first, preferably with something heavy like a battering ram"
- Daemor saying.

I've been a flyer all of my life. I have flown under my own power. Also on a flying horse, a flying motorcycle, on the back of a dragon and even the occasional aircraft, but believe me when I tell you flight by hammer is an entirely new ballgame. The power of Mjollnir is unbelievable. The longer it was in the air, the faster it went. It would probably be less of a thrill to ride a missile. The fear of heights and falling in a non-magical environment was quickly replaced by a fear of hitting something and being squished at this speed.

On the plus side, the trip back to Asgard was proving to be a fast one.

Heimdal grinned and waved at me as I flew by, yelling "Good luck." I'm sure he understood why I didn't wave back.

As I approached the Golden City, I eased up on my grip of the hammer and let my gauntleted hand catch it. That stopped the propulsion, but not the inertia. I had adjusted the trajectory slightly upward so I was able to ride out the momentum and didn't have to let my wings kick in until I started my downward arc. I lowered myself to the ground in front of Tyr, who was still pulling guard duty and had already closed the gates.

He looked with wide-eyed horror as he realized that I was now holding Asgard's mightiest weapon. Then his eyes shifted to my chest and he was again lost to the magic of the necklace.

"Open the gates, Tyr. One-Eye and I have something we need to discuss," I said.

"Wotan has banned you from the Golden City. Forgive me, beautiful one, but you may not enter," Tyr said, staring at my bra.

"I wasn't asking," I said, holding up the hammer. The god took a step back and his eyes actually left my chest. Tyr looked like he was wishing he was on the other side of the gate. "You have to know Brokk was using mind control over One-Eye. I beat Brokk. Let me free One-Eye."

Tyr shook his head. "Some forms of mind control are not reversible. That means I may have to deal with this Odin for millennia and I am not going to cross him."

"I thought you were supposed to be the brave one, the one who put his hand in Fenrir the wolf's mouth in order to trick him into being bound."

Tyr laughed. "I admit the story makes me look better than I should.

Odin, Balder, and Loki all refused to do it. Thor offered, but Odin said his hands were too valuable to the realm. Odin ordered me to do it and I was more afraid of old One-Eye than I was of the wolf. I still am."

And by saying old One-Eye's name more than three times, he made sure he had warned him of my arrival. Slick.

"There is afraid and then there is terror. Beyond terror, there is Terrorbelle," I said trying for dramatic as I threw the hammer where I knew the hinge was on the upper left part of the gate and followed that by doing the same on the other five hinges. Each time the hammer returned to my gloved hand. Finally, I threw the hammer at each giant-sized gate and they fell inward like rotten trees in a thunderstorm.

I walked slow and steady up to Tyr, pulling my gun with my left hand as I approached. I locked eyes with the god and he blinked, scurrying out of my path.

And that is how I stormed the Golden City. The place was not without its defenders, although not as many as I expected. Jerkgunner had a handful of others ready and waiting, none of whom I had met before. I hoped that was a good sign and Rudy had saved the warriors of Valhalla from their final death.

"You shall not pass, Daemor," Jerkgunner said holding up a sword that crackled with mystic energy.

"I guess you lost that loving feeling," I said. The Valkyrie wasn't looking at me the same. I guess Brokk's second dose with his ray must have worked. She seemed beat up, her skin singed

"Odin is furious. He attacked me. I will not make him any angrier," she said.

"Angrier than betraying him and helping kill Adar and spiking the horns with crux? The lowest thing a soldier can be is a traitor and that, Jerkgunner, is just what you are. You betrayed the Valkyries and all of Asgard. I have no idea what you could possibly do that would be worse than that," I said.

I had nothing else left to say. There was a time for talk and there was a time for fighting. I let the hammer fly and it hit the Valkyrie in the chest. She was knocked off her winged horse, flew thirty feet and crashed into a wall, then through it. The horse was unhurt. I'm no monster.

Mjollnir flew back to my hand and the Valkyrie lay motionless in the rubble. I could get used to having this power at my beck and call. I'd win almost every fight. It was amazing Thor, at least on Earth, was as humble as he was.

I turned to the other assembled defenders of the realm.

"I have come to free Odin," He knew I was here. No harm in letting him listen in. Maybe it would reach his subconscious and help him take it easy on me. "Not harm him. However, anyone that gets in my way is going down. I suggest you all step aside." A few were smart enough to listen, but most held their ground. I threw the hammer at an angle, managing to hit four on the away trajectory. I flew back and forth so the hammer took out three more on its way back to me.

That was enough to make the rest run for cover.

Time to move on to Valhalla.

"I've always said that you should walk a mile in a man's shoes before you judged him. That way, you have his shoes and a good head start."
    -Loki, Norse trickster

The flying Caddy smacked the serpent's head around like a boxing glove punching a speed bag. The snake staggered, then fell.

The Caddy pulled alongside the bartender and opened a door. "Murphy, get in," Paddy said.

The bartender scrambled toward the door just in time to see the serpent was down, but not out.

"Boss, it's coming back," Murphy said.

Paddy hit the gas and smashed his car into the serpent's nose, but this time the fender crumbled.

The door still open, the Caddy swung back around to pick up Murphy, who scurried inside.

Paddy drove back to the gods and leapt out with a homemade lock pick kit. He went straight to Loki.

"Ye give me your word that ye'll go back when it's time. And safe," Paddy said.

"Murphy's okay?" Loki said.

"Fine and likely as obnoxious as ever. Give me your word," Paddy said.

"I give my word, Moran. Now hurry, it's not done with us yet," Loki said.

Seconds later, his chains popped off and Loki leapt up and saw the damage to the Caddy's front end.

"Paddy, I'm sorry about what it did to Baby," Loki said.

"Had to lower the shields to get Murphy. I can replace the fender," Paddy said. "But not Murphy."

"I knew you cared," Murphy said. "I'm sorry about Baby. I guess this was her day of wreckoning."

"Of course, now I wonder why I thought that was such a good idea," Paddy said, moving on to Thor's chains.

"You really auto know that by now," Murphy said, as the trickster moved to the edge of the drop off just in time to see the serpent rise up.

The trickster smiled and cracked his knuckles. "You try to kill my friend? After all you've done to me over the centuries, I'm going to enjoy putting you down."

Behind him Paddy worked his magic again and Thor's chains came off. The thunderer got up quickly and put his hand on the trickster's shoulder.

"Brother, let me," Thor said.

Loki turned to look the thunderer in the eyes. "It tried to kill Murphy. It has to pay."

"Oh it will, I promise. Let me. Pretty please with a cherry and sprinkles on top," Thor said.

"Well, since you put it that way, how can I refuse?" Loki said with a smile, bowing with a flourish of his arm toward the beast.

"Thank you," Thor said, leaping up toward the serpent who snatched him out of the air with its jaws like a dog catching a biscuit.

The maw closed and from the look on the serpent's face it thought it had won. Then its jaws were not only forced open, but snapped back hard enough that the lower part dislocated as the red-bearded thunderer pushed from the inside like a jack.

Next Thor rammed his fist up into the soft palate of the serpent mouth, ripping through tissue. Next he climbed up to the outside of the head and ripped its remaining eyeball out, then worked his way down, damaging each section of the snake as he went.

"Should we stop him?" Murphy said.

"Best not to. You joke, he fights. This is actually therapeutic for him," Loki said. "Although you might want to look for a couple of sacks to put the goats' bones in so they will revive in the morning."

"Ye didn't have to give him a straight line, did ye?" Paddy said, rolling his eyes at Loki.

"Loki, I thought you had changed, but after everything you've been through, you still want to get Thor's goat," Murphy said.

"He's your friend," Paddy said.

"Hey, you're the one that saved him," Loki replied.

"It's great to be loved," Murphy said as he got a couple of bags out of the back of Baby and went down to gather goat bones.

"Magic is not the solution to every problem, but it sure helps in eleven out of ten cases."

-Ganieda, twin of Merlin, mage of Camelot, agent of Nemesis & Co.

"That's the last one," Mista said. "All the heroes are healed and have the crux out of their system. Except for Argus."

"Thank heavens," Gani said, floating down to the ground. "I'm exhausted and oddly craving a cigarette."

"Do you smoke?" Mista said.

"Only if a spell goes really wrong," Gani said, then tilted her head back and shivered as the lust goddess screamed in pleasure.

"What about Argus?" Mista said. "He drank the poisoned mead and has crux in his system too."

"Freyja's unrelenting orgasms already burned it out of the hitman early on," Gani said. "He's fine. In fact, being that close to the generation of manna will likely make him able to survive a long time without the ram's horn's manna."

"Maybe we can sneak the warriors back to Valhalla before she's done and we won't even have to worry about dealing with her," Mista said. "Gani, can you get her gates open?"

"As tapped in as I am to her power and as distracted as she is now, I'd say yes," Gani replied.

"Won't do us any good. Grandfather has surrounded us in a sphere of woe," Rudy said. Munin flew into the arena and went to a high perch, planning to stay out of sight, but was spotted by Freyja's flying cats who began to stalk him.

"Bad news. Deadly mystic energy bubble. Not many could manage even a small one," Gani said. "To make it big enough to envelop this hall must have cost One-Eye a lot of power, unless he tapped into the half sphere around the city, but that would weaken the city's defenses."

"Can you get us through it?" Rudy said.

It blocks most teleportation, even body slides. If I went immaterial and tried to slide out, it would still cook me like a nuclear powered microwave," Gani said.

"Can you punch a hole in in?" Rudy said, as the raven dove in front of her, the two flying cats in hot pursuit.

"If I was at my best and able to focus, maybe. But…" Freyja screamed as the lovers changed positions yet again. Gani trembled and would have fallen on the ground if Rudy hadn't caught her. The white-haired mage trembled and squeezed the Valkyrie tightly. "… as you can see, I'm a wee bit distracted."

"Then we best get ready to fight," Mista said, the raven landing behind her in hopes that the Valkyrie's size would frighten the airborne felines off. Instead they landed and crept around her, one on each side.

"Why?" Rudy asked.

Mista pointed to the hitman. "Judging by the look on Argus' face, I'd say the perseverance charm Gani gave him just gave out and he's done."

Argus gave a loud scream which Freyja joined in, then both collapsed. The raven used the distraction to get airborne again.

Gani frowned as her safety window started to slam close and drew as much power to her as she could manage before it shut completely. Her amorous activities ended, Freyja finally sensed the draining of her power.

"Witch! You dare steal from me?" Freyja rose naked off of the hitman and waved her hand. The floor flowed up like mercury rising until Gani was completely enveloped within it.

"The warriors from Valhalla are now mine by right. I will choose their fate. Whether they live or die will depend on whether they denounce Odin and swear fidelity to me," Freyja said.

"You're a little late – you already missed that bus," Rudy said.

Freyja looked around at the thousands of healed warriors. "How is this possible?"

Gunshots burst out of Gani's shell, cracking it. Next, the shell exploded outward, freeing the white-haired mage.

"All part of our deal, strumpet," Gani said.

"You tricked me," Freyja said.

"Nope. You were just thinking with the wrong body part when you made the deal," Gani said, pointing the gun at the lust goddess. "Now you can surrender and we can work together to try to get through the sphere of woe around your hall."

"Nonsense, Odin would never do that to me," Freyja said, but she still reached out with her mind to survey her domain. Meanwhile the raven landed behind Rudy, who actually waved her hammer to shoo the cats away. "That bastard!"

"Men. Can't live with them, can't turn them into rats when they cheat on you. Well, actually I can. Not that I would. At least not again. Probably," Gani said. "So, truce?"

"Truce? You and your truce can go straight to Hel!" Freyja said. "You think you have the power to stand against a goddess of Asgard?"

"Damn skippy," Gani said. "You may have more power, but I have the advantage in knowledge and I'm smarter than you."

"You think so?" Freyja said, waving both hands. The floor rose up and enveloped Rudy and the rest of the Valkyries, as well as the hiding raven. The cats moved in to swat at the bird, but it was like hitting a statue.

The floor tried for Gani again too, but this time she was prepared and it didn't rise above her chest. Before it did, she saw her cell phone on her belt blink with the message "Turn off the lights and let me in." It had been in total darkness while she was enveloped the first time.

Freyja laughed and started glowing. Even with all the manna Gani had siphoned off, the lust goddess still had plenty left. Plus she was in her place of power. "Tell me, how do you plan to stop me before I slay your friends?"

Gani answered with a hand wave of her own. The stadium faded to darkness and she whispered a name three times.

"You think I'm frightened of the dark? That shadows will make me tremble?" Freyja said, her hands lighting up to banish the darkness.

Her answer was the barrel of a gun placed at the base of her skull and the sound of the hammer of said gun being cocked.

"Actually, what is in the shadows should make you tremble and be very afraid," said Nemesis.

"How did you get through the sphere of woe? Nothing can teleport through and survive," Freyja said.

"Funny thing about shadow stepping. It's not really teleporting so much as opening doors in the dark to a realm of night. It doesn't have to go through so much as it travels completely around it," Gani said. And it helped with cell reception too if the mystic circuits were attuned to channels of darkness.

"Release my people and the others or die," Nemesis said.

"I don't fear some woman with a gun," Freyja said.

"That's no ordinary woman. That's our boss," Gani said. "Maybe you've heard of her – enforcer for the Council of Thrones? Daughter of Nyx? Or as some who have faced her call her – No, please don't kill me!"

Freyja became very pale. "Nemesis, the god slayer?"

"I've been called that too. Although I do prefer the last one Gani mentioned. Always loads of fun. You have until I count to one to free them," Nemesis said. The shells cracked and fell in giant flakes to the ground. The cats made a dive for the bird, but he leapt between Rudy's feet. "One."

"Very well, sister of Merlin. I accept your truce and offer to help circumvent the sphere of woe," Freyja said.

"Sorry dearie, but that boat has sailed. My ride's here," Gani said. "You're on your own."

"Boss, we need a mass evac," Rudy said, kicking a cat that was still trying for the raven.

Nemesis nodded. "Have the Valhallans and Valkyries join hands and make sure they keep their eyes shut. The dead don't do well in Nyx's realm."

Argus picked up his coat, put it and his holsters on and carried the rest of his clothes as he walked up to an amused Nemesis.

"Argus."

"Nemesis. A pleasure to see you again," the Soul For Hire replied. "You have good people."

"I do. I suspect there is an excellent reason for your lack of clothes?" Nemesis said.

"There is," Argus said, offering his hand to Nemesis. "Just helped save a bunch of lives and probably the world. You know, the usual."

"Right," Nemesis said. "I can see in the dark. You reach for a gun and I'm leaving you in the darklands."

"Fair enough," he replied.

Nemesis looked at Argus, then at the naked Freyja and guessed part of what happened. She donned a leather glove before taking the hitman's hand.

"Is everyone ready?" Nemesis asked.

Munin landed on Rudy's shoulder, minus a few feathers. Mista and the other Valkyries nodded to Rudy. All the souls they had come with had their hands linked up.

"We're good to go, boss," Rudy said. "But we'll have to stop for Morningdour. She's outside the hall."

Nemesis nodded and turned to Gani. "Make it dark."

Argus turned to Freyja. "I had a great time. I'll call you."

The flying cats dove one last time for the Raven on Rudy's shoulder. Gani raised her arms and the lights went out. When they came back on, the Valhallans and the great escape party were gone. And the flying cats had crashed into the floor.

"Sometimes the little guy or gal wins for no other reason than overconfidence on the part of the big bad. I'm pretty sure Goliath figured the shepherd kid didn't have a chance right up until the rock hit him in the head."
-Terrorbelle, agent of Nemesis & Co. and former Daemor soldier

I used the hammer and glove method to fly to Valhalla. It seemed abandoned, almost waiting for tumbleweeds to roll by. There were no Valkyries guarding it, no one at all to stop me from entering. I landed, then walked in and slowly made my way through the great hall.

I was half expecting Odin to be gone as well, but instead he was sitting on his throne, as immobile as a statue. His two wolves sat on either side, but they were whimpering like they had recently been kicked. One of his ravens was pecking at the golden strap of his eyepatch. Odin reached up to swat it as if it was a fly, but the raven was quicker than his hand and got away, but was missing a few feathers. Seems his totems had been trying to free him and gotten hurt for their troubles. Not yet knowing the other had gone to spy on Freyja, I wondered if he had killed the other bird.

Odin glared at me with an anger that made my common sense scream at me to get away. I didn't because sometimes it doesn't matter if you run, because trouble will chase you down and find you anyway.

"I see you defeated Brokk," Odin said.

"Quite handily I might add," I said.

"I will not be beaten. I will give you a chance to lay down that hammer at my feet and maybe I will let you leave Asgard unharmed," Odin said.

"Such a tempting offer. Are you sure you can manage that 'maybe'?" I said. "Where are Rudy and Gani?"

"My treacherous granddaughter and Merlin's twin are no longer your concern. They are lost to you for eternity," Odin said.

The problem with talking to those with a lot of power is very simply put, they have their own way of speaking. Many of them make up their own meanings for phrases. I didn't know if he meant he was going to punish them for all eternity or he had killed them. At the moment it didn't matter. Don't get me wrong – personally to me it meant the world. However, I learned even as a child that during a battle, one's personal feelings have to be swept aside to be sorted out later. Survival is always the priority and victory the second goal. If they were dead, there was nothing I could do to change that. If they were imprisoned, the best thing to do was to defeat their warden.

"Since you were nice enough to offer me a deal, let me make a counter one, but I am only doing this because you are Rudy's grandfather. You take off that eyepatch and throw it away and I will give you the hammer." I said it into the thumb of the gauntlet like I had seen the dwarf do in hopes that would make it an order.

"I will not be told what to do by some wench who fancies herself a warrior. You are not fit to fasten the bootstraps of one of my Valkyries. You will give me the hammer anyway," said Odin.

So much for being able to hack the dwarf's mind control mojo. I pulled my gauntleted hand back. "You got that right."

I threw the hammer. I didn't have the skill that Thor did, so Odin was able to stand up from his throne and step aside before Mjollnir struck him.

The one-eyed god laughed. "You will have to do far better than that."

"I will," I said using my wings to dart to the side with my hand out. The hammer's return trip changed course and struck Odin in the back of the head, knocking him face first into the stone floor, then landing back in my hand.

With Odin's power levels, I had seconds, maybe less. I dropped the hammer and pulled my Daemor badge off of my belt with my left hand. It was a work of magic artistry that even Gani was impressed by. It had charms to protect a Daemor against many things a soldier would face on and off the battlefield, including a strong spell breaker.

I was fairly certain that Brokk would have made the patch almost impossible to take off by normal means so I pressed my Daemor badge up against it. My hand pulsed as the magics warred with each other, but the corner of the eyepatch came loose from the Norse All-Father's skin. I wedged my finger underneath and pulled for all I was worth. The eyepatch barely budged, but I was able to get another finger under it. I repeated the process over and over until I got it off his eye. Odin screamed and raised his hands. At first I thought it was to hit me, but instead he grabbed hold of the golden straps and helped me pull. His wolves and raven even joined in the fun.

The golden eyepatch now sported roots that literally bored into Odin's skull and scalp, so pulling it out wasn't pretty. Wasn't pretty wasn't something that scared me. I'd been that way all my life. We pulled and got the straps off, but the roots started growing in an attempt to sink themselves back into the one-eyed god's head. I managed to get both hands on either side of the patch, which was already half way off. I put my foot on the side of Odin's face and pulled for all I was worth. Then I pulled some more. There was a horrible ripping sound and I was thrown backwards, landing on the floor. Odin had blood pouring out in a crimson silhouette where the golden patch had been.

I leapt to my feet and picked up the hammer from where I had put it down. I threw the eyepatch far away from both of us and tossed the hammer at it. Mjollnir hit it with enough force to shatter it into pieces, but the pieces still moved, writhing in an attempt to join back together again.

I reached back for another toss, but Odin stood up and raised his palm. "Stay your hand, Daemor."

Odin pointed his index finger at the mass of writhing gold. A crimson bolt of mystic energy shot out and started to disintegrate the remains of the eyepatch. It seemed almost to scream as it writhed, then stopped moving before turning to dust.

Odin turned toward me and I took a step back, not sure if the spell had been broken and even if it had, if that changed matters.

"My thanks, Terrorbelle. You have freed me from Brokk's control. Since you have his gauntlet, may I assume he is dead?" Odin said.

"Not dead, just missing both hands. I left him in Paddy Moran's custody," I said.

Odin nodded and held out his hand. "I would like Mjollnir to be returned to me now."

I shook my head. "Not a chance." The one-eyed god narrowed his brow and started to say something, but I cut him off. "This is Thor's hammer. I give it back only to him."

Odin nodded. "That is how it should be."

"Don't you think it's about time that you started freeing a bunch of people that are wrongly imprisoned," I said, hoping I guessed right and they weren't dead.

I heard the clicks of the automatics before I saw Nemesis step out of the shadow behind Odin's throne. Her automatics were both trained on the back of Odin's head. Shadow stepping is a handy talent that the daughter of night can use to get into almost anywhere that has even a piece of darkness.

"The important prisoners have already been freed," Nemesis said with her dark and scary voice set on maximum fear. "The question remains as to what punishment you get for turning against my people, One-Eye."

I had to give Odin credit. Nemesis had made the god Zeus flee Earth and Olympus for parts unknown. Odin simply turned to look at her and raised an eyebrow. Both of his wolves growled.

"Only two guns and three possible attackers. Not a good situation," Odin said.

Nemesis moved her guns and shot both wolves, then trained them back on Odin. I recognized the sound of the ammo. She used mystic tranquilizer bullets.

"Not really a problem. I think you better start explaining what happened before I send you to see Hel," Nemesis said. "As I understand it, the pair of you are not too fond of each other. "

"Boss, he was under mind control." I pointed to the ashes on the floor. "It has been taken care of."

"That gives us the reason, but it doesn't excuse the behavior."

There was a honking from an old fashioned car horn. I looked up to see Paddy Moran driving his 1930 Caddy through the throne room door. Although driving wasn't entirely accurate as it was floating in the air behind us.

"Nemesis and Wotan, if I may suggest we do this without any fighting. I would be happy to broker an agreement between you," Paddy said, landing his car. I could see through the windows that Loki, Thor, and Murphy were inside. I smiled and winked at Murphy as my gut unclenched. I know I did the right thing in not going after him, but I would never have forgiven myself if anything happened to him.

Nobody got out – probably safer that way – but Murphy smiled and winked back. Loki smiled like he was the cat that swallowed the canary and fourteen of the canary's cousins and washed them down with a gallon of heavy cream.

"That shan't be necessary. Nemesis is correct. I have to make this right to her. Daughter of night, what would you ask of me?"

"Safe passage for my people and Moran's would get me to put down my guns so we can discuss matters," Nemesis said.

Odin nodded. "You have my word that none of your people will be subject to any further harm during their visit."

Nemesis put the hammers back down and put her guns into her holsters under her trench coat. "First off, un-exile Rudy."

Odin bowed his head and there was a great look of sadness on his face. "Alas I cannot. Her exile was because I gave my word and even though I was under another's control, I cannot break it." An instant before he started speaking, Rudy, Gani and Morningdour all body slid into the hall seemingly appearing out of nowhere. With the body sliding you can always tell because they are blurry for an instant before they become solid.

They all recovered from it faster than I usually did. None of them even threw up.

Rudy and her grandfather exchanged looks. Thor got out of the car and joined the look exchange.

"However, I could see fit to undo it if my granddaughter manages to perform a feat of such great valor that it cannot be ignored. I'm certain that during her time with Nemesis & Co. that will occur."

Nemesis nodded.

"Grandfather, you are well now?" Rudy said, the raven leaving her shoulder for that of the one-eyed god.

Odin nodded toward me. "Thanks to your friend's intervention."

"And you are still exiling me from my home?" Rudy said, a look of great sorrow on her face.

"I am truly sorry, but as I just said, the word of a god, especially the head of a pantheon, must be followed or all within the realm lose power, yourself included. Twilight would destroy all if I did that. I am saddened to say that you also must leave Morningdour and that forgery of a hammer."

"What?! Leave Morningdour? " Rudy said. The horse reared up and whinnied. "We've been together since I was a child. You don't deserve her. You were going to have her killed. I won't allow it."

Odin's face was a mixture of anger at the disrespect and sorrow of what he was putting his granddaughter through. "All the Valkyrie mounts belong to me. You have them only though my good graces and there is already a great shortage. The winged horses are too valuable to not be in the services of Asgard. Morningdour will serve another Valkyrie. Now give me the hammer."

Rudy straightened her spine and looked her grandfather in the eye, pulling the hammer to her chest. "Morningdour may be yours, but the hammer is not. I found it and bound it, so it belongs to me now, Grandfather. You want it, you can try to take it from me."

Even from the little I had seen of Odin, I knew a direct challenge was not the way to get what you wanted. One-Eye reached out towards Rudy, which had instant reactions from several people in the room and three people in particular.

Rudy brought the hammer back, ready to use it as a weapon. Thor stepped up behind his daughter, both hands crackling with lightning and Nemesis pointed both guns at his face.

"By the spoils of war, the hammer is hers," Nemesis said.

"Rudy keeps the hammer," said Thor. "And just so you know, as long as her exile lasts, I will not return to the Golden City."

"What!?" Odin said truly shocked. "But the defense of Asgard depends heavily on both you and the hammer. If Twilight should fall …"

"Tough," Thor said. "I have dealt with your manipulations for more centuries than I care to count, but now you're going after my daughter. A parent is supposed to protect their children, apparently something you in all your wisdom never learned."

"Then I insist the hammer be returned to …" Odin said. Before he could finish the sentence, I handed Mjollnir back to Thor. I also gave him the gauntlet that the dwarf used to control the hammer.

Sighing, the one-eyed god put down his hands and Nemesis put down her guns. And everyone pretended that all was happy in the land of Asgard.

At this point, the Caddy emptied as Paddy, Loki and Murphy got out. Loki was dressed this time, as was Thor. I guess both were able to conjure up clothes.

Decorum be damned. I ran over and hugged Murphy so hard his back popped.

"I'm so glad you're okay," I said.

"Back at you," Murphy said. "Although I think I may not be okay. There must have been too many people in the car, because when we flew through the tunnel that leads to the cave, my hands and wrists got numb. I think I might have carpool tunnel syndrome. And on the way over here we almost got creamed by a milk truck."

"You must have been udderly terrified," I said.

Murphy smiled and kissed me on the cheek. Loki stepped up as I lowered Murphy to the ground, then Murphy started to stare at me like he never had before.

"He hasn't stopped since we left the cave," Loki said, grinning. He leaned in and whispered in my ear. "And you still have the harlot's necklace on. Murphy is still only human. A few more seconds and he could be all yours."

I realized what the trickster said was true. No more waiting. No more beating around the bush. With Freyja's necklace Murphy would be mine. But it would be cheating. He wouldn't be mine because he chose it, but because the lust magic overwhelmed him. It would be the mystic equivalent of giving him a Rufie. Of date rape. I wanted Murphy more than anything, but not like that. Never like that. I couldn't put someone else through my nightmare. I wanted him to want me too. For real and forever. I took the necklace off and put in in my pocket.

Murphy's stare became less intense, as did everyone else's. Loki nodded approvingly. I nodded thanks and got back to the conversation we were having.

"It was that bad, huh?" I said. The more scared Murph is, the more he makes bad jokes. Helps him function despite his fear.

Loki nodded, his face suddenly serious.

"I suggested we pick up this hermit we passed and let him have a turn at the wheel, but Paddy was afraid he'd be charged with recluse driving," Murphy said.

When he was like this it was best to let him keep going and work it out of his system. Murphy has done and seen things that would break normal people. I've seen soldiers get drunk, fight and worse to cope. I still have nightmares, so I figure Murph has a pretty mild – if annoying – coping mechanism in comparison. And sometimes I even help him along. "I thought Paddy didn't let anyone else drive Baby."

"Not true. He used to have me drive him around, but I stopped," Murphy said.

Loki sighed. "Why's that?"

"At the end of the workday, I had nothing to chauffer it," Murphy said. "And it was rough at first, trying to figure out how to drive a stick shift. No one would teach me and I couldn't find the manual. And then Paddy thought I was addicted to brake fluid, but he was wrong. I told him I could stop any time."

I looked around and realized everyone was staring, including Odin whose mouth was literally open. He wasn't exactly used to Murphyesque behavior.

Murphy had to shut up, whether he wanted to or not. I leaned in and kissed him hard on the lips. That stopped him short. I pulled him in for another hug.

"The damn snake almost ate me," he whispered as he shivered in my arms.

I whispered in his ear, "It's okay. You're safe now." Murphy pulled back and started to open his mouth. "And if you try any combination of safe cracks, you'll have to deal with me."

Murphy shrugged and straightened a green scaly thing on his neck.

"What are you wearing?" I asked.

"Thor made it for me. You like it? It's a boa tie," Murphy said.

"Why would you wear such a thing?" Odin asked.

"Because boa ties are cool," I said. I caught the reference because it was from one of our favorite TV shows that we sometimes watched on movie night, but nobody else got it. However, I got a huge smile from Murphy.

"Yes, he keeps saying that, although I have no idea why," Thor said, then turned to his father. "It is a battle trophy for Murphy to commemorate his glorious fight with the serpent beast."

"He survived a battle with the serpent?"

"More than that. He protected we two gods from it," Thor said. Odin looked doubtful. "Murphy is most impressive for a human."

"Murphy is most impressive for anybody," Loki added.

"Will the lot of ye quit swelling his head. I'm the one who has to deal with him when we leave here," Paddy said.

Having had his will stymied, Odin was looking for another target to turn his attention on and Paddy had just given him an opening.

"Padriac Moran, you have freed Loki without my leave? Moran, you try my patience," Odin said.

"Excellent," Murphy said. "You must really come by Bulfinche's Pub sometime and try ours. I think you will find it simply sublime, especially if you put a little hot fudge on top."

Both Odin and the leprechaun glared at Murphy.

"Murphy, hush," Paddy said.

"We have an agreement that allows Loki's freedom once per Earth year. Have I so lost track of time that I missed what the mortals call Halloween?" One-Eye said. "Or is there some other reason you would have for freeing that treacherous son of a dog?"

"Well I am your adopted son, One-Eye," Loki said.

"Loki, hush or I will make you and Murphy wait in the car," Paddy said.

"That's no fun. You won't even let us change the radio station," Murphy said. "Of course, I still have some mileage left on some car puns. Only used by a little old lady on Sundays when she went to Bingo."

Paddy put a hand over his bartender's mouth, then turned back to the one-eyed god. "Your guardian serpent had gone berserk and was trying to kill my bartender and both your sons. Do we not have an agreement of safe passage for those who wish to man the shield station for Loki?"

"We do, against my better judgment," Odin said.

"Then would ye kindly explain to me why ye would let your serpent try to kill John Murphy? On the orders of a dwarf named Brokk as I understand it. Obnoxious as he may be, Murphy is still under my protection and that of many, many others," Paddy said.

"Including mine," Nemesis said.

"And mine," I said.

"And not least of all mine," Loki said. "Trust me, Father, you do not want to deal with me if you had allowed or done anything to harm my friend. Or do so in the future."

"Terrorbelle had alerted me to the crisis, so I simply came to the aide of those in danger, including both of your sons," Paddy said. "Thus preserving your guarantee on safe passage. 'Tis ye who should be thanking me from saving ye from embarrassment and oath breaking."

"Be that as it may, 'tis almost as if you knew how to undo Loki's chains," Odin said. "Like you had had prior experience."

It was the great unspoken non-secret that Odin realized that Paddy had been freeing Loki for the trickster competition on Fools' Day for years coming to a head. Of course, if Odin acknowledged it, he'd also have to address the fact that Loki had continuously returned to his imprisonment, despite Loki having the chance to escape forever to a place far enough away that Odin would never have found him.

"I can be quite creative when I need to be. Years of practice escaping from mortals who were trying to steal me pot of gold. Including some of those present who have managed to get me in handcuffs." Paddy looked at Murphy.

"Hey, it was only the one time. And I let you go," Murphy said.

"That ye did. And I did get Loki's word that he would return before I freed him," Paddy said.

Odin turned and looked Loki in the eye, as two was beyond his ability without a lot of side to side pupil movement.

The trickster god smiled and wiggled his eyebrows. "It's true, I am dumb that way. I did indeed give my word to return."

"Your word? Hmm. Very well. I shall take care of the serpent so that Loki can return to his punishment," Odin said.

"No need. I took care of it," Thor said. His father turned to stare at the thunderer. "Permanently. Your guardian is no more, with the exception of Murphy's boa tie. And furthermore, I can assure you that I will not be going back there."

Odin started to open up his mouth with a sharp retort then became silent. One-Eye thought a moment more before he spoke. "No, you shall not. I was under Brokk's influence when I gave you that punishment and it was wrong of me. Let us bid farewell to these strangers and deal with our family business."

"As far as I am concerned, Father, our business has been dealt with and I will be leaving with my daughter," Thor said.

The pair stood and glared at each other with stares icy enough to make a frost giant feel at home. One-Eye broke off first.

"Is there nothing I can do to change your mind on this?" Odin asked.

"Nada," Thor said.

Odin's face went from being a mask of pride and anger to that of a sad old man for just the barest instant. "I would like to convince you otherwise. But if that is what you wish, I will not stop you. Nemesis, let us conclude our business. What is your price for erasing the debt between us for me imprisoning and attacking your agents?"

Nemesis walked up to the one-eyed god and whispered in his ear. His eyebrows rose then fell. "Very well. You shall have it, provided it does not run counter to stopping the Twilight. That leaves two pieces of business before this matter concludes. Moran, I would like Brokk the dwarf returned to my custody for punishment."

"I'm sure ye would. When ye have your house in order, come by Bulfinche's Pub for a drink and we will discuss the matter further," Paddy said.

One-Eye nodded. He turned to Rudy. "My Thrud, I truly regret your exile, but I would ask you to do me one favor before you go."

"Why would I do you any favors, Grandfather?" Rudy said.

"Because it is one that will bring you a moment of happiness, which you more than deserve. Hladgunner has betrayed us all and appears to have fled Asgard. I ask you and whomever you would like to assist you track her down and return her to me for punishment."

"I will do the favor if in return you give Morningdour back to me," Rudy said.

"I will allow you to retain Morningdour until Hladgunner is returned."

"Fine, although I may wait a decade or so before I start looking then," Rudy growled through gritted teeth.

"You have three days," Odin said.

Rudy moved to her horse and hugged it around the neck. Morningdour used her chin on Rudy's back to return the hug. There were tears coming from both their eyes.

"And last but not least, I owe a great debt to you Terrorbelle. Without your intervention, my mind would not be my own and my realm would still be in great peril from my clouded actions. What would you ask of me?"

I looked at my friend who was hugging her horse and crying after losing her home. "Undo the exile."

"I have already said it will only be undone when Thrud performs a great act of valor, not before. It is the best that I can do," Odin said.

"Standing up to you and saving the Valhallans wasn't valorous enough?" I said.

"They were done prior to my stating the need for an act of valor," he said.

"Then let her keep the damn horse," I said.

"Daemor, you know my debt is great and I would have to give you any magical item or any amount of wealth that you ask for. We have belts that would double your strength…" Apparently Thor used one to hold up his jeans. "… and weapons that put Nemesis' guns to shame. Are you certain that a horse for someone else is what you want?"

"Damn skippy," I said, using Gani's favorite phrase.

"Very well. I hereby transfer ownership now and forever of Morningdour to Thrud, daughter of Thor, granddaughter of Odin."

Rudy and Morningdour broke up their sad embrace. Rudy came to me and put one hand behind my head and pulled in to kiss me on the cheek. "Thank you, Belle."

"You're welcome." Morningdour came over and got her two cents by licking my face. It was somewhat disgusting, but touching just the same. "You're welcome too, Morningdour."

"Our business is concluded," Nemesis said. "That leaves what we do next up to you, Rudy."

The now former Valkyrie grinned darkly. "Let's go get Jerkgunner."

"You can never make up for a lost childhood, but sometimes you can do something that makes the bad things in the past matter less."
-Rudy, Norse storm demigoddess, Valkyrie, agent of Nemesis & Co.

Rudy of course picked the rest of Nemesis & Co. to help her. And Thor. Those didn't surprise me at all, but her including Murphy, Paddy and her Uncle Loki did.

Especially since Odin was against it, insisting that the trickster return immediately to his punishment.

"Grandfather, you did say whoever I would like to assist me," Rudy said.

"It's true," said Loki. "We all heard it."

Odin smiled darkly. "Very well. I did say that. Here is what else I have to say – I am also banning anyone from manning your shield station for two weeks."

"Petty and vindictive as ever I see," Loki said.

"People do not change," Odin said.

"Except when they do," Loki replied, taking Rudy's arm in his and escorting her to Morningdour.

"I heard what you did for Father," she said, kissing her uncle on the cheek. "Thank you."

Loki's pupils got wider and he tried to hide a smile as he petted the red horse as his niece mounted Morningdour. "I wish I could have done more."

"I believe you, Uncle. Would you like to ride with me on Morningdour?" Rudy said.

"Nothing would please me more," Loki said, getting on behind her.

"Any suggestions where we should start our search for the traitor?" Rudy said.

"It's said that someone always finds something in the last place they look, although a wise prey will make it a place which their pursuer is unlikely to consider. Hladgunner would not stay in Asgard because she would not be able to hide long from One-Eye and her horse is able to travel to any of the nine worlds. She would likely try to hide in the last place she thinks we would think to look for her," Loki said. "Suggestions for last place you'd look?"

"With your daughter Hel?" Rudy said. "Or among the giants?"

"Thor's living room?" Murphy said.

"Gani's shoe closet," I said. It's bigger than my apartment.

"The night realms," Nemesis said.

"Under One-Eye's throne," Paddy said.

"Bulfinche's Pub," Thor said. "We would never think of looking for her there and it is where Brokk is."

"Ding," Loki said, pointing at Thor. "The woman likely thinks she is in love with the dwarf and will try to rescue him. The question is, does she know that Paddy's bar is a mystic null zone?"

It turns out the answer to Loki's question was not so much judging by her approach. It only re-enforced my view that Daemor were better than Valkyries. To become a Valkyrie, a woman had to excel at fighting and be willing to dedicate her life to a cause. Daemor had to do that too, but we had to demonstrate intelligence and excellence in other areas as well. And we trained in more than just fighting, as we were each expected to lead parts of Mab's army if the need arose. Most notably lacking from the Valkyrie's training was a knowledge of global tactics.

There is no other way I can explain Hladgunner literally storming Bulfinche's Pub.

Fully armored, she kicked open the door, a sword in one hand, one of her expandable spears in the other.

"If you bring me Brokk, I'll let you live," she said to the assembled staff and patrons.

Their reactions were not what she expected. Rebecca, a homeless woman who was called the Mother of the Streets because she could allegedly hear the city speak to her and use what it said to help others, burst out laughing.

"If we bring you a brick, you'll leak like a sieve?" Fred the satyr said, trying to be funny.

And Hercules simply stood up quietly, preparing to disarm the woman.

Hladgunner pushed a gem on the hilt of her sword, most likely more of Brokk's handiwork and pointed it at the demigod bouncer. Nothing happened. From her repeated pushing of the jewel, it was obvious she was expecting something to shoot out the end of it and vaporize Herc.

Nothing continued to happen, which is when the rest of us arrived.

None of us pulled a weapon. Guns don't work in Bulfinche's, same as magic, something Jerkgunner would have learned if she had bothered to do any recon.

"Give it up Jerkgunner. You're outnumbered and outmatched," Rudy said.

"I'll kill all of you, then step over your corpses as I take my love out of here," Jerkgunner said.

Hercules laughed and stepped forward.

"Herc, mind if I take care of this? Me and Jerkgunner have a history. She used to bully me back when I was a kid. I've dreamed of the day when I could take her down without my Grandfather protecting her," Rudy said.

Herc looked first to Paddy who nodded his consent. Next he looked to Thor. The two were old friends and drinking buddies. Herc wasn't about to risk the thunder god's daughter getting hurt if Thor wasn't okay with it. Guns and magic might not work in Bulfinche's Pub, but blades and spear points still did.

Thor nodded his okay.

Lastly, Herc looked at the boss. Nemesis and the Greco-Roman pantheon go way back, even if she was the one who sent Daddy Zeus running for the Otherworlds. Her nod was barely perceptible, but Herc picked up on it and stepped back. The rest of us followed his lead.

Rudy still held her hammer in her right hand. She hadn't let go of it since we left Odin's throne room.

"Odin protected me from you? You are delusional. He always made things so easy for you, Sipill," Jerkgunner said, dropping into an attack stance with both blade and spear pointed toward Rudy.

"You're wrong. I was stronger than any Valkyrie when I was just a girl. Grandfather forbade me from striking any of you outside of training for fear I would hurt you," Rudy said, moving her hammer back and forth. "Today, you're not so lucky."

"Lucky? You are joking. I've never been lucky whenever you were around. Did you know that hammer was to have been mine? Brokk promised it to me for helping him. With it, I would have been able to join the upper pantheon," Jerkgunner said.

"Pity. It'll never be yours now that I've bonded with Róta," Rudy said. She had named the hammer. It translated as sleet and storm. She almost went with Mickle which means mighty, but I couldn't see anyone ever quaking in fear at the hammer Mickle, so I talked her out of it.

"It will be mine when I pry it from your lifeless hand," Jerkgunner said, stabbing her spear forward. Rudy grabbed hold of the shaft with her left hand and yanked her forward, while bringing the hammer up with her right. It connected with Jerkgunner's chin and the disgraced Valkyrie crumbled to the floor.

I went up to Rudy and lifted her hand above her head. "And the winner by a two move knockout, Rudy Thorardottir!" Yeah, Rudy's last name was unfortunate too, but meant daughter of Thor.

Rudy took a bow to some applause. Next she pulled out a pair of charmed handcuffs and locked the unconscious Jerkgunner's wrists behind her back. Rudy then disarmed her, including her belt pouch of collapsible spears.

"I'd like to buy the house a round," Rudy said. And she did, but before anyone took a drink she raised her glass. "I'd like to toast Adar, a good man whose afterlife was cut too short."

"To Adar," I echoed. The rest of the bar did the same.

"Since Adar won't likely get a memorial service, I was hoping maybe to have one here if that was okay with Paddy," Rudy said.

"'Tis more than okay," Paddy said, laying a hand on Rudy's shoulder. "I'd be honored."

"And it would keep me out for even longer," Loki said. "I knew him. I'd be happy to give a backup eulogy. After the main one by my niece of course, who knew and loved him best."

"You will be vacating long before that," Odin said as he walked in the front door.

"You always were a party pooper, old man," Loki said.

"Are we going to have a problem, great deceiver?" Odin said.

"What part of giving my word don't you understand?" Loki said.

Odin made some noise in his throat and turned to Rudy. "You did well, Thrud."

"Quite an act of valor, huh Grandfather?" Rudy said.

"Nice try, granddaughter. I will take Hladgunner now. Moran, may I also take Brokk?" Odin said.

"First, we'd have to discuss my feelings on capital punishment, but right now we're in the midst of a memorial service for one of your own. Ye are welcome to stay and say a few words," Paddy said.

Odin lifted Hladgunner off the floor. "I appreciate the offer, but I must be going. My sight is crippled in here so it is dangerous for everything for me to stay too long. I will return to discuss matters. Loki, come."

"Woof," Loki said, but stood.

"I didn't know you did tricks," Murphy said.

"Yeah, I'm good. Never did get the hang of rolling over, however," Loki said. "I'm trying though."

Odin ignored the exchange as well as Loki's farewells. He walked to the door, dragging the disgraced Valkyrie, and paused.

Odin turned back. "However, I would be remiss to not say a few words about one of Valhalla's finest. Adar was a strong and valiant warrior and he shall be missed. And I would return him to life if I could for that alone. The fact that I cannot do so for the sake of my granddaughter who loved the man makes me sadder than I have been in a long while. My Thrud, I trust I will see your beautiful face again soon."

"Bet on it," Rudy said. And Odin left with Hladgunner and Loki in tow.

Which is when Rudy began her eulogy. "I first met Adar when I was only a girl…"

"Being a good father is even harder than being a good king."
-Odin, King of the Norse gods

Loki was returned to his cave of torments. Odin found another acid drooling serpent to take the place of the one that Thor killed. This one was a child of the first and while immense, was not quite the giant that his father was. Still, its spittle was just as powerful at dissolving flesh and Odin had banned anyone from manning the shields that protected the trickster for two weeks.

So once again the mountains around the cave of torments shook with the screams of the tortured trickster.

After the first day of the renewed torture, Odin again returned to the cave of torments, but this time he was not alone or empty handed. Following in his wake were Brokk the dwarf and Jerkgunner the former Valkyrie leader. Odin had used dark magics to make their wills not their own. They followed him into the cave with looks of terror upon their faces. The serpent turned at the invasion of his lair, posed to attack. Upon seeing it was Odin, the serpent bowed its head and came over to be petted by the one-eyed god as if it were a pet of some sort. Odin obliged and gave it a treat, an entire ox which it swallowed in one gulp.

With the serpent's attention turned away from the trickster, Loki's body began to heal almost instantly and he turned to watch what was unfolding. Odin had a large burlap sack tossed over one shoulder and he walked past Loki without acknowledging him. Brokk and Jerkgunner trailed in the one-eyed god's wake.

As the dwarf passed Loki, the trickster's first instinct was to shout something mocking, but did not. Loki realized what Odin was going to do to them and neither of them was a mighty god or a shape shifter, so the trickster held his tongue.

Odin stopped on the opposite side of the cave and turned to the two criminals. "Lay down here alongside each other, but do not touch," Odin said to the lovers, knowing full well the agony they were about to endure would be made worse by not being able to take comfort from one another.

The pair did as they were told and Odin pushed his wide brim hat back. He took out shackles and a non-magical hammer from the burlap sack. One-Eye attached one to the dwarf's elbow and hammered it into the stone and did the same on the other side. For Hladgunner, he did the same thing but around her wrists as she still had her hands. He repeated the process around their waists and ankles.

Odin put the hammer back in the sack, returning his wide brim hat to its normal position over his forehead and stood looming over the two.

"You may now both speak if you wish to," Odin said.

"Odin, you don't want to do this. I can still create great marvels. My brother can build me artificial hands that will work better than the ones I lost. I can still build you wondrous weapons to help you win at Ragnorak," Brokk said.

"I believe you. You could still make wondrous weapons, but they would most likely be used against us whether we had them or others did," Odin said.

"All-Father, I have served you faithfully for centuries. Please do not do this to your loyal and humble servant," Hladgunner said.

While it was obvious to Loki from the look One-Eye gave the dwarf that he despised him, the look in his eye for the Valkyrie seethed with the kind of hate that can only come from the death of destroyed love.

"You dare use the word faithful to describe your service? You almost destroyed the heroes of Valhalla. Centuries of training and planning in hopes of saving the lives of all in Asgard and the nine worlds, and you toss it away on what? A whim? The illusion of love? A play for power?"

"I served you faithfully and got no thanks for it. We haven't a hundred new warriors in three times as many years. I led the Valkyries and what did you do for us? You trained us as warriors and then turned us into serving wenches and prostitutes to keep some dead humans happy? That is the true betrayal. My body is my own and having to use it like a common whore to please lowly humans was the ultimate insult. You talk of betrayal, but it was you that betrayed us first, choosing dead mortals over your own." The former Valkyrie spat at Odin, but it did not even reach his knee.

"You were given much power. You could have asked to leave my service. It has happened before and I have let Valkyries go, one even to marry a mortal. You had options other than betrayal and destruction. Make peace with yourselves and each other for your death is nigh."

Hladgunner turned to the dwarf by her side. "Brokk, I love you."

The dwarf turned to Hladgunner. "I never loved you. You were just a means to an end. A cheap whore with an easy asking price."

"I gave up everything for you," she said, tears streaming down her cheeks.

The dwarf smiled. "And I thank you for it."

The former Valkyrie spat at the dwarf, but her final act also fell short, instead catching her on the arm. Odin walked away and nodded toward the serpent who had been waiting obediently in the corner where they first entered, nibbling on his ox carcass. At the gesture, the serpent slithered until it was over the pair. The son of the first beast began its diabolical drooling. The acid came in drips and drabs at first, searing skin and dissolving clothing. But soon that became a steady stream. The screaming of the dwarf and the former Valkyrie did not have the power of the gods and failed to shake anything. Their death cries merely echoed throughout the cavern until they stopped abruptly, replaced with the empty sizzle of flesh. Odin stood and watched until there was nothing left of the pair but a gooey, toxic mess.

Odin walked past Loki, but the trickster was not one to be ignored.

"I'm surprised you didn't ask them who their partner was," Loki said.

"I am no fool. Crux in my horn. I know who it was. I shall deal with him," Odin said.

Loki laughed. "Good luck with that. And good luck with ever dealing with Padriac Moran again."

"What do you mean?" Odin said.

"That had to have broken your agreement with Paddy," Loki said.

Odin turned and looked at the trickster. "Why would you say that?"

"I know Paddy. He would not have given Brokk back to you without assurances that you wouldn't kill him. The leprechaun values life above almost all," said Loki.

Odin shrugged. "I told him that I would not kill Brokk and I did not. He was killed by a wild beast. Hardly my fault."

"If bespelling his mind and shackling the dwarf to stone so he couldn't run away doesn't give you contributory negligence, what would?" Loki said.

"Do you believe that I should have let the treacherous cur live?" Odin said. "He had no further part to play in slowing or stopping Twilight, but he could have played a part in speeding its arrival."

"For all my faults, I have never been a murderer," Loki said.

Odin laughed. "Look at the pot calling the cauldron black. What do you call what you did to Balder then? You made sure that mistletoe could hurt him."

"You know as well as I that your wife's invulnerability spell had to have one weakness. It's the nature of magic – it hates absolutes. I just made sure I knew what it was," Loki said.

"And do you find any difference between how you tricked Hod into killing Balder with a dart any different than what happened here?" Odin said.

Loki was silent a moment. "I suppose not. I guess then I too am a murderer, but only the one time. We both know that is a distinction you cannot make. And I did not break a vow to a good man to do it," Loki said.

"These words seem odd coming from your mouth, Loki. For it has been your words over the centuries that has caused us no end of pain or trouble," Odin said.

"True, but I also got you out of all of that trouble, usually better off than when you went in. And perhaps if you had treated me better or listened to what I had tried to tell you, I would not have gone down the paths I did. And for that I am truly sorry," Loki said.

"I almost believe you," Odin said.

"I do believe him," Thor said from the mouth of the cavern.

Odin and Loki turned to the thunder god as he leapt to land beside them, covering the length of the cavern in a single bound. He held his hammer in one hand and a picnic basket in the other.

"I am surprised to see you my son. I thought you vowed never to return to Asgard until your daughter could," Odin said. He was loathe to point out that his son had stopped short of actually swearing it or giving his word.

"You know as well as I that I specified the Golden City. This cave is nowhere near it."

"Why are you here? I banned Loki from having any assistance for this time," Odin said.

"You banned anyone from manning the shield station." Thor looked at the replacement serpent and sparks flew from his eyes. It slithered back quickly. "I won't need to even touch it."

Odin nodded. "You are learning. You are using your mind more than your brawn. It is both surprising and refreshing. There was a time when you simply would have thrown down with me instead of making a rational argument."

Thor tapped his head, where there was only the faintest hint of a scar on his scalp. "A lot easier to think these days. I think you'd best be going, Father."

"Very well. But I would still like to speak with you about matters. Privately," Odin said.

"You can send one of your ravens to make an appointment to meet me at my home. On Earth," Thor said. "In two weeks."

The one-eyed god nodded, then walked away, stopping once to look back at his two most prized remaining sons. Thor had sat down beside Loki and pulled out a blanket. The thunder god laid it on the ground beside the trickster. Despite himself, Odin smiled as he left.

"Murphy sends his greetings. And he also sent Nasher and Grinder a thank you basket of fruit and gourmet food," Thor said.

"Well, they did save his life," Loki said. "I trust they regenerated well."

"Better than well. Nasher has had a limp for years because of a badly healed break while he was dead. Murphy had Hermes re-break and reset it. The goat's leg is as good as new," Thor said, pulling out food.

"Duck a l'Orange? Petit Fours? This is what you're spending your time on these days? What's next? Quiche?" Loki said.

Thor pulled out a pie plate filled with a yellow and green concoction. "As a matter of fact, yes. Now if you are implying it is too girly, I would be happy to pack it all up and go."

"Nonsense. You went through all the trouble for me, so the least I can do is taste your girly food," Loki said.

Thor sliced a piece of quiche and held it out for the trickster, who took a big bite. "This is delicious. I am impressed," Loki said.

"Thank you," Thor said.

"You are going to make somebody a good little wife someday," Loki said.

"I already tried that when you made me dress up as a bride to get Mjollnir back from Thrymr," Thor said.

"All because he wanted Freyja as his bride and she refused to even help out. She was trouble even then," Loki said.

"Maybe we should have listened to you," Thor said.

"You're finally making sense," Loki said. "Did Odin take down his sphere of woe?"

"I don't know," Thor said.

"One would think you'd keep better track of the only woman who you'd dress in drag for," Loki said.

"Cross dressing didn't really work for me. Or being a bride. Besides you actually were a bride, remember?"

"It was only the one time. And I wasn't exactly myself," Loki said.

"You turned yourself into a mare. And you not only got pregnant, but you gave birth to an eight legged horse. That is a lot more girly than making a quiche," Thor said.

"I don't know about that. Motherhood is one of the most beautiful things in creation. And damn painful too. Besides I heard about the aprons you wear and that you've been mistaken for a transvestite in them. A very large, muscular transvestite, mind you. Although it's rumored that a certain Isabella finds you quite fetching in them."

"You know of Isabella? Tell me what else you've heard," Thor said.

Which is where Loki stopped telling me his version of his visit from his brother. I don't know what happened after that, but the trickster did seem quite pleased with himself about it. Especially since he mentioned that Thor managed to intimidate the new serpent enough that it stayed away from him simply by changing his shape to look like Thor. Apparently, Paddy had "broken" one of the charms allowing Loki to shape shift just in case he needed to. Although it didn't make the chains any easier to break.

"Sometimes a kiss is just a kiss. And sometimes it's not nearly enough."
-Terrorbelle, agent of Nemesis & Co. and former Daemor soldier

Murph and I decided to go classic on movie night. "Casablanca" followed by the Marx Brothers' "A Night In Casablanca." I had seen the first, but not the second. Murphy was a big Marx Brothers fan.

We ordered a pizza and made some popcorn.

"So how are you holding up?" I said.

Murphy shrugged. When we were alone he didn't always go right for the jokes.

"This one hit me hard. This is the closest I've come to dying," he said. "Except for the time I sort of did."

Murphy had sacrificed himself to save Paddy and the world in order to stop Lovecraftian chaos spawn from taking over. It's a long story that involved him hatching, or perhaps detonating would be a better word, an egg laid by Manuk Manuk. She's the blue cosmic chicken that laid the egg that hatched this universe. Apparently that hatching was the cause of the big bang. Murphy stepped through the portal of darkness before he opened the second egg. The light from that big bang drove back or destroyed the dark invaders and jump started a new universe. The explosion also either destroyed Murphy's body or transformed it into energy which was turned back into matter when the blue chicken laid another egg that hatched a fully grown Murphy back into this universe. Did he really die or did something else happen? Well, he's never been able to get a totally straight answer on that one, especially regarding the dreams he sometimes has about the other universe.

Yeah, sometimes I have trouble believing everything that happens around me too.

"I'm a little messed up I think," Murphy said. "If you hadn't sent Paddy and he didn't get there when he did…"

"But he did," I said.

"Not that I should complain. I just had to deal with a giant snake. You had to fight a king of a pantheon, a lust goddess and a dwarf that had stolen the power of a god," Murphy said. "How are you holding up?

"Good," I said, not exactly lying. I've suffered from what they are calling PTSD - or Post-Traumatic Stress Disorder - since I was eleven. I sometimes wake up screaming from nightmares and other night terrors. Not all the time, but too often for my tastes. I didn't think this case was going to give me more, but I did have a dream last night where I was back on the battlefields of Faerie. The other Daemor and the rest of Mab's army, along with Rudy and some scattered Valhallans, were dying all around me and there was nothing I could do to save them. It took me several minutes after waking to convince myself it was a dream, not a memory.

"New nightmare?" Murphy said, able to read my face too well.

"Yeah," I said.

"Bad?"

"Not so much," I lied, trying not to remember the giant snake that slithered among the dead and dying as it swallowed them whole.

Murphy sat next to me on the couch. He opened his arms and I laid my head on his shoulder.

"I'm supposed to be the one comforting you," I said.

"No reason we can't comfort each other," Murphy said.

"So you're not mad at me?" I said.

"For saving the day? And my life? And those of thousands of other dead guys. Well, their afterlives at any rate," Murphy said. "What kind of guy do you think I am?"

I kissed him on the cheek. "A great one, but I mean that I didn't save you instead."

"But you did, at least by proxy," Murphy said. "So let's see. In the middle of a battle with old One-Eye and a dwarf with one of the most powerful weapons on Earth or Asgard, you managed to hold them off and figure out a way to save me at the same time. Why would I be mad?"

"Well, when you put it that way," I said and smiled, snuggling in closer.

"So what was it like riding a rainbow?" he said.

"Fantastic. Almost as good as flying by hammer. More terrifying though. I at least had control of the hammer. Wanda did right by me though. I like her a lot," I said.

"She's all right. Her brother is a bit of a jerk though," Murphy said. "Wanda drops in to Bulfinche's from time to time – think maybe she'll give me a ride?"

"Murphy, I don't want you riding any other woman," I said and instantly regretted it. "Sorry."

"Why? You are just being honest. And by the way, class act for taking the necklace off," Murphy said.

"How…"

"Did I not notice you suddenly transform into the hottest woman in the universe and then back to…"

"The ugliest," I said. My self-image has improved of late, but I still hear the soldiers who destroyed my childhood telling me how ugly I am and it's hard to get past their voices in my head."

Murphy grabbed hold of my chin and pulled me up so I was looking him in the eyes.

"I don't want to hear that again. If anyone else said it, them and I would be having words. What makes you think I'd let you get away with it?" Murphy said.

"So you wanted me when I had the necklace on, but only then?" I said.

"Hardly. I'm a man and despite what you may think to the contrary, you are a beautiful woman," Murphy said.

"Not compared to Nemesis or Gani or even Rudy," I said. "Forget about lust goddesses."

"There's the problem. Stop comparing yourself to other people. You are never going to win that mind game. No matter who you are, you are always going to find somebody who is better looking, smarter or funnier. Look at where I work. If I compared myself to the gods and mystic folk who came to Bulfinche's Pub, I'd be so afraid of measuring up that I'd never show up for work. I'd probably never even get out of bed. In the long run, who cares? None of us are just one thing. We are the sum of all our parts - good, bad, beautiful, ugly and everything in-between. What's important is that we try to be the best we can be, not the best there is," Murphy said.

"How'd you get so wise?" I said.

"All part of the Zen of bartending. Plus, spouting this stuff really helps me get better tips," Murphy said with a wink. "And as far as I'm concerned, there is nobody who could be a better Terrorbelle than you."

"Thanks. But just to be clear, you totally wanted to do me when I was wearing the necklace," I said with a grin. A girl had to enjoy even the small victories.

"Yes, I did," Murphy said, then saw me frown. "But it wasn't the only time."

"Really? When else?" I said.

"You really don't think the thought hasn't come up? Not to mention other parts?" Murphy said. "T-Belle, you are one of the most beautiful people I know, inside and out."

"Then why haven't you…"

"It wouldn't be right. I'm still not ready for a real commitment and for me to take advantage of you just for my own manly needs would be wrong. I'm not built that way. And I know how you feel and what you've been through, which would make it far worse," Murphy said.

"Maybe I want to be taken advantage of," I said.

"We both know that's the last thing you want. If we take this to the next level, I have to be all in. And so do you. No games. No maybes. No just for tonight's. I know I have issues. I still miss Elsie. I know she would want me to be happy, but part of me feels like I would still be cheating on her even though she's dead. And part of me is terrified that I'll fall in love with someone else and they'll get taken away from me too. I guess inside I'm a real mess. I'm sorry. You deserve more," Murphy said.

"Yes I do. We both do and together I think we could get it. And let's not forget you aren't the only one who is a mess. And if you think I would ever get taken away from you, I'm here to tell you I would never let that happen," I said. I sighed and stood up. "I'm sorry to do this, but I'm going to ask you to leave."

"Why?" Murphy said, a little shocked.

"Because I… care about you. And to be honest, some of the necklace's lust magic has lingered in my system. If you stay, I will seduce you and rock your world. But if the next day it's going to have been rocked the wrong way or with regrets, I can't risk it. I can't imagine my life without you in it," I said. "So for the sake of our friendship, you need to go."

Murphy nodded and stood up. I walked him to the door and opened it. We hugged and I kissed him on the lips.

"Murphy, I love you. And I will wait for you to figure things out. But I won't wait forever. If the opportunity to date someone else I like arises, I'll do it. So don't wait too long," I said.

"Okay," Murphy said solemnly. "See you Saturday at the game?"

"Murphy, you are not going to see any less of me. And I'm not about to let the team down," I said. Bulfinche's Pub has its own softball league, primarily because the type of folks that frequent the place would have advantages over any other team, including the Yankees. I was the pitcher on Murphy's Marauders. Murphy played catcher. We were up against Herc's Hammers for the playoffs. Considering not only did they have Hercules, but Thor and Mista as well as Kintaro – a super strong samurai; Fin MacCool – a super strong Irish warrior of legend; Samson – blind, but super strong biblical hero – well you get the idea. Think people who could hit the ball out of the park – Central Park. The lot of them are basically most of Herc's warrior training circle. We were the underdogs, but were still hoping to win.

"And I hope I don't let you down," Murphy said, stepping into the hallway.

"You never have before," I said. Murphy smiled and closed the door.

I was shocked. I was expecting a joke.

There was a knock on the door. I still check the peephole and the security camera because in my line of work you can never be too careful. It was Murphy and he was still alone.

"Who is it?" I said.

"Who's on first," he said as I opened the door. "I just wanted to make sure you understand that hitting a home run tonight and on Saturday mean two very different things, right?"

"Yes, Murphy," I said. He stood staring at my eyes and smiling. "What?"

"He's on second," Murphy said.

"I don't know about you sometimes," I said, feeding him the line he was hoping for.

"Third base," he said.

I rolled my eyes and pushed him out the door. "Say goodnight, Murphy."

"Goodnight Murphy," he said and leaned in and kissed me on the lips, then took off for the stairs.

I shut the door and leaned my back against it before sliding to the floor.

Then I realized three things. One, that was the first time he initiated a lip kiss where there wasn't any danger involved. Two, for him to be joking so much meant he was nervous. Hopefully a good sign. Three, I pulled the necklace out of my jeans pocket. I didn't plan to use it, but then again I still kept it nearby. I resolved to give it to Gani for safekeeping in the morning. She'd been bugging me about studying it since we got back anyway.

I turned on "A Night In Casablanca" and ended up laughing as the cop who was rounding up the usual suspects asked Harpo if he was holding up the wall. The silent comic nodded. The cop, not believing him, yanked him away and the building fell down behind him. I smiled. It was something that might happen to Murphy.

Halfway through I paused the movie and decided to put on the necklace and look at myself in the mirror. I was hoping maybe it would work on me and change my poor self-image. I looked at my reflection. Still had broad shoulders, big muscles and a plain face. I guess it didn't make the person wearing it more attractive to themselves.

Pity.

Then there was a knock at the door. I rushed over and did my security check. It was Joe Hannk with a dozen roses.

I threw open the door.

"Joe, I wasn't expecting to see you," I said.

"I have a layover in New York and I don't leave until noon tomorrow. I have one of your friend Sydney's limos and thought we could paint the town pink if you were up to it…" Joe stopped mid-sentence and his jaw dropped.

Damn, I forgot I was still wearing the necklace. I slammed the door.

"Terrorbelle, you look amazing. Please, let's go out. Or stay in, if you want," Joe said. "Anything you want, actually."

I sighed. The necklace started working on me, playing on my feelings for Joe and my frustrations with having kicked Murphy out. I was thinking of doing things I would never normally do at this stage of a relationship. Not that Joe was a bad choice for any of that. He was a hunk with a hot body and the looks of a movie star. Of course, that might be part of why he was a movie star. To be honest, he had a better body than Murphy, although that was mainly because he worked out with a personal trainer two hours a day. Part of his contracts with the movie studios required it. Murphy did other things with his time, but still had a solid build. Of course, Murphy wasn't here and he had his chance. Not my fault a hot, willing man just showed up…

That wasn't me talking inside my head. I quickly took the jewels off and returned the necklace to my pocket.

I took a couple of deep breaths and opened the door again. Joe was still staring, but now the stare seemed confused, trying to merge the image of me from a moment ago with the one he was seeing now.

"Actually, Joe, I can't tonight," I said. "But I'd love to do breakfast in the morning."

"Okay, if that's what you want," Joe said, leaning in to kiss me on the cheek. His lips lingered hungrily. The necklace might be away, but it had already started something in both of us. It was all I could do not to rip off his clothes. I took a giant step back, then another.

"Yes, please," I said.

"Seven?" he said.

I laughed. Joe didn't know me well enough yet to realize I wasn't an early riser by choice. I didn't have to be in to work until ten.

"Let's try for eight," I said.

"It's a date," he said and handed me the roses.

"I suppose it is," I said, feeling guilty and excited at the same time. "See you then."

Joe said goodbye and left by the stairs.

Wow. Kicking two great guys out of my apartment in one night. Definitely a record for me. Usually I feel like I need to knock guys on the head and drag them inside my place.

I sat down on the couch and watched the rest of the movie and at the end still had no more idea about how to land a funny guy than I did at the beginning. Or a movie star. I don't know whether it was me or the necklace, but I really regretted my nobility in sending both guys on their way. Although part of me was picturing the scene had Joe arrived when Murphy was still here. That could have got ugly fast. Or if I was wearing the necklace, it could have been something else entirely. I shivered and decided Gani was definitely getting the necklace before my date with Joe.

I fell asleep on the couch holding a throw pillow that still smelled like Murphy, but visions of two men danced in my head. On poles and wearing thongs.

I was actually hoping that tomorrow was a busy day at work so my mind would focus on other things.

There was one bright spot. Despite all of Thor's cooking – and several generous doggie bags – I had actually lost weight.

I guess all that flying was good for more than just fun.

"Before the Twilight of the Gods there will be a brief intermission."
-Loki, imprisoned Norse trickster god

Sadly, we didn't take our investigation into Thor's framing as far as we should have, but once he was cleared, there seemed little point.

We showed that Brokk was the culprit with help from Jerkgunner. Although we had our suspicions, we never did prove who his other accessory - the clapping man - was. Accessory might have been the wrong word. Mastermind would be better. I only found out about this much later on from Murphy when it came to a head. It's an adventure that he hasn't written yet, but has referred to as Before Twilight.

The blonde man in the expensively tailored suit appeared again, this time on the plains of Asgard, seemingly out of nowhere. He hadn't used the Rainbow Bridge Bifrost. Nor did he seem to utilize any of the branches of the World Tree. After appearing, he walked calmly and with great confidence, as if he was master of all he surveyed, right up to the newly repaired front gate of the Golden City. It had been reinforced with even more hinges. It was still dented, but functioning. For the time being Tyr had moved his guard post to the inside of the gate. The knock hole had been sealed shut and had been replaced by the more Earthly invention of a camera and video screen. There was even a button to ring to get the guards attention. The blonde-haired man didn't bother with it and instead rapped on the giant gates with his knuckles. The gates should not have made a sound from such a small action, but they did. The sound boomed through the entire city, shaking everything within it as if by an explosion. The outside video screen blared to life.

"Who goes there?" Tyr was nothing if not a traditionalist.

The Devil smiled. "Gee, and here I was hoping you would guess my name." The musical Earth reference went over the Asgardian's head.

Tyr was on his guard as Heimdal had not notified him of anyone approaching. "What do you want and why are you here?"

"I just came to pay my dear friend Odin a visit."

"If you give me a name I can check if he will see you," Tyr said.

The Devil smiled. "You can tell him that Nick stopped by to visit and remind him that he has something that belongs to me. Because of that I did something that almost took everything away from him. He still lost his son and his granddaughter and with them Asgard's greatest protector. If Twilight should happen to arrive sooner than later... Well, wouldn't that just be a pity. Please tell him that if my property is not returned to me, I will make it a priority to ensure that Ragnarok will be on its way shortly."

"What property?"

"The soul of Vince Argus, which is mine by contract. It was stolen from me by one of his Valkyries, Mista by name. No matter. All One-Eye needs to do is return this soul to my possession and all will be forgiven. I will give him a day to think it over. He knows how he can reach me."

And with that, the Devil disappeared to where not even Heimdal could see or hear him.

There has long been a debate among certain obscure and drunken literary scholars about whether **PATRICK THOMAS** was raised by Cthulhu, a leprechaun in a Manhattan bar, or two human parents. What there is no arguing about is that Patrick is the award-winning author of 40 books including the beloved fantasy humor *Murphy's Lore series* (9 books from *Tales from Bulfinche's Pub* to *The Mug Life*), as well as 2 books in the future space adventures in the *Startenders* series.

The Murphy's Lore After Hours spin-offs star the half pixie/ogre Terrorbelle (*Fairy With A Gun, Fairy Rides The Lightning,* and *Terrorbelle The Unconquered*); the former demon-possessed serial killer Agent Karver of the Department of Mystic Affairs (*Dead To Rites, Rites of Passage*); the cursed magi Hex (*By Darkness Cursed* and *By Invocation Only*); Vince Argus, the Soul For Hire (*Greatest Hits*); and Negral, a forgotten Sumerian god who works as Hell's Detective (*Lore & Dysorder, Bullets & Brimstone,* and the graphic novel *The Moon Maniac* with Blair Webb).

His *Mystic Investigators* paranormal mystery series includes *Shadows & Brimstone* (omnibus of *Bullets & Brimstone* and *From The Shadows* with John L. French), *Once Upon In Crime* (omnibus of *Once More Upon A Time* and *Partners In Crime* with Diane Raetz) *Mystic Investigators,* and *Mean Streets. Assassins' Ball* is his first traditional mystery, co-written with John L. French. He co-edited *Camelot 13, New Blood, Hear Them Roar* and was an editor for the magazines *Fantastic Stories of the Imagination* and *Pirate Writings.*

His other works include the steampunk *As The Gears Turn.* the space epic *Exile & Entrance,* and the *Bikini Jones* series. Patrick's darkly humorous advice column *Dear Cthulhu* has been running since 2005 and has 6 collections including *Cthulhu Knows Best* and *What Would Cthulhu Do?* The Dear Cthulhu advice empire has expanded from magazines and books to radio as Dear Cthulhu now broadcasts monthly on the show Destinies: The Voice of Science Fiction which is hosted by Dr. Howard Margolin.

Over 100 of his stories have been published in magazines and anthologies. His noir novella appears in *Murder in Montague Falls.* A number of his books were part of the props department of the *CSI* television show and *Nightcaps* was even thrown at a suspect's head. His urban fantasy *Fairy With A Gun* had been optioned for film and TV by Laurence Fishburne's Cinema Gypsy Productions. Top Men Productions has turned his *Soul For Hire* Story, *Act of Contrition,* into a short film.

He also writes books for kids as PATRICK T. FIBBS including the YA *Emotional Support Nifghtmare,* the midde readers *Undead Kid Diaries: Over My Dead Body, the Babe B. Bear Mysteries: Bad Hair Day, Joy Reaper Checks Out,* the picture book *Fushcia The Mermaid Who Loved Pink,* and *the Ughabooz* picture books *5 Silly Monsters Jumping On The Zed* and *On Top Of A Yeti,* and the early reader *Soggy Goes to the Beach.*

Please drop by www.patthomas.net or follow him at I_PatrickThomas at Twitter or www.facebook.com/PatrickThomasAuthor to learn more.

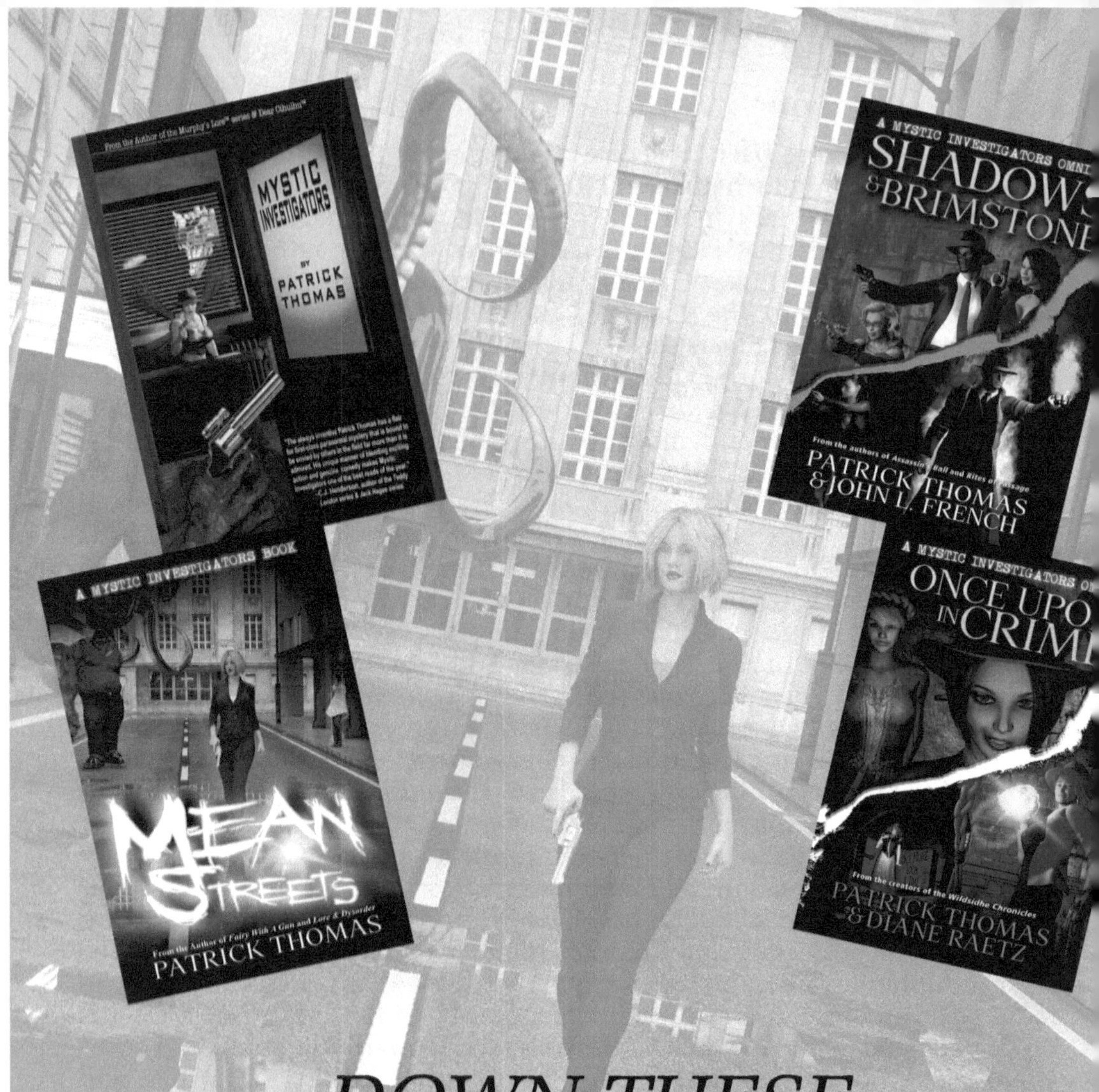

DOWN THESE
MEANS STREETS
of Magic & Monsters walk the

MYSTIC INVESTIGATORS

**Being *CURSED* to wear a bikini
Won't stop this Hero
From *SAVING* the world**

**THE ADVICE
COLUMN TO
END ALL
ADVICE COLUMNS**

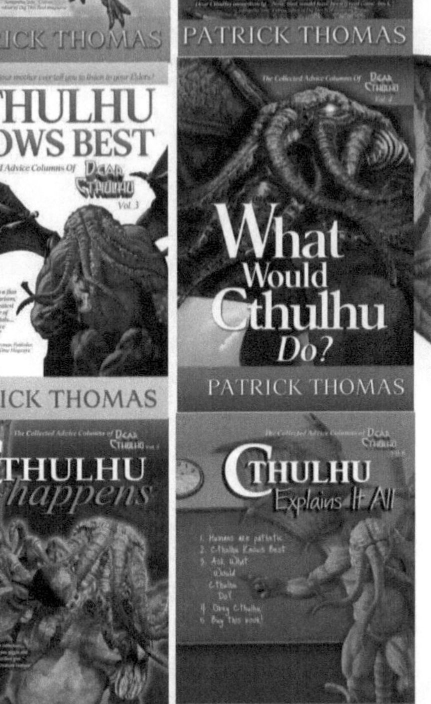

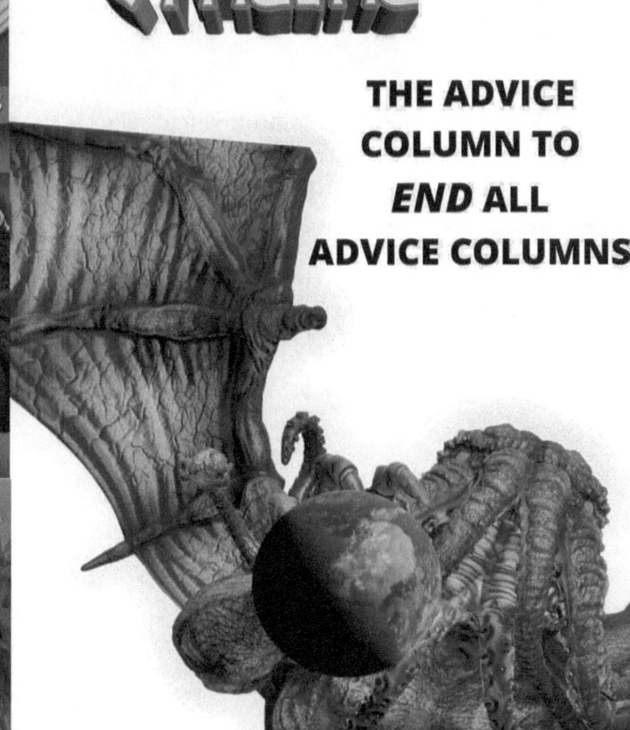

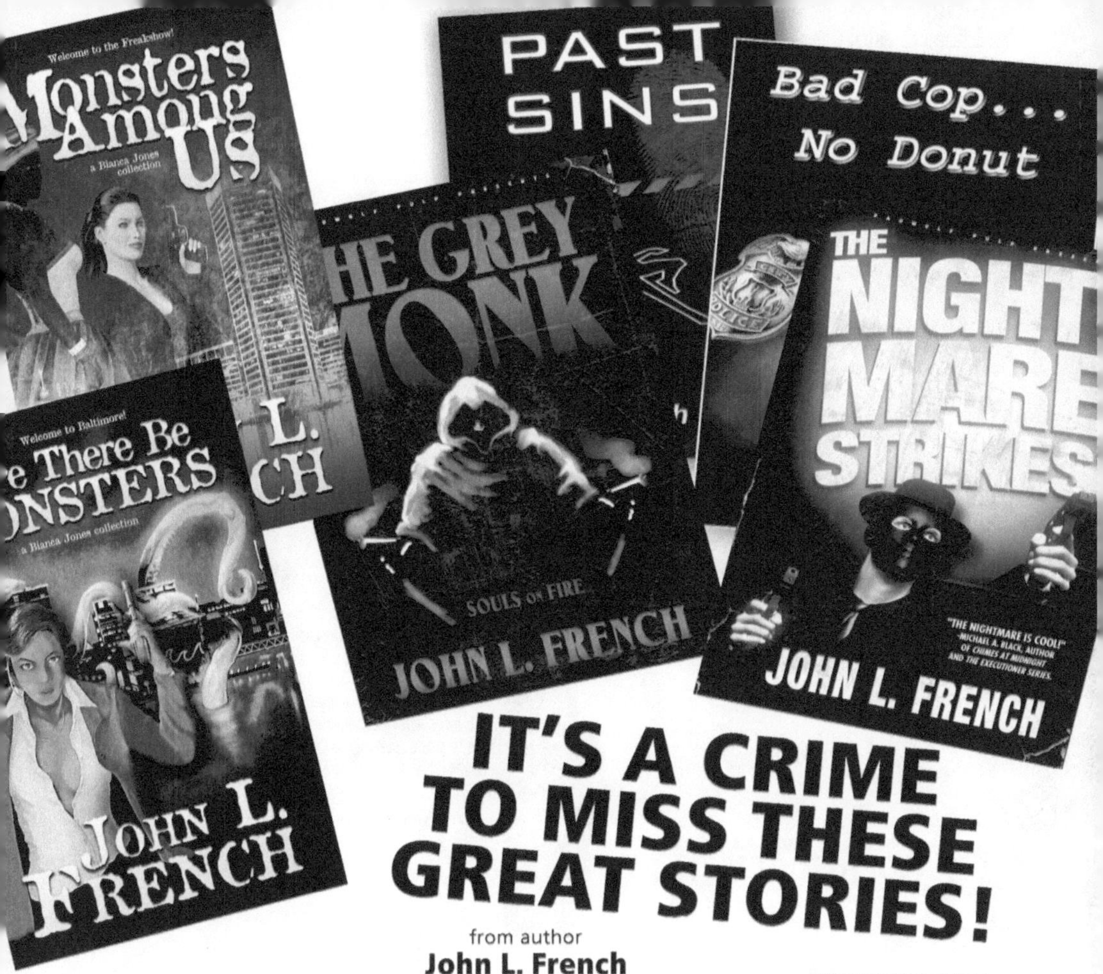
Welcome to the Freakshow!
Monsters Among Us
a Bianca Jones collection
PAST SINS
Bad Cop... No Donut
THE GREY MONK
SOULS ON FIRE
JOHN L. FRENCH
THE NIGHTMARE STRIKES
"THE NIGHTMARE IS COOL!" -MICHAEL A. BLACK, AUTHOR OF CHIMES AT MIDNIGHT AND THE EXECUTIONER SERIES.
JOHN L. FRENCH
Welcome to Baltimore!
a Bianca Jones collection
JOHN L. FRENCH

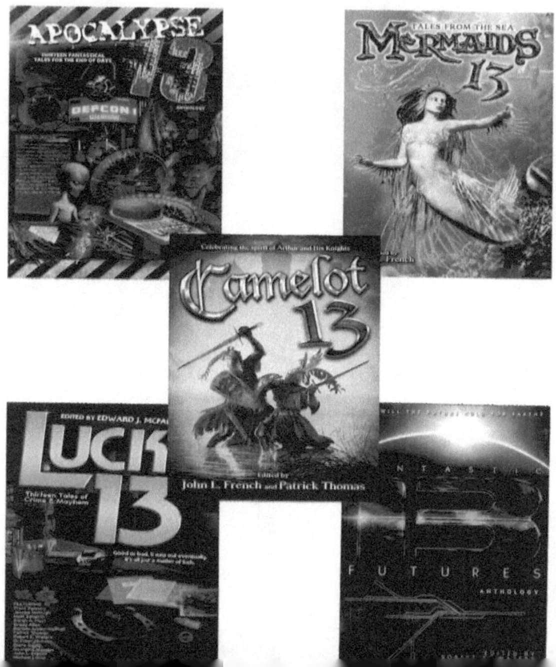
APOCALYPSE 13
THIRTEEN FANTASTICAL TALES FOR THE END OF DAYS
DEFCON 1
TALES FROM THE SEA
MERMAIDS 13
Celebrating the spirit of Arthur and His Knights
Camelot 13
Edited by
John L. French and Patrick Thomas
EDITED BY EDWARD J. MCFADDEN
LUCKY 13
Thirteen Tales of Crime & Mayhem
FUTURES
ANTHOLOGY

"Patrick Thomas is... so believable it's unbelievable."
-Ida Vega-Landow, The Journal of the Lincoln Heights Literary Society
DEAD TO RITES
Patrick Thomas
C.J. Henderson
rites of passage
John L. French
Patrick Thomas
When Darkness Falls
The Department of
Mystic Affairs
Picks up the pieces
From The Murphy's Lore Universe of
PATRICK THOMAS
www.patthomas.net
Find us on Facebook!

Even the things that go Bump in the night
will learn that you DON'T mess with...
Terrorbelle

Fairy Rides the Lightning
PATRICK THOMAS
Fairy With A Gun
PATRICK THOMAS
Terror the Uncon
PATRICK TH
"Thomas certainly brings the goods to the table
when it comes to writing urban fiction...I promise, you will love...
Terrorbelle: Fairy With a Gun. Who doesn't love a well-stacked,
ass-kicking, gun-toting, woman with bullet-proof, razor-sharp win
that investigates all manner of supernatural spookiness? I know
and Thomas's humor shows through in every tale. Jim Butcher an
Laurell K Hamilton have nothing on Thomas." The Raven's Barro
From The Murphy's Lore Universe of
PATRICK THOMAS

Shape up...
You only get
ONE Warning
By Invocation Only
Hex Factor
PATRICK THOMAS
Darkness Cursed
Hex marks the spot
PATRICK THOMAS

Hell's Detective
No One Is Above The La
Even In
LORE & DYSORDER
PATRICK THOMAS
SHADOWS OF BRIMSTONE
PATRICK THOMAS
CASE OF THE MOON MANIAC
"Dark... and charming."
- Ellen Datlow,
The Best Horror of the Year Vol 4
"Gritty, snappy, very dark

One Last Chance to Save Happily Ever After

Can a group of heroes including Goldenhair, Red Riding Hood and Rapunzel help General Snow White and her dwarven resistance fighters defeat the tyrannical Queen Cinderella? And will they succeed before a war with Wonderland destroys everything?

Their only hope to stop Cinderella's quest for power lies with a young girl named Patience Muffet who carries the fabled shards of Cinderella's glass slippers.

Roy Mauritsen's fantasy adventure fairy tale epic begins with *Shards Of The Glass Slipper: Queen Cinder*.

"Fantastic...
A Magnificent Epic"
-*Sarah Beth Durst* author
Into The Wild & Drink, Slay, Lov

"The Brothers Grimm
meets
Lord Of The Rings!"
-*Patrick Thomas*, author
of the *Murphy's Lore* series

"Shards is a dark, lush
full-throttle fantasy
epic that presents
a bold re-imagining
of classic characters."
-David Wade, creator of
319 Dark Street

"Roy Mauritsen's
enchanting epic
comes at a time
when fairy tales
are back in the
forefront of
our collective
imagination."
-Darin Kennedy,
short fiction author

PADWOLF PUBLISHING

In paperback & e-book
Find out more at
shardsoftheglassslipper.com
padwolf.com

Features all
6 books in the series in
one deluxe volume!

NO TEACHERS.
NO PARENTS
SCHOOL IS OUT....
OF THIS WORLD

www.talehaven.com

"If you don't got the cash, we can take it out in trade," Ponytail said, leering at the woman who was already in the van.

"That's my wife!"

"Don't worry. We'll let you watch," Ponytail said.

I lived through soldiers manhandling my Mama up to and beyond the point of death. And they made me watch.

No child was going to see someone hurt their parents while I was around.

I yanked Ponytail's hair back so hard he probably got whiplash. It was enough to make him let go. I reached forward and grabbed him by his large metal belt buckle. A second later I had lifted him over my head. I used my left arm this time.

I turned to the father and smiled. "Don't worry about this, sir. We'll take care of it, too. You and your family go ahead and get back on the road."

"Bless you," the father said gratefully, but that didn't stop him from locking the doors of the van once he was inside. The kids waved from the back row as they pulled away. I waved back with my free hand.

The other two biker boys moved towards me, having taken issue with me laying hands on their friend.

"Put him down," Longbeard said.

"Before we hurt you," Bushy added.

They weren't the only ones taking issue with the way things were going down. Rudy came up behind them, spun them around and grabbed their oversized belt buckles. She bent her knees and, with a clean and jerk, got both men over her head.

"Show off," I said.

"Well if you got it, flaunt it. I have lots, so please notice the flaunting. But don't despair, Terrorbelle. If you spend years working out and practicing, well you still won't be as strong as me, but you will be better off then you are now," Rudy said with a smile.

Sadly, she was right. I was strong, but the daughter of Thor had me beat. Not by a tremendous amount, but it was enough that any strength contest would come out in her favor.

"Yeah, but I can take you in a fight," I said

"Keep thinking that if it helps you get through the night," Rudy said.

"My nights are fine because a Daemor –" My old unit in Faerie. We were the elite female soldiers of Mab's rebel army. "Will kick a Valkyrie's butt any day of the week and three times on Sunday."

I guess we were spending too much time on friendly bickering and not enough concentrating on the bikers we were teaching a lesson to. Like most men, they needed to be the center of attention or they just weren't happy.

Showing them up on the road and with changing the tire wasn't enough humiliation for the day. Nope, Ponytail was hungry for more slices of degradation pie. That was the only explanation I could come up with why he would be dumb enough to take a swing at my face from the position he was in.

Sometimes you just can't save people from their own stupidity. And sometimes you don't even want to try. I didn't bother to try to block the blow, instead smashing my forehead into his fist. It hurt me a little, but I heard a crack and it didn't come from my skull. Ponytail grabbed his broken hand and screamed like a baby.

I've got a very hard head.

OTHER BOOKS BY PATRICK THOMAS

MURPHY'S LORE™: TALES FROM BULFINCHE'S PUB - FOOLS' DAY - THROUGH THE DRINKING GLASS - SHADOW OF THE WOLF - REDEMPTION ROAD - BARTENDER OF THE GODS - NIGHTCAPS - EMPTY GRAVES

MURPHY'S LORE STARTENDERS™   STARTENDERS - CONSTELLATION PRIZE

MURPHY'S LORE AFTER HOURS™ UNIVERSE:

TERRORBELLE: FAIRY WITH A GUN - FAIRY RIDES THE LIGHTNING TERRORBELLE THE UNCONQUERED

AGENT KARVER: RITES OF PASSAGE (with John French) - DEAD TO RITES

HELL'S DETECTIVE: LORE & DYSORDER - BULLETS & BRIMSTONE (with John French) - THE CASE OF THE MOON MANIAC (graphic novel with Blair Webb)

HEXCRAFT: BY DARKNESS CURSED - BY INVOCATION ONLY

SOUL FOR HIRE: GREATEST HITS

XILES: EXILE & ENTRANCE

BIKINI JONES: BIKINI JONES VS. THE BRAINNAPPERS FROM OUT SPACE BIKINI JONES VS THE SEA MONSTERS - BIKINI JONES VS THE EMPEROR OF PLANET Z

THE JACK GARDNER MYSTERIES: THE ASSASSAINS' BALL (with John French)

GRIFFIN, BATSQUATCH, & DINGBAT: CRYPTID FIGHT CLUB

DEAR CTHULHU™: HAVE A DARK DAY - GOOD ADVICE FOR BAD PEOPLE - CTHULHU KNOWS BEST - WHAT WOULD CTHULHU DO? CTHULHU HAPPENS - CTHULHU EXPLAINS IT ALL - CTHULHU TAKE THE WHEEL

MYSTIC INVESTIGATORS™: MYSTIC INVESTIGATORS - MEAN STREETS - ONCE MORE IN CRIME with Diane Raetz - SHADOWS & BRIMSTONE with John L. French

AGENTS OF THE ABYSS™: FRANKENSTEIN: MONSTERS OF THE ABYSS - DETECTIVES OF THE ABYSS (both with John L. French) - STARING INTO THE ABYSS (Editor)

YA: THE WILDSIDHE CHRONICLES OMNIBUS (contributing author)

ANTHOLOGIES AS CO-EDITOR   NEW BLOOD (with Diane Raetz) - CAMELOT 13 (with John L. French)

WRITING AS PATRICK T. FIBBS

YA: EMOTIONAL SUPPORT NIGHTMARE

MIDDLE READERS:
UNDEAD KID DIARIES™: OVER MY DEAD BODY - IT'S MY PARTY AND I'LL DIE IF I WANT TO
BABE B. BEAR MYSTERIES™: BAD HAIR DAY - AIN'T SEEN MUFFIN YET
JOY REAPER CHECKS OUT

YOUNGER READERS:
UGHABOOZ™ PICTURE BOOKS: 5 SILLY MONSTERS JUMPING ON POOR ZED - ON TOP OF A YETI - SOGGY GOES TO THE BEACH an Ughaboos™ early reader

FUSHIA THE MERMAID™ PICTURE BOOKS: FUSHIA: THE MERMAID WHO LOVED PINK